Like the Wind

Also by Robin Lee Hatcher

I'll Be Seeing You
Make You Feel My Love
The Heart's Pursuit
A Promise Kept
A Bride for All Seasons
Heart of Gold
Loving Libby
Return to Me
The Perfect Life
Wagered Heart
Whispers from Yesterday
The Forgiving Hour
The Shepherd's Voice

LEGACY OF FAITH SERIES
Who I Am with You
Cross My Heart
How Sweet It Is

THUNDER CREEK SERIES
You're Gonna Love Me
You'll Think of Me

KINGS MEADOW ROMANCE SERIES
Love Without End
Whenever You Come Around
Keeper of the Stars

Like the Wind

A NOVEL

ROBIN LEE HATCHER

THOMAS NELSON
Since 1798

Doubleday Large Print Home Library Edition

Published in Nashville, Tennessee, by Thomas Nelson. Thomas Nelson is a registered trademark of HarperCollins Christian Publishing, Inc.

Scripture quotations in the historical portions of the novel are taken from the American Standard Version. Public domain.

Scripture quotations in the present-day portions of the novel are taken from the New American Standard Bible®, Copyright © 1960, 1971, 1977, 1995, 2020 by The Lockman Foundation. All rights reserved.

Publisher's Note: This novel is a work of fiction. Names, characters, places, and incidents are either products of the author's imagination or used fictitiously. All characters are fictional, and any similarity to people living or dead is purely coincidental.

ISBN 978-1-63910-422-2

Printed in the United States of America

This Large Print Book carries the Seal of Approval of N.A.V.H

**To the One who calms the wind
with just a word.**

Like the Wind

Prologue

BETHLEHEM SPRINGS, IDAHO

A strong March wind buffeted Olivia Ward's back as she climbed the steps to the deck of her friend's cabin.

"Olivia?" Sara Cartwright's voice came to her through a fog of thoughts. "Are you all right?"

She turned. "I'm fine." It was a lie, of course. She wasn't fine. She would never be fine again. Her life was in tatters.

Sara closed the door, plunging the living room of the aging log house into shades of gray and muting the wind outside. With resolute steps, she walked to the nearest lamp and turned it on. "Let me show you around."

Olivia nodded.

"There's one bedroom down." Sara pointed toward a short hallway. "And the bath is next to it. Kitchen and eating nook are right through there. And upstairs there are two small bedrooms and a half bath. You can use those bedrooms to store things if you need to." She faced Olivia again. "Do whatever you want. Rearrange the furniture. Move it all out and bring in what you have. Paint the walls and cabinets. Hang new curtains. Anything that makes you feel at home."

Tears welled in Olivia's eyes. "I'll never be able to thank you enough."

"Don't be silly. You've already thanked me enough. Besides, this is what friends do. They help each other out. I've got this old place that's just sitting empty. We haven't come up to stay here in over two years. And you need a home."

Throat too tight to speak, Olivia reached out and embraced her friend.

When they separated at last, Sara had tears on her cheeks too. "Do you need anything before I go?"

"No. Really. I'll manage."

"You've got my number. Don't hesitate to call for any reason. I'm only an hour away if you need me." Sara set the keys on the entry table near the door. "Any reason at all," she repeated.

Olivia nodded, both relieved and saddened by her friend's departure.

Once alone in the house, she went to the sofa and sat. The silence swirled around her, strange and disconcerting. No, it wasn't the silence that felt strange. It was the lack of something more to do. There was nothing more to do. For more than a year she'd fought in every way she knew how to keep from losing what mattered most. She'd researched. She'd met with her attorney. She'd talked to family and friends. She'd met with her attorney. She'd gathered statements. She'd met with her attorney.

All to no avail.

Two days ago the judge had not only ended Olivia's thirteen years of marriage to Daniel Ward, he'd given primary custody of their nine-year-old daughter to Olivia's now ex-husband. With a stroke of his pen, the judge had destroyed her life.

"Don't You care, God?" she whispered, not for the first time since her world had spun out of control. "Don't You care what's happened? To me and to Emma."

Silence.

Daniel didn't want custody of his daughter because he desired more time with her. He wanted custody so he could hurt Olivia by taking Emma away. He'd said as much to her months ago, and because he had lots of money and plenty of power, he'd succeeded.

"No, You don't care." Olivia covered her face with her hands.

God hadn't stopped the lies her ex told to get what he wanted. He hadn't stopped the deceit, the trickery, or the betrayals that had brought her world crashing down.

Why don't You care?

One of Olivia's so-called friends had said that everything happened for a reason.

What's the reason for all of this? For taking Emma away? For everything?

Olivia no longer had a home of her own. She would see her daughter only every other weekend—and then only if Daniel didn't take Emma with him on his frequent business trips. Olivia had lost her job after too many absences as she'd fought Daniel in court. She had nothing left in savings. Her bank account had run dry long ago. Her parents had helped her as much as possible with attorney fees, but even that hadn't been enough. Daniel had too much money, too much clout, too many favors he could call in with people in power.

Olivia lay on her side and curled herself around a throw pillow. "Just let me die. Please. Just let me die."

Chapter 1

SIX YEARS LATER

Olivia ignored the phone when it rang at 7:30 a.m. She ignored it again at 8:00 and 8:20. She hated to be interrupted when she was working on a new design for a client. Much easier to let callers leave a message. Only no one had left a message, and when the phone rang again at 8:35, she lifted the handset from its cradle. "Olivia Designs," she all but snapped.

"Mrs. Ward?"

She hated to be called that. **Ms.** suited her much better. "This is Olivia

Ward."

"My name is Savannah Hodgkiss. I'm a counselor at Blakely Academy. I'm calling about your daughter."

Her heart almost stopped. "Has something happened to Emma?" She clutched the handset tighter.

"No…but there's been an accident."

"An accident? Is she in the hospital?" Olivia looked toward her computer screen. How long would she have to wait for a flight? It was over an hour's drive to the Boise airport, and there wouldn't be a direct flight from there to Orlando. A layover would add another hour or two or more to an already lengthy flight. When could she get there? Maybe before midnight?

"Mrs. Ward, Emma is fine. She wasn't with her father."

She drew a deep breath. "Daniel?" Why would the school call her about Daniel having an accident?

"Mr. Ward was killed late last night in an accident on the freeway."

Olivia almost dropped the phone.

"As you can imagine, your daughter is rather distraught. I believe she needs you."

Olivia didn't ask if Emma had actually **asked** for her. She suspected she hadn't. She looked toward the computer screen again. "Please give me your contact number. I'll book a flight, then call you to let you know when I'll arrive. How long a drive is it from the airport to the school?"

"About an hour and a half with traffic." The woman gave Olivia her phone number.

"Okay. I'll call back as soon as I'm able."

"Thank you, Mrs. Ward."

Olivia set the phone in its cradle.

Daniel dead. Gone, just like that. His life over. There had been moments in the past when—in her anger—she'd wished him dead. Now he was. What should she feel? What **did** she feel? She didn't know. She wasn't sure.

Drawing a deep breath, she closed her eyes, then slowly exhaled. After a moment more, she looked at her computer again and focused her attention on her most pressing need. Fifteen minutes later she had her flight booked without maxing out her credit card, as she'd feared it might. Soon after, she contacted her virtual assistant so the young woman could advise Olivia's clients of the situation. The next call was back to Savannah Hodgkiss with her estimated arrival time. After that she began to pack, taking far more than would likely be necessary.

It had been nearly a year and a half since Olivia had seen her daughter in person. The last two summers the girl had refused to come for the month-long visit agreed upon after Daniel relocated to the far side of the country, and more often than not, Emma had an excuse for why she couldn't FaceTime with her mom either. Emma had changed a great deal in the six years since her parents' divorce. The distance between Olivia and her was far more than mere miles.

"She's fifteen," Sara liked to say. "All girls are impossible at fifteen. It'll get better."

Bitterness left a bad taste in Olivia's mouth.

She knew Daniel delighted—correction, used to delight—in doing whatever he could to drive a wedge between mother and child. Worse still, he'd succeeded. Olivia was rushing to Florida to see a daughter who had become almost a stranger to her. And it was all **his** fault.

"He's dead," she whispered to herself. She tried to feel sorry about that. She couldn't. Not with anger roiling in her chest.

Once upon a time, she'd loved Daniel Ward. She knew that was true, although it was hard to believe today. She'd fallen hard for him when she was a sophomore in college. Daniel had been nearly seven years older than Olivia and already a successful businessman. She'd never met anyone quite like him. So handsome. So charming. So in control.

He'd controlled her, too, although she hadn't realized that at first. Perhaps she hadn't let herself realize it.

Her parents had expressed concern when she'd wanted to marry Daniel before they'd dated even a year, but nothing could have stopped her from going through with it. Nothing. And she'd been blissfully happy. She hadn't minded when her new husband asked her to quit college and stay at home. She hadn't minded when she lost touch with most of her friends. Daniel had wanted her all to himself. Wasn't that how it was supposed to be?

Things had started to go wrong after the birth of Emma, and it had taken her years to understand why. She'd finally understood that Daniel hated that he was no longer the very center of her world.

And so he'd torn everything apart.

Her thoughts continued to churn during the hour-long drive from her home in Bethlehem Springs, a former gold-rush town in the Idaho mountains, to the Boise airport. She left her car in long-term parking and pulled her rolling suitcase toward the terminal, wondering what awaited her at Blakely Academy. She ached to hold her daughter in her arms. Would Emma allow it?

At the counter she checked the larger bag, then headed for the TSA screening area. Fifteen minutes later she settled onto a chair to await the call to board. As she withdrew her mobile phone from her carry-on, it began to vibrate. Sara's picture appeared on the screen.

"Hi, Sara," she answered.

"What was that message I got on your answering machine at home? You're out of the office?"

"I'm at the airport. I'm flying to Florida."

"Florida? Good grief. What's up now?"

Sara Cartwright was one of the few friends who had stuck with Olivia through her marriage to Daniel, the messy divorce, and the grizzly past six years. Sara knew all the details of Olivia's life, had witnessed many of her meltdowns, and had loved her at her most unlovable points—of which there'd been plenty. Bless her, she still put up with Olivia's foul moods. A more loyal friend couldn't be found. The only thing that would have made the friendship better was if they lived in the same town. Get-togethers were too few and far between.

"I don't know any details," Olivia answered, glad there was no need to pretend with Sara. "Just that Daniel was killed in an accident on the freeway. I'm headed for Emma's school now to get her."

"Oh, Olivia. I'm sorry. Will Emma come home with you?"

"Of course," she answered, but doubt

was already causing her to wonder.

Would Daniel have done something to prevent her from taking Emma back with her to Idaho? **Could** he have done anything? She was Emma's mother, but that hadn't been enough six years ago. Daniel had a string of lawyers on retainer to make sure things happened the way he wanted them to. Would he have prepared the same for after his death? Or had he thought his wealth could prevent even death?

"I'll pray for you," Sara said, intruding on Olivia's thoughts.

"Thanks." She'd stopped believing in prayer. She hadn't stopped believing in God, but she'd stopped asking Him for anything. He hadn't cared when her world fell apart. She didn't imagine He would care if it should happen all over again. But Sara believed both in God and in the power of prayer, and it was easier to simply thank her than to say not to bother.

"When will you and Emma be back?"

"I don't know. I really don't know anything."

"Did you talk to Emma yourself?"

"No. Just to the counselor at the school."

"Is there anything I can do to help while you're gone?"

"Not that I can think of. Not now. But I'll let you know if anything comes up."

"Be sure you do." Sara paused, then asked, "Would it be okay if I prayed for you now?"

Her pulse quickened, almost as if she were afraid. "Sorry. I can't. I need to go."

"Okay. Safe flight. Text me when you land."

"Will do."

"I'll be praying. I love you, Olivia."

"You too." She pulled the phone from her ear and ended the call.

December 10, 1931
Thursday

I'm twenty years old today.
Isn't that something to write? I'm
no longer teenaged. Not that it
should matter. I've been married
three and a half years now. I'm
not a little girl. Haven't been for a
long time. I've got a husband and
two sweet daughters. Still, I like
writing that I'm twenty. Makes
me feel more grown up.

This is my first entry in this
new diary. Harry gave it to me
this morning for my birthday,
although he probably shouldn't
have spent the money on it. I
plan to keep it out of reach of my
girls. Gladys took my last diary
(the one my mother gave me the

last Christmas before I married)
and scribbled on nearly every
page. The pages I'd filled with
writing and the blank ones too.
I scolded her, but I'm not sure
she understood what she did
wrong. She's only two and a half.

Dottie ran a fever again today.
Dr. Harper wants to put her in the
hospital to do tests. She's so
little. Much too young to be
apart from me. She wouldn't
understand the separation.
Neither would Gladys. The girls
are only ten months apart in age.
Almost like twins, they are so
inseparable.

Harry says I worry too much.
About Dottie. About money. But
it's hard not to worry, what with
so much hardship all around us.
It's been two years since that
New York stock market crashed.
I don't pretend to understand
what that has to do with us here

in California. The orchards need sunshine and water, and we've got those. But I guess it does matter because we've got neighbors who have given up and moved away. And because Harry worries, too, even though he tells me not to do the same.

Life doesn't always go the way we think it will. Mother told me something like that before Harry and I left Iowa. But I don't think I believed her then. I do now.

January 1, 1932
Friday

A new year.

The house is quiet. I am the only one awake at this early hour. Even Harry is still asleep. That's unusual for him. I have put the coffee on so that it will be ready when he rises. For now, I sit at the table with this new diary.

A new year. 1932. What will it bring?

When I was a girl, I thought I wanted to be an actress. I told Mother I wanted to go to New York City and appear on the Broadway stage. That was the same year a company performed **H.M.S. Pinafore** at the theater in town. Afterward I got to talk to the actress who played Little Buttercup. Oh, how I longed to be like her. To get to perform. To get to travel the country. I was determined to leave home as soon as I finished school.

But then I met Harry and everything changed.

I'm not sorry everything changed. But I miss having that dream of being on the stage. Aunt Tess liked to do dramatic readings. She performed in Grange halls and schools. Maybe I could do that, once the girls are older. Aunt Tess memorized **The Gift of the Magi**. That was my favorite of her performances. Maybe because I love the O. Henry short story so much. I have a copy that I brought with me from Iowa. I think I'll take it off the shelf and try to memorize it.

Chapter 2

Tyler Murphy drove his black SUV slowly along Main Street. Bethlehem Springs had retained much of its Old West appearance over the past century and a half, but it wasn't a ghost town or a tourist trap trying to entice visitors to the mountains of Idaho. It was a small community with its own schools, churches, a bank, a grocery store, a gas station, a movie theater that was open on the weekends, a café, and the municipal building that housed the courthouse, sheriff's office, and jail. Residents tended to be of the independent sort, and yet they formed close relationships at the same time.

One thing the town lacked was a motel. While his house to the north of town was undergoing some remodeling, Tyler planned to stay in one of the two bed-and-breakfasts. That would serve his purposes well since he'd heard Mary Ellen Foster loved to gossip. That might be helpful for his new assignment.

He turned right on Bear Run Road and followed it past the firehouse. A left onto Shenandoah Street took him by the three schools on his right—elementary, middle, and high—and the town park on his left. At the corner of Shenandoah and Wallula, he saw the sign for the Parker Bed-and-Breakfast and pulled into the gravel parking area behind the two-story house.

A woman, perhaps in her late fifties or early sixties, looked up from behind a counter when he entered through the front door. A smile instantly wreath her face. "Hello. You must b

Murphy."

"I am." He nodded.

"It's nice to meet you at last. I'm Mary Ellen Foster."

He glanced around the front parlor. While not shabby, it appeared to have been decorated at the turn of the twentieth century rather than the twenty-first.

"If you'll sign the register…"

He returned his attention to Mary Ellen and nodded once again, then looked down at the book that had been turned toward him. The sight of it amused him. She really did want her guests to feel transported back in time.

He scrawled his name and put down the pen.

"Remodeling is such a pain," Mary Ellen said. "When I redid the bathrooms, th— —e was at sixes and sevens for— oh my. The construction dust. — everything. Took me forever —use shipshape again."

— sound of agreement to let

her know he listened.

"Well, I shouldn't keep you standing here. Follow me. Your room is right at the top of the stairs." As she led the way, she rattled off a few rules of the house and the window of time when breakfast was served in the mornings. "You're our only guest at the moment," she finished as she used a key to open the door.

"There's wired internet in the room," Tyler said. "Is that correct?"

"Yes. The connection's in the wall above the desk, there by the window, and the password's in that book next to the phone."

Tyler knew without looking that his mobile phone wouldn't have any bars in this location. When the wind was right, he could get service out closer to the two-lane highway. Hopefully the new cell tower would be completed in another week or two, bringing better cellular service to folks in town. B most people in Bethlehem Sprin the surrounding area would continue to rely on landlines, Tyler included. It was one of the downsides of mountain living.

"There's Wi-Fi in the parlor and dining room," Mary Ellen continued. "Different password from the wired. You'll see a sign with the password for Wi-Fi on the welcome counter."

"Thanks. Good to know." He dropped his bag onto the floor next to the bed, then turned and held out his hand for the key. "I appreciate your help, Mrs. Foster."

"Mary Ellen, please. After all, we're pretty much neighbors even if we've never had the chance to meet." She placed the key on his palm. "Homebaked cookies are available in the dining r___ at five o'clock."

___ knowledged her words with ___ nod as he reached to close ___ few moments later he car___ p to the small desk near ___ d proceeded to get connected to the internet through his own secure router. While he doubted Mary Ellen knew how to access other people's computers remotely, he took no chances. A habit born out of his profession.

A quick check of his email showed nothing that needed his immediate attention. He already knew Olivia Ward and her daughter wouldn't land at the Boise airport until four thirty this afternoon, assuming their flights were on schedule. Adding time to collect luggage and the drive up to Bethlehem Springs, he didn't imagine they would roll into town until six o'clock at the earliest.

Not that it mattered much to him what time they got back tonight. He wouldn't try to arrange a "chance" meeting for another day or two. He had other work to accomplish first.

He opened the brief on his lapto and perused the information wit was a different kind of assig him, one that he'd acquired based on his residence in Bethlehem Springs more than because of his qualifications as an investigator. He was tasked with learning more about Olivia Ward and her daughter but asked not to surveil them in the usual fashion. No taking photographs of their every move. No following around. "I don't want to violate their privacy," the client had told Tyler over the phone.

It was difficult to obtain information without prying, but he would do his best to comply with the client's request. Besides, in a small town like this, it could get back to his subject that he was asking about her. That wouldn't serve his purposes. No, he would have to proc ed slowly and carefully.

ed the brief and opened the begin.

the parking garage and enly unsure where she'd le. A long day of travel, piled upon the stress of the past two weeks, had left her brain foggy.

"Where are we going?" Emma asked, her tone sullen.

Thankfully, her memory returned. "This way." Olivia started walking, accompanied by the sound of small wheels crossing pavement. After the luggage was loaded into the back of the Subaru, Olivia looked at her daughter. "Are you hungry?"

"No."

"Maybe you'd better rethink that. There won't be much waiting for us at home. I'll need to do some shopping."

"It isn't my home."

Olivia swallowed a reply as she moved toward the driver-side door. Even after she was settled behind the steering wheel, she had to wait for Emma. Her daughter was doing everything possible to irritate Olivia. And it worked. She closed her eyes, remembering the nine-year-old who had clung to her so tightly, tears in her eyes.

"Don't go, Mama. Please don't go."

The other door opened, and Emma plopped onto the seat. "I guess I could eat," she mumbled.

"We'll grab a hamburger at a drive-through."

"How long does it take to get where we're going?"

"About an hour. Don't you remember your last visit?"

"Not really."

The words hurt Olivia more than she wanted to admit. Were they true? Had Emma truly forgotten her few trips home to see her mom?

To make matters worse, when not in school, Emma was used to living in a mansion with hired help, a tennis court, and a swimming pool. A far cry from the quaint log house that Olivia called home. She'd bought the cabin from Sara a few years ago and, with her dad and some of his friends doing the labor, had added a room on the ground level to use as her office and studio. Other repairs and updates had been made as she could afford them. Still, the entire house would have fit into half of Daniel's garage.

She released a breath as she blinked back tears of frustration.

It wasn't as if Emma had spent a lot of time in her dad's home either. Daniel had placed Emma at Blakely Academy, a posh boarding school, soon after their move to Florida. He'd said it was good for her, but the truth was he hadn't had the time to be bothered with parenting.

And this is the result.

Olivia started the engine and backed out of the parking spot, trying not to let bitterness overwhelm her.

Emma stared out the window at the passing terrain, the road winding between tall mountains on both sides. Everything looked very different from Florida. It was all so...brown. Brown and narrow, the sun blocked out by those same tall mountains. No endless blue sky. No ocean lapping at a shore or salty breeze filling her lungs, the way it was at her dad's house.

Of course Emma remembered more about Idaho than she'd let on to her mom. She even remembered that she hadn't always hated coming for a visit. But that had been when she was a little kid. It was different now. She had a **life** in Florida. She had friends there. Mom never should have dragged her off to Idaho. There must have been some way she could've stayed at Blakely Academy for another few years. There must have been enough money for that. After graduation she could have made up her own mind where to live—and it wouldn't have been **here**.

But no. Others had made those decisions for Emma. Blakely Academy had more or less kicked her out, and the corporate lawyers had taken just about everything else that she'd thought of as her dad's if not hers. The house. The cars. The boat. It was all gone. Apparently there was nowhere to go except to Idaho.

She ventured a glance to the left. Her mom's gaze was locked on the road ahead. Tension made her expression hard.

She doesn't really want me. Nobody wants me.

Emma turned her eyes out the passenger window again.

I wish I' d died with Dad.

The hamburger Olivia ate in Boise felt like a rock in her stomach by the time she drove up to her house in the pines. Turning off the car's engine, she dared a glance in her daughter's direction.

"You've gotta be kidding me." Emma leaned forward for a better look through the windshield. "You're still living **here**?"

"Home sweet home," Olivia replied, trying to keep her voice light.

"I thought you got a new place. Someplace...better."

"I decided to buy it instead of move."

"It's a dump."

"Maybe. But it's our dump." She opened the door and got out.

Emma stayed in the car.

Fine. Let her sit there as long as she wanted. All night, even. No skin off Olivia's nose, as her mother liked to say. Perhaps she should be ashamed of her attitude, but she was too tired to care at the moment.

She retrieved her own suitcase and carry-on from the back of the Outback and carried them onto the deck, setting them down near the front door. It took a few moments to retrieve the key from the pocket of her travel bag.

Heaven help me, she thought as she glanced back toward the car.

Emma hadn't budged.

Olivia turned the key in the lock, opened the door, and rolled her luggage into the house and straight to her bedroom on the main floor. Minutes later, a quick look in the kitchen told her that Kathy Dover—the only person who had a spare key to the house, so it had to be her—had brought food to restock the refrigerator and pantry. They wouldn't go hungry after all.

Bless you, my friend.

She went to the windows in the living room and opened them, letting in fresh air. The vantage point allowed her to look down at the Subaru in time to see Emma emerge, a scowl on her face. When she wasn't crying, a scowl was the girl's most common expression.

It was something of a shock to learn that Daniel had left this earth owning very little to pass along to his only child and heir. The house, the cars, almost everything he'd possessed, had been in the name of the corporation. Olivia didn't understand all of the legal details, but she did understand what that coven of lawyers had meant when they said there was no inheritance for Emma, that no provisions had been made for Daniel's daughter to continue her education at Blakely Academy or any other private institution. That he'd left her nothing at all. That there'd been nothing to leave to her. He'd tied everything up, as if to keep it to himself even after he was gone.

Olivia understood what that meant, but she didn't think Emma had grasped it yet. Emma still expected to live the way she'd been living. While her dad hadn't given her much of his time, he had given her most of what she'd wanted. The clothes. The technology. The trips. All of the trappings of wealth. Even that boarding school had made the girls who lived there feel privileged and better than others.

Had Daniel made his selfish choices because he truly didn't care about Emma, or had he done it to punish Olivia, even after all these years? She hoped it was the latter. But neither she nor her daughter would ever know for certain.

She pressed her forehead against

the glass. **Please don't let this hurt linger**.

The words in her head sounded suspiciously like a prayer.

January 20, 1932
Wednesday

Dottie is in the hospital. The doctors cannot decide what is wrong with her. They suspect. They discuss. They use words I don't understand. They have ruled out scarlet fever and measles. Or I think they have. But it seems to be a mystery, what is causing her high fever and other symptoms. They have isolated her from other children in the ward. She cries, and I am not allowed to go to her.

Please, God. Please help Dottie get well. I feel so helpless.

February 10, 1932
Wednesday

We brought Dottie home from
the hospital today. She is so frail,
a wisp of the chubby toddler she
used to be. Her second birthday
is a little more than two weeks
away. And I am afraid to write
the question that screams in
my heart.

God, will she?

May 10, 1932
Tuesday

We have lost the lemon orchard.
We have lost our home. What
this Great Depression, as
President Hoover has called the
financial panic of the past few
years, hasn't taken from us,
Dottie's illness and medical
expenses have. We have nothing
left after paying the doctor and
hospital what little we had.
Nothing.

Tomorrow morning we leave
California for Idaho. Harry's
brother says there is a tenant
farm waiting for Harry to work,
with a house for us to live in.
Most of what we can take with
us is already piled onto our Ford.

There is little room left for Harry, Gladys, Dottie, and me. Not to mention Scruffy. A neighbor offered to take the dog, but the girls were heartbroken at the idea of leaving him behind. They have already said goodbye to the horse and the two milk cows and the chickens. We couldn't make them say goodbye to Scruffy too. And so he will go into the automobile with us, and God willing, we will all survive the long journey to Idaho.

When Harry and I married, I didn't know we would soon after move to California to begin a new life. How could I know? I was only sixteen and a half and so innocent about anything beyond our small town, despite my girlish dreams of performing on the stage. What did I know of big cities and Broadway? When we arrived in California, I didn't know what it would mean to own a lemon orchard and a fine, big house. Again, how could I? My parents never owned their own place. It seemed impossible that we could be so blessed. Gladys was born before our first anniversary and Dottie came before our second. But Harry worked hard from dawn to dusk, and the orchards thrived, and I thought we would always have what we needed. I never imagined everything could be taken away so quickly. We were blessed.

How could we lose it all?

I have asked God to show me why these things have happened. If He has answered, I have not heard or understood.

We are not alone, of course. There is hardship all around us. People are suffering, believers and unbelievers alike. As the

Bible tells us, it rains on the just
and the unjust.
So why does it feel as if we are
the only ones?

Chapter 3

"This quite a spread," Tyler said to Mary Ellen as she set a platter of breakfast meats in the center of the table between the bowl of scrambled eggs and a basket of breads.

"I hope you find something to your liking." The woman stepped back, her hands folded over her stomach, a pleased smile curving her lips.

He reached for the bowl. "I'm sure I'll like it all." He spooned fluffy eggs onto his plate. "Will you join me?"

"Heavens, no. I wouldn't think of intruding on your morning."

Tyler smiled as he reached for the

platter of ham, bacon, and sausage. "You wouldn't be intruding. You'd be company. I eat alone all the time at home. Wouldn't mind someone else to talk to for a change."

"Well…" She took a step closer to the chair at the opposite end of the table. "If you're sure."

"I'm sure." He waited until she sat down before asking, "How long have you lived in Bethlehem Springs?"

"All my life. This house has been in my family for more than a hundred years. It was a boardinghouse back in the early days, then a private home again. I decided to turn it into a bed-and-breakfast when the last of my lot headed off to college."

He wondered if there was a Mr. Foster in the picture.

As if reading his mind, Mary Ellen said, "My husband passed on when my youngest was still in high school."

"I'm sorry for your loss."

"Thank you, but that's been many

years ago now. The sorrow is gone, and the memories are sweeter. Time has a way of doing that."

Tyler hoped she was right about that. His sister had died several years before, and he still wrestled with his emotions, with his doubts, with the lingering guilt that maybe he could have done more to help her.

"Mr. Murphy?"

He blinked, his thoughts brought abruptly to the present. "Sorry."

"I asked what brought you to Bethlehem Springs."

"I grew up in Boise," he answered, knowing that sharing a little about himself could often garner more information from others. "I camped in this area a lot in the summers, and I hunted up this way most autumns. When I was looking to buy a place of my own, I liked the idea of living up here. I can work remotely some of the time, and it's not a bad commute down to Boise when it's required."

"What is it you do?"

"I work for a law firm."

"You're an attorney?"

"No. I investigate for them. Research and such. Spend a lot of time on the computer."

"Oh."

He decided to steer the conversation away from his occupation. "Another reason I wanted to live up here is I'm a bit of an Idaho history buff. I love learning new things about this state."

"Ah. Well, there's plenty of that to be found. I guess you know there's a museum where the Washington Hotel used to be."

"I've been in the museum. Not sure why, but I didn't realize it used to be a hotel."

"Saints alive, yes. But I think the hotel closed down around the start of the Second World War. Or maybe it was soon after the war was over. I can't be sure. It's been a museum as long as I can remember."

Before the food on his plate could grow completely cold, he decided to encourage Mary Ellen to do most of the talking. The best way he knew was to ask the right question. "What's your favorite historical location up here?"

"That's easy. The New Hope Health Spa. Have you been up there?"

He brought a forkful of eggs to his mouth, an excuse not to answer her.

"You should go explore the site. The spa was in operation for more than fifty years. The hard financial times in the seventies spelled the death of it. A shame because it was a magnificent place." She began to describe the setting and buildings.

Tyler wasn't ignorant about the New Hope Health Spa. Back in college he'd done some research into it for a paper he'd written. But that wasn't pertinent. It was current residents of the town who interested him now. Or rather, one particular resident. It was time to bring Mary Ellen's thoughts a little closer to home.

Between bites of his breakfast, he began to ply her for information. It didn't take much to get her talking and keep her talking. Most of what she said would mean nothing to his investigation, but he'd learned to take it all in. He never knew what might turn out to be relevant later on.

Olivia was wiping the counter with a cloth when Emma stepped into the kitchen. Her daughter wore an over-sized T-shirt and a pair of baggy shorts. Her long dark hair was disheveled, and her feet were bare despite the chill in the morning air. "What's for breakfast?" she mumbled as she pushed hair back from her face.

"I made pancakes and bacon earlier. The extra batter's in the fridge. It won't take you long to warm the skillet."

Emma stared at Olivia as if she'd sprouted another head.

There had been a time when Emma

loved to help Olivia in the kitchen. The little girl would stand on a stool and complete whatever task her mama asked of her. Usually it was to stir something in a bowl. Judging by Emma's expression, those fun times had been forgotten, along with most of her childhood in Idaho.

It was difficult for Olivia not to curse Daniel Ward one more time. But what purpose would that serve? Daniel was dead, and the damage he'd desired was done. Olivia had to concentrate on how to heal the relationship with her daughter. Hating Daniel wouldn't help. In fact, it could only make things worse.

Emma sank onto a kitchen chair. Was she stubbornly refusing to make her own breakfast, or did she simply not know what to do? She suspected it was the latter.

Olivia drew a deep breath. "I'll make your pancakes. You can pour your own orange juice." She opened the refrigerator and removed both the batter and the bottle of juice, setting them on the counter before retrieving the skillet. "Do you remember where the glasses are?"

"No."

She pointed. "That cupboard there."

Emma grunted but didn't move.

Olivia pretended not to notice as she whisked the pancake batter. "I made an appointment for us to meet with the school principal later today. We need to get you registered for the fall."

"I don't want to go to school in this stupid place."

"I'm afraid there isn't any other option, Emma. This is where we live. This is where you'll have to go to school."

Emma leapt up from the chair. "You don't understand anything," she shouted before fleeing the room in tears. Soon after, the door to her upstairs bedroom slammed closed.

Olivia turned off the heat beneath the skillet, then went to the table and sat in the chair Emma had occupied moments before.

What am I going to do? She covered her face with her hands.

She could sell the log house in the pines, she supposed, but she would never get enough money for it to buy a suitable place in Boise. The cost of housing in the capital city had skyrocketed in recent years. As for finding a rental, that would be next to impossible. Especially affordable housing. It simply didn't exist. She'd read that a person could spend years on a waiting list before something became available.

Here in Bethlehem Springs, Olivia's income from website design and book-publishing services was adequate. Her home was snug, the payments small, and she had a decent, reliable automobile. She lacked for nothing she truly needed, and sometimes she had enough left over for a few wants as well. Now that there were two in the household, money would have to stretch a little farther, but she could manage in

Bethlehem Springs. In Boise her income wouldn't be anywhere near enough. No. Moving was not an option. Emma would have to learn to be content with things as they were, not as she wanted them to be.

Taking a deep breath, she lowered her hands to the table.

The first time Emma had spent a weekend in Olivia's home in the mountains, not long after the divorce was final, she'd loved it. Olivia had imagined the day when her daughter might live there with her. **This** was not the way she'd pictured it. The smiling, laughing, adventurous girl of nine had disappeared, leaving a beautiful but spoiled, scowling, disapproving teenager in her place.

"It wasn't supposed to be like this."

More than one person over the past two weeks had advised Olivia to take it one day at a time. **Don't borrow trouble. Deal with today. Live in the present.** But what if the present was impossible?

She drew in a quick breath and released it. "I'm the mom. Emma's still a child, even if she doesn't think so." She stood. "We'll get through this."

May 16, 1932
Monday

We are here. Harry told me when
we crossed into Idaho. The
countryside didn't change. It
was the same on one side of the
state's border as it was on the
other. Still, there was something
good about knowing we'd
reached Idaho at last.

We were a tired and dirty group
of travelers after all those days
on the road, camping under the
stars at night. The girls didn't
seem to mind the inconveniences,
although I worried how the heat
and dust would affect Dottie.
She still doesn't seem strong to
me. I worry so about her.

And there is another worry as

well. One that I haven't shared with Harry yet. One I only began to suspect in the days before we left our home. I'm pregnant. I'm sure of it now. The morning sickness has begun. Outside of when I am carrying a baby, I am never sick in that way. I suppose the baby will arrive right after Christmas or maybe in the new year.

I want to be happy about it. I love my daughters so much. When Harry and I married, we talked about the large family we wanted. But now, with things as they are, what if we fail as tenant farmers? What if we can't feed the children we have, let alone another?

Don't worry about tomorrow, Jesus told His followers. Tomorrow has enough worries of its own.

I know this is true. I know I should heed those words. But how can I keep from it?

May 19, 1932
Thursday

The house on the farm is very small. There are two bedrooms upstairs, and the stairway going up is so narrow Harry feels the need to turn his shoulders. The girls share a bed in one bedroom. Harry and I are in the other. There will be room enough for a crib if we can afford to buy one when the time comes. The one we had for the girls was left behind. There wasn't room for it. Perhaps the baby will have to make do with a dresser drawer. That is enough for many newborns.

I still haven't told Harry that I am pregnant.

We are farming forty acres.

The land is in corn. Harry's father raised corn back in Iowa, so Harry isn't a stranger to it. Although that was dry farming, and here they irrigate. Across the road is a dairy farm. Holsteins. I rather like the sound of their lowing in the mornings. Scruffy feels the need to bark as the cows come in to be milked. I hope we can teach him it isn't necessary to warn us of their movements. Back home he never barked at our Jerseys, but we only had two.

"Back home." I must stop that, mustn't I? This is home now. This little house outside the small town of Thunder Creek. This is where we live. This is where our children will grow up. God willing.

It's pretty here. There are many fruit orchards. Not lemons. Lemons wouldn't grow in Idaho,

Harry says. I suppose because it is too cold in the winters. But cherries and apples and apricots and peaches all grow here. Many farmers raise corn and alfalfa for hay and sugar beets. Irrigation with water from the rivers and canals has made this land come alive. Harry says the volcanic soil is rich with the nutrients required to grow healthy crops. He is hopeful. So hopeful.

Please, God, help Harry. Strengthen and encourage him. And make Dottie strong too. She remains frail. The doctor warned it would take time for her to get better, but it hurts to see her like this. Touch her as only You can. Amen.

Chapter 4

Inside the high school the air felt cool. Lights were off in the hallways, and the building seemed eerily silent without students roaming around. Olivia walked toward the school administrative offices with purpose in her steps. Emma followed, but at a slower pace.

"Hi, Olivia," the school counselor greeted as they entered the front office.

"Hi, Tammy." She knew the younger woman slightly from church. "Is Rachel available?"

"Yes. She's waiting for you both." Tammy Anderson's gaze shifted beyond Olivia's shoulder, and her smile blossomed. "We're so glad to have you here, Emma."

Emma didn't respond, and Olivia could only guess what her expression must be.

Rachel Hamilton, the school principal, appeared in a doorway. "Good morning."

Olivia didn't know Rachel well. They'd met a few times at community events over the years, but that was all. Her impression of the woman was that she was both kind and no-nonsense. Olivia also knew that Rachel, a widow, had raised three sons and a daughter, all of whom had gone on to college and careers beyond the boundaries of Bethlehem Springs.

"Emma," Olivia said, drawing her daughter forward with a hand on her arm, "this is Mrs. Hamilton, the principal." She nodded in Tammy's direction. "And this is Miss Anderson."

Tammy said, "I'll be the one who helps you get registered for all of your classes."

"But we can do that in a bit." Rachel motioned with her arm. "Come into my office so we can get acquainted."

Although Olivia knew Emma hated it, she put her hand on the girl's back to propel her forward. Otherwise, she was afraid Emma might bolt.

Once everyone sat, Rachel asked Emma how she was doing. She got nothing more than a shrug for an answer. With a nod, Rachel glanced at Olivia, the same question in her eyes. Olivia answered with a slight shake of her head. That seemed enough for the principal. She opened a file on her desk and perused a few sheets of paper, then said, "It's obvious that Emma loves English and history and struggles a little in science and math. But her grades from Blakely Academy are solid. I anticipate she will do well at Phoebe Simpson High."

Olivia could only hope Rachel was right.

"Emma, would you mind waiting outside? I would like to speak privately with your mother for a few minutes."

Without answering, Emma rose and left the office.

Rachel got up and closed the door. Turning, she asked, "How is she **really** doing?"

"She's angry and confused. She doesn't want to be here. She liked her boarding school in Florida and the life-style her dad provided." The words tasted bitter on Olivia's tongue. "I've become a stranger to her. I think she blames me for the choices her dad made. She doesn't understand that I had no control over anything he did."

"You'll have the summer to get used to each other before school starts. But if I may, I suggest the two of you get some counseling. As soon as possible. She's grieving, and moving back to Idaho is an enormous change on top of losing her father."

Olivia nodded.

"Perhaps you know Adam Green."

This time she shook her head.

"Adam is a licensed counselor. He had his practice in eastern Idaho for many years, but when he retired, he moved back to Bethlehem Springs. He still sees the occasional client here in town. I think he could help Emma get through these difficult first months." Rachel's expression softened. "And he should be able to help you as well. If you like, I can give him a call."

"Yes. I...I'm willing to try anything."

Rachel returned to her chair behind the desk. "It will get better, Olivia. It may not feel like it now, but it will."

From his SUV in the parking lot, Tyler saw the girl exit the high school. Before she turned away, he caught a glimpse of her face. Enough to know it was Emma Ward and that she was angry. Obviously the meeting with the principal hadn't gone well. At least not in her mind. He watched, but Olivia Ward didn't follow through the doorway. Not yet, anyway. Emma walked toward the track and football field behind the building, disappearing from view. Perhaps this was the opportunity he'd hoped for when he'd learned the Wards had an appointment at the school today.

He got out of his vehicle and strolled toward the track and field. He wore running shorts and shoes, attire that he often found helpful when attempting to meet strangers. Without looking to where Emma now sat on a set of silver bleachers, he stretched before starting his run. After running twice around the track, Emma was still in the same place. He slowed and began to walk. Twice around the track wasn't even a half mile, but another time around might cost him a chance for an introduction.

Reaching the end of the straightaway, he turned and started back. That was when Olivia Ward appeared. She walked toward her daughter, said something, then sat on the row in front of

Emma. Even from where Tyler was, he could read misery on both of their faces.

Questions filled his head. Tyler hadn't learned much of any use from Mary Ellen Foster. Apparently Olivia Ward didn't do a lot of mingling with the locals, although she didn't sound completely antisocial. He knew she had her own business and worked from home. He knew she sometimes attended Cornerstone Community Church, the place he called his church home. In fact, he'd noticed her there even before he'd been assigned this case, although he hadn't known her name. Everything else he knew had come from Peter Ward, the firm's client, and experience had taught Tyler not to take everything he heard from the client at face value.

Now all he needed was a reason to talk to the mother and daughter. He glanced at his wrist, then quickly removed his watch and slipped it into his pocket, all the while moving slowly closer to the bleachers. When Olivia made eye contact with him, he said, "Morning."

Olivia gave him a curt nod.

"Could I trouble you for the time?"

Emma glanced at her phone and answered him.

"Thanks." His gaze shifted back to Olivia. "I'm Tyler Murphy." He had better sense than to offer his hand. "I live just outside of town."

Olivia didn't introduce herself, but she did give him another nod.

He smiled, as if not noticing her lack of reply or the cool reception. "Thanks again." He gave a small wave and walked away, headed for the parking lot. At least she knew who he was now. The next time they met would be easier.

He got into his SUV. He could have walked to the school from the B&B if his only goal had been to create a chance meeting with the Wards. But he wanted to drive to his house today to check on the remodel. He should go now. He didn't want Olivia to catch him lingering in the parking lot.

Still, he didn't start the engine at once. Instead, his thoughts shifted to his sister. Christa Murphy, three years younger than Tyler, had been a sullen, angry teenager. Maybe that's why he'd easily recognized the expression on Emma Ward's face. It was a look that Christa had worn often. As a teen. As a young adult. He'd loved her, but he'd failed her. If only he'd known how to help. If only he'd done more. If only he could have stopped her before it was too late. If only...

But there was no going back. He couldn't change the difficult childhood they'd both endured. He couldn't change the injustice or the instability. Nor could he change the path she'd chosen. The past was what it was.

He released a breath and reached to turn the key in the ignition, wanting to drive away from the painful memories.

Tyler's house was not quite three

quarters of a mile outside of town. The conifer forest thickened as the road climbed steadily upward. Homes of varying shapes, sizes, and ages were tucked in among the lodgepole and ponderosa pines, the Douglas firs, and the western larch. The air coming in through the open window smelled fresh. No hot city odors here. That was only one of the reasons he'd relocated a year ago to this community in the mountains.

Three trucks were parked in his driveway when he arrived, and two men were up on the roof of the house while two more stood on the deck. Tyler parked the SUV and got out of the vehicle.

"Hey, Tyler," Bert Collins, the contractor, called to him.

"Hey, Bert." He strode toward the house.

"Glad you came by. We've got a question for you."

Emma picked at a hangnail on her left

thumb, fighting against the tears that threatened.

"Emma," her mom said at last. "I know this is hard for you. Your whole life has changed. Suddenly and completely. I know you loved your dad, and you haven't had time yet to grieve his passing. I know you feel like a stranger, with me and in your new home. I want to make things easier for you. I want to help you get through all of...this. But I need you to meet me partway. Just be willing to try."

"Why couldn't we stay in Florida? You could work there."

"You know why. We couldn't afford it. We wouldn't have anyplace to live. No car. No home. Nothing. And you couldn't stay at Blakely either."

"I don't believe it. There must've been something you could do."

"You're wrong. There wasn't anything. Your dad...Your dad didn't leave any provisions for you to stay."

Emma sucked in a breath, willing

anger to replace sorrow. "I hate this place. There's nothing to do here."

"You don't know that. We've only been back one night."

"I don't know anybody."

Her mom shifted position. "You'll make friends. You just need time and opportunity."

"Why won't you let me go home?"

"Because you don't have a home in Florida any longer. The house belongs to...to someone else now."

Anger fled, and Emma had to choke back her tears. "Why did Dad do that to me?"

"He didn't do it to you, honey. He didn't know he was going to die. He didn't plan for it. It just happened."

He didn't love you, a voice whispered in Emma's head. **He didn't really want you.**

Mom hadn't wanted her either. That's what Dad had told her, time and again. Dad had taken her to Florida because Mom didn't have room for her and didn't

want her around. And now Emma had
landed back in her mom's lap, wanted
or not. Mom pretended it was okay, but
how long would that last?

**I don't have anybody who cares.
Not anybody.**

May 22, 1932
Sunday

At church this morning, I finally got to meet six more members of Harry's family: Fred and his wife, Rose, and their children. The brothers look a great deal alike, despite the thirteen years in age that separates them. Fred and Rose weren't able to be at our wedding. They already lived in Idaho by then, and that was too far and too costly to travel, especially since Rose had just had a baby.

While the brothers have the same height and coloring, Fred is heavier than Harry. He smiles more and laughs more too. Despite the hardship of these times, Fred seems to put more trust in God to see him and his family through. Harry often seems drained of his faith in the Almighty. It hurts me to see him like that. When I first fell in love with him, he seemed to bubble over with the love of God. (He would want me to find a more dignified way to describe him.)

Harry says he wishes now that we'd moved to Idaho in the first place, instead of going to California. He says maybe things would have been different here, better here. Maybe we wouldn't have lost everything. But I wonder if that's true. Would Dottie be healthier if she had been born here instead of California? Would we have been able to buy our own land, to build our own house? There is no way to know the answers to such questions, and it serves no purpose to wonder what might have been. I try to tell him that, but he doesn't seem to hear me.

After church, Fred and Rose took us to their farm for Sunday dinner. It was good to sit around a large table, to eat with members of our family, to talk about something more besides the Depression. I loved seeing my girls with their older cousins. Fred's oldest boy, Freddie Jr., took both Gladys and Dottie for a ride on one of their horses. A big old draft horse called Sunrise. Dottie squealed with delight because of how high up she was. Oh, it did my heart good to see her so happy. There was color in her cheeks and a sparkle in her eyes. Something I haven't seen in far too long.

Thank You, Father, for Your mercy. Thank You for the gift of

children. They truly are a blessing, as the Bible says.

May 25, 1932
Wednesday

The corn is only a few inches high at this time, so the fields around our little house look almost bare. Harry says it should be about knee-high by the Fourth of July, and we'll be harvesting in August or September. With the permission of the land owner, he may change to another crop or even two next year. Fred has done well in alfalfa hay, even with the Depression. Those who have cattle and horses must feed their animals.

I try to be content, but I miss stepping out my front door and seeing the orchards, the straight rows of fruit-bearing trees. I didn't know how much I loved the sight of them until they were gone. There are two apple trees and three cherry trees on this property. I don't know how much fruit grows on them, and there is no one to ask. So I must wait and see.

I planted a vegetable garden that will produce food for us in late summer and early autumn. I hope I will get to see Harry's crops grow for a good spell to come. But our lease is from year to year. That does make me feel less anchored and secure. I want to feel safe here. I don't.

But weren't those feelings of permanence and security false anyway? Even though we owned our land in California, we found ourselves adrift.

We must be anchored in Christ, not in the things of this world. Christ is the only security.

Help me, Father, to remember that Jesus is my security, not the things of this world. Not even the people of this world. Only You.

Chapter 5

Tyler called Peter Ward on Friday morning. "I'm afraid I don't have much to report," he said after they'd exchanged greetings. "Emma and her mother have been back in Bethlehem Springs for three days. On Wednesday they went to the school to register for next year, and I managed to arrange an opportunity to introduce myself. A chance encounter, as far as they knew. Ms. Ward seems to be well liked in the community. She doesn't socialize a lot, but she isn't a stranger around town either. She occasionally attends the same church I do. I could be wrong, but I don't believe she recognized me from there."

"And the girl," Peter asked. "What about her?"

"From the little I observed, I would say she isn't happy at the moment. But that's to be expected, given the circumstances."

"Yes. I suppose it is."

Tyler's employer had been retained to learn more about Olivia Ward, to see if she was a fit mother for Peter Ward's granddaughter, but Tyler wished to know more about the client as well. Peter was a man in his seventies and had money of his own, although nothing that came close to the wealth Daniel Ward had acquired in his lifetime. Or at least appeared to have acquired. He knew that Peter and Daniel had been estranged for more than two decades, and that had kept Peter from knowing his daughter-in-law or granddaughter. What had caused that estrangement? Was the man trustworthy, or was he more like his son?

Tyler gave his head a slight shake, clearing the questions. "As we discussed before, Mr. Ward, finding the information you want is going to take time. Especially given the parameters you've set."

"Yes, yes. I understand that. I'm willing to wait. I've waited fifteen years already."

"Have you considered driving up and introducing yourself? You might get your answers sooner rather than later."

"I have considered it, but I'm convinced this is the better way. At least for now."

The firm wouldn't like Tyler talking a client out of work that generated billable hours. It was time to keep his opinions to himself. "All right, then. I'll call with another update next Friday."

"I'll look forward to it."

They said their goodbyes, and Tyler placed the handset back in its cradle. Afterward he opened his laptop, checked and answered emails, then made a few more notations in the Ward file before opening his browser and doing relevant searches for another case he was working. An easier case than the one involving the Wards. He just wasn't sure...

He'd met Peter Ward not long after the man received the news about his son's death. Tyler's instincts told him Peter was well intentioned. But that didn't mean Tyler thought he was right to interfere in his daughter-in-law's and granddaughter's lives. If Emma was in danger, that was one thing, but nothing he'd uncovered about Olivia would suggest it. Emma's way of life had been dramatically altered. That was true. But did that mean it was for the worst? He didn't think so.

On the other hand, he knew only too well that appearances could be deceiving. He'd watched his last foster parents put on a good show for others, then turn into monsters when no one else was around. If that personal experience wasn't enough, his years as an investigator had taught him even more about the dark underbelly of the world. His work too often included custody cases, and he'd seen some ugly divorces. Daniel and Olivia Ward's divorce had been contentious in the extreme, and it didn't take an expert to know that wealth and political power had won the day. Olivia hadn't stood a chance. She could have been a bona fide saint, and it wouldn't have made any difference to the outcome. She'd lost everything— home, money, friends, and custody of her daughter. From what Tyler had uncovered thus far, she hadn't deserved any of it. Not in the slightest.

He rose from the chair and went to the window of his room in the B&B. Outside, Bethlehem Springs lay quiet. From where he stood, he could see the band shell in the park as well as the high school across the street from it. Maybe he should go for another run. A real one this time. Clear his head. Most of the time, Tyler managed to keep an emotional distance from the cases he worked. That wasn't proving true for the Ward case. It felt...personal. He wasn't sure why.

No. Not entirely true. He knew what it was like to lose everything. Everything. Home. Security. People he loved. Sure, he'd been a kid when it happened to him, and he'd understood less of what was happening at the time. But he could still tap into those feelings. Even from a distance, he'd recognized the same emotions on the faces of mother and daughter when he'd seen them at the school track.

He returned to the desk and reopened a website on his laptop browser. The photo of Olivia staring back at him looked to be fairly recent. She was an attractive woman. No denying that. And she looked younger than her thirty-nine years. Her long dark hair was curly, and she wore it swept up on her head. Her hazel eyes looked more brown in this photograph. Too bad the photographer hadn't captured the glint of gold he knew was there.

Something he did see in the photograph—unwanted, no doubt—was a shadow of sorrow. Olivia Ward had slowly remade her life over the past six years, but the absence of her daughter had left an ache she couldn't hide. Maybe now that Emma was back, she wouldn't need to hide it. It would be gone for good.

Unless Tyler found something he didn't want to find.

"I'm going to the store," Olivia called up the stairs. "Do you want to go with me?"

At first there was no answer, but finally she heard Emma reply, "No."

She shook her head. For the past two days she'd listened to her daughter complain that there was nothing to do. Yet when invited to get out of the house, she refused.

Maybe it was just as well Olivia could get away by herself for a few minutes.

She grabbed her car keys and purse and headed outside. In the winter she parked her Outback in the small detached garage. But in the summer it sat in the driveway, shaded by the tall trees. That allowed her to be on her way into town in a matter of minutes.

The Merc sat on the corner of Wallula and Idaho Streets. Like much of the town, it retained its Old West appearance, but in most ways it was a modern grocery store. It had good produce, meat, and bakery departments. It carried all of the required snack foods to clog one's arteries and enough sweets to give one a sugar high that would last a week. Olivia headed for those two aisles first, feeling a desperate need for things both sweet and salty and not necessarily good for her.

As she moved a bag of barbecue chips into her cart, she wondered if Emma liked them. She used to, but did she like them still? Maybe girls who lived in elite boarding schools didn't eat chips. Maybe it was all health foods or gluten-free or low-fat or low-carb.

She stopped still and closed her eyes. **I don't know my own daughter. God, help me.**

Would He? Would God help her? After so much silence on her end. After so much anger. Also on her end.

A cart rounded the end of the aisle and nearly collided with hers. "Sorry."

She looked up at a man who seemed familiar, although she couldn't place him. He was about average height with thick brown hair and a close-trimmed beard.

He grinned. "Well, hello again."

She looked at him, still unable to place where she'd seen him.

"You were at the track the other day. With your daughter or your kid sister." He placed his hand on his chest. "I'm Tyler Murphy. I was running laps that day."

"Yes, I remember now, Mr. Murphy."

He watched her with expectation in his chocolate-brown eyes.

Reluctantly she answered, "I'm Olivia Ward."

"Nice to meet you. Are you new to Bethlehem Springs?"

She shook her head. "No. I've lived here for six years."

"Wow. Can't believe we've never met." His smile broadened. "I moved here a little over a year ago. Wanted to escape the rat race."

"Did you?"

"Did I what?"

"Escape the rat race."

He laughed. It made the corners of his eyes crinkle. An appealing look. "Afraid not."

Olivia returned his smile. She couldn't help it. It was somewhat contagious.

Tyler Murphy pulled back his cart, then rolled it around her. "Hope to see you again, Ms. Ward."

It wasn't until after he'd turned at the

far end of the aisle, disappearing from view, that she realized she hadn't let him know Emma was her daughter and not her kid sister. Not that it mattered. If they'd gone a year without meeting each other, she might very well never see him again.

She resumed her shopping, steering her cart toward the produce area. She already had enough junk food to satisfy the cravings she'd felt upon entering the store. Now it was time for some "real" food. She would start with fresh fruits and vegetables.

Tyler Murphy was also in the produce department, testing the firmness of plums. So much for not seeing him again. She acknowledged his presence with a quick but dismissive smile before turning her attention to celery hearts and organic carrots.

"Can I bother you a second?"

Startled by his sudden nearness, she turned to face him.

"Do you know anything about cantaloupes?"

"Cantaloupes?"

He held one up in his right hand. "How do you know if they're ripe? I usually buy them already cubed, but sometimes those aren't very good. Not to mention they're pricey."

Men. She took the melon from his hand. "You want one that's oblong or round. Avoid anything that has dents or punctures." She moved it up and down in the air. "It should have a good weight. If it feels hollow or too light, it isn't any good." She held the fruit closer to her ear and rapped it with her knuckles. "You want a low, deep sound when you knock on it." Finally, she held it toward him. "This one should be good."

"So I was right. You're a cantaloupe expert."

The notion made her laugh, and as his smile broadened, her pulse quickened. The reaction surprised her. It had been a long time since she'd felt a pull of attraction to a man. Any man. She took a step back, the laughter dying in her throat.

He sobered as well. "I appreciate your help. If I can ever return the favor..." He let the offer drift into silence before turning and walking back to his own shopping cart.

"If I can ever return the favor..."

The memory of Tyler's voice resonated deep inside of Olivia, and she felt the need to flee the store as quickly as she'd wanted to flee her daughter less than an hour before. She selected vegetables with haste and hurried toward the checkout aisles.

May 28, 1932
Saturday

I told Harry about the baby.
I didn't have a choice. He
came back to the house and
heard me being sick. But it was
time he knew. With my other
pregnancies, I couldn't wait a
second to tell him. This time feels
so different. He seemed happy
with the news, and yet I am not
sure. Does the news only add to
his burden? The Bible says that a
man is blessed with a full quiver.
Children are a blessing from the
Lord. But does Harry worry, like
I do, that we might not be able
to provide for our little ones? Will
there be enough food, enough
heat, enough clothing? I think he

does worry, although he doesn't speak such things aloud. Not to me.

I will see the local doctor next week. His name is Dr. Redenbacher. Rose tells me he is nice and has a comforting manner. He delivered three of her four children, and all of them are healthy and thriving. I will take Dottie with me to the appointment. She seems better, but I would like to hear that a doctor believes the same.

Dr. Hazelton back home was rather taciturn. He wasn't the sort of man one wanted to share stories with. But I trusted him as a physician. He was the first to realize how sick Dottie was. If we hadn't taken her to the hospital on his advice, she wouldn't have lived through the next few days. She definitely wouldn't be with us now.

"Back home." I'm still writing that. I must stop. I must redirect my heart. I must stop longing for what used to be.

June 1, 1932
Wednesday

Dr. Redenbacher is as nice as Rose said. And he is younger than I expected. Perhaps he is in his late thirties. I am used to physicians with graying beards and thinning hairlines. Dr. Redenbacher is clean shaven, handsome, and has a full head of dark-brown hair. And he's kind. Very kind.

He listened so patiently as I detailed Dottie's history. After his examination he told me some ways to encourage her to eat more, as she remains under-weight. He said that isn't un-expected, given what she went through, her many days in the hospital and how sick she was.

But he would like to see her put on a few pounds. He also recommended that she play out in the sunlight for thirty minutes to an hour every day. She will think that is a wonderful prescription. She is tired of being told to rest.

As for me, the doctor sees no reason to expect anything other than a normal pregnancy and delivery. As I suspected, the baby should come around the first of the year.

I am hoping for a son for Harry. He says it doesn't matter to him. He loves his daughters, a truth that I see every day. Still, the time will come when a boy would be such a help in working the farm with Harry. Such is the way of the world, a son following in his father's footsteps. It was that way with my family and with Harry's family. So it will be with ours, God willing.

June 12, 1932
Sunday

I have successfully memorized
The Gift of the Magi. It took far
longer than expected. I thought
about memorizing it months
ago, but with Dottie's illness
and our move to Idaho and all
of the other upheaval in our lives,
I forgot to even try. But I started
working on it a few weeks ago,
and finally I've done it.

Today, after church, I recited
it for Rose while we prepared
Sunday dinner for our families.
Before I reached the end, she
sat down at the table to listen
undisturbed. She applauded
when I reached the end and
insisted I must perform it in

December at the Christmas Eve service. I am not sure that is a good idea. After all, I will be in my ninth month of pregnancy by then. But Rose refused to take no for an answer. She said it will bless everyone.

Is it sinful, how proud I am that I could recite the entire short story from memory?

Chapter 6

Junk food—whether sweet or salty—didn't help Olivia when it came to dealing with Emma's moods.

In the following days she felt her nerves fraying with each encounter. Her daughter spent most of the time shut in her bedroom. But when forced to come down the stairs to get something to eat, she was either silent or surly. Olivia longed for the cherubic girl of her memories, the smiling, agreeable, laughing child who'd wanted to spend time with her mama. But that girl had disappeared while in Florida and wouldn't be returning. Even if Emma suddenly decided she loved her mom again and loved living in Bethlehem Springs—oh, if only she had enough faith to believe those things would happen—that little girl of her memories was gone for good. She needed to accept that fact.

Adam Green, the counselor recommended by Rachel Hamilton, called Olivia on Friday morning. "I can meet with the two of you on Wednesday mornings at ten, if that's a good time," he said after a brief conversation.

"Yes, that's a good time." She was so desperate she would have met with him at midnight, but she didn't tell him that.

He gave directions to his office on Bear Run Road, and then they ended the call.

After placing the handset in its cradle, Olivia looked up at the closed door to Emma's room, wondering if she should tell her daughter in advance that they would meet with a counselor together or if she should wait and spring it on her next Wednesday morning.

"I'll wait," she said aloud before heading into her work studio.

For several hours she managed to lose herself in a current project, not even stopping long enough to refill her coffee mug. It was the doorbell that broke her concentration. She'd risen from her chair when she heard the sounds of Emma's rapid descent on the stairs. Olivia smiled. Something more than hunger had brought Emma out of her lair. Good to know.

Olivia stepped into the kitchen in time to see Emma open the front door. Whoever was on the deck said, "A package for Emma Ward."

"That's me."

"Sign here."

Curiosity pulled Olivia into the living room as Emma signed the electronic pad. "What is it?" she asked a moment later.

"It's from a friend at school." Emma

clutched the medium-sized box to her chest and headed for the stairs.

"Emma, wait."

Her daughter stopped and turned, defiance in her eyes.

"I'd like to know what's in the box."

"It isn't any of your business."

It was tempting to give in, to let it go, to be left in the dark. But something told her she had to be firm. "You're wrong there. I'm your mom. It is my business what comes into my home. I don't know your friends. I don't know what they might send you."

"Whose fault is that?"

Your dad's. Somehow she stopped the words in her head from leaving her mouth.

Emma turned as if to start up the stairs again.

"Bring it to the kitchen table. I have a box knife. You can open it there."

After releasing a huff of air, Emma did as she was told.

Olivia wasn't sure why she was determined to see the box's contents. It was probably nothing. And perhaps it was wrong to insist. Emma was fifteen. She should have some rights to privacy. But the past few weeks had filled her with not only frustration but distrust. Daniel's betrayal of Emma shouldn't have surprised Olivia, but it had. And to make matters worse, she found herself living with a stranger. An angry, petulant stranger.

Emma took the box knife Olivia provided and sliced open the tape. Olivia resisted the urge to step forward and peer inside the box once the lid was open.

"Go on. Look." Emma began removing items and setting them on the table. "Regina borrowed this sweater so she returned it. They found this necklace under my bed after I was gone. These are some books I missed when I left. And I did these paintings in art class." She held up the box to show it was empty, shaking it over the table. "Satisfied?"

Olivia wouldn't let herself feel guilty. "Yes." She motioned to a chair. "But sit down. We need to talk."

"You always want to talk," Emma grumbled.

"And yet somehow we rarely do." She pulled out a chair for herself. "Please."

With another huff, Emma complied.

"Sweetheart, please listen to me." Olivia paused, hoping for a nod or anything that signaled consent. Nothing changed. Not her daughter's posture or expression. Not a sound. Nothing. She drew a breath and began. "Emma, I can't change what happened in the years since your dad took you away from Idaho. If he hadn't taken you to Florida, you and I would have been together every other weekend. I would have come to your school events. We would have known each other so much better. Do you remember what it was like, right after the divorce when you came to stay with me in this house?"

Emma shrugged, her gaze locked on the table.

"It wasn't perfect, but we had fun when we were together. Then your dad moved across the country and took you with him. I didn't have the money to fly to Florida to see you the way I would have liked. I was barely getting by. And when you came to see me those first few summers, the visits were so short. Then you stopped coming altogether."

"I was busy."

"I missed you. I waited the whole year for those weeks in the summer."

A look of surprise crossed Emma's face. As if she didn't believe what she'd heard.

Olivia swallowed the resentment that rose inside. This was about her relationship with her daughter, not about the wrongs Daniel had done. "You and I used to FaceTime each other every weekend. Remember? And then you stopped that too."

"I had a life."

Olivia took another slow, deep breath and released it. "Believe it or not, I had a life too. A very different one from what I expected when I married your dad and then had you, but it was still a life. And now we can make a new one together. You and me."

Emma grunted.

She counted to ten in her head. Maybe it was time to offer something she hoped would interest Emma. "There's a play at the community amphitheater tonight. I can get us tickets."

"A play?" Emma glanced up, a glimmer of curiosity in her eyes. But it vanished quickly as she crossed her arms over her chest. "I don't want to go."

Olivia felt her own temper about to snap. "You're going anyway. Sometimes in life we don't get to choose. This is one of those times for you. You need to get out of your room and off your devices. You need fresh air and to meet some people." Olivia knew her daughter had been in several plays at school in the past two or three years. Not that she'd seen the plays in real time, but she had seen photographs after the events and even a couple of short video clips. Last year, the drama instructor had told Olivia in an email that Emma was a talented young actress. Hopefully this was something that would bring Emma out of herself.

As if in answer to that thought, Emma said, "Couldn't be any good. I won't like it."

"Perhaps not. Although I know the company has quite an excellent repu-tation. People drive up from Boise to see these productions all summer long."

Emma's eyes narrowed.

"We'll pack food to eat for our dinner and go early. Everyone does. You'll want a jacket and blanket, as it will get cool after the sun goes down."

"All right. If I have to go, I guess it's okay."

Olivia hid her relief. "Be ready to leave at five."

Tyler hadn't been to a Bethlehem Springs Mountain Theater production in years. Over a decade. He'd purchased two tickets last summer, planning to bring a date, but the woman he'd been seeing at the time had canceled at the last minute, and Tyler hadn't felt like going alone.

He wouldn't have a date tonight, either, but he was going for a different purpose. A little bird—by the name of Mary Ellen Foster—had told him he should go, and then had told him the names of local residents she'd sold tickets to that very same day. Olivia's name was among them. That was all he needed to hear to fork over the price of one ticket.

The amphitheater was located on Skyview Street. A gentle slope closest to the stage had been tiered, making it easy for the audience to use short-legged lawn chairs or to place blankets on the ground for seating. Higher up, there were rows of plastic chairs on concrete for people who didn't want to bring their own. The forest provided a partial backdrop for the stage already set for the opening scene of the play.

When he entered through the side entrance at 5:15 p.m., he found many were there before him. The air was alive with voices and laughter as people ate picnic dinners and drank wine and other beverages.

"May I help you find your seat?" a girl of about seventeen asked. She wore attire straight out of the late eighteen hundreds, no doubt meant to go along with the play for that night, **The Importance of Being Earnest**.

Tyler showed her his ticket stub.

She smiled. "Right this way."

He followed, carrying his blanket, jacket, and the fried chicken and four-bean salad, along with eating utensils, that Mary Ellen had graciously provided.

"No need for you to go buy something to eat," she'd said. **"I've got extra."**

The volunteer usher stopped. "This is your seat." She pointed to the grass right next to the aisle. On a concrete strip at the edge of the tier was a marker with row and seat position on it.

"Thanks." As he put his blanket on the ground, his gaze fell on the people in front of him, and he felt his breath catch in surprise. How perfect was that? Olivia and Emma Ward. He couldn't have planned the setup better.

"Hey, Tyler."

He looked to his right to find Greg Dover, a friend from his Tuesday-morning men's group.

"Haven't seen you here before," Greg added.

"No. It's been a while." He frowned in thought. "Last production I came to was **The Tempest**. At least ten years ago."

Greg looked to his right. "You remember my wife, Kathy."

"Yes, of course." He smiled at her. "We've talked at church a few times."

Greg said, "Kathy serves on the theater company's board of directors." There was a note of pride in his voice.

From the corner of his eye, Tyler saw Emma turn to look behind her, taking in both him and the Dovers. It was an opportunity he couldn't let pass. "Well, hi there." His gaze moved to Olivia, who had turned her head as well. "Good to see you again. Tyler Murphy, in case you forgot." He put his hand on his chest, looked at Emma again, then motioned to his side. "And this is Greg and Kathy Dover."

Olivia's smile was tight. "Kathy and I are friends."

That was information he'd somehow missed, and for a moment he couldn't think of what to say.

"And I'm Emma." The girl's eyes went to Kathy. "So you work with the company? I didn't know that when Mom introduced us."

"Yes, I volunteer with them. We attend each play every summer. They do four. One each in June, July, August, and September."

"Is the company made up of all local actors?"

"Not all. Some of them live in the valley, and they come up for the season. But many of them live here year-round. The director of the company does." Kathy's gaze swept the theater, then returned to Emma. "I remember your mom telling me that you were in a number of plays at your old school."

"Yeah." Emma turned to put her knees on the seat of her chair, giving her a better view of Kathy Dover.

And Tyler a better view of Emma.

"Do you know if they're still looking for cast members for this summer?" the girl asked.

That morning, he'd told Peter Ward that Emma was an unhappy girl, but she didn't look unhappy now.

"I can't say for sure." Kathy leaned slightly forward. "But there's the director over there. Would you like to meet him? He doesn't look overwhelmed with duties at the moment."

"Could I? I'd love to meet him." Emma turned the opposite direction to look at her mom. "Is it okay?"

Olivia's smile told the story of her relief. "Of course. Go ahead. Thank you, Kathy."

As soon as Kathy and Emma moved away, Tyler said to Olivia, "Your daughter sure got excited. She must want to be an actress."

"Looks that way, doesn't it?" Her gaze followed Emma to the far side of the amphitheater.

"She sounded like she doesn't know anything about the company. Hasn't she been to any of their productions before tonight?" He knew the answer, of course, but he tried to sound puzzled.

The smile on Olivia's face faded. "No, she's never been. She was with her father in Florida for a number of years, but now she's come back to live with me."

Tyler noticed that she didn't mention the death of Daniel Ward as the reason for her daughter's relocation. Not that she should have talked about it to a stranger. Still, he wondered what her feelings were about her ex-husband's demise and the shambles he'd left behind.

Greg interrupted Tyler's thoughts when he asked Olivia, "How is Emma adapting?"

"It hasn't been easy." Her shoulders rose and fell on a sigh. "She's been angry and confused, and she blames me for how much her circumstances have changed."

"Big adjustment," Greg remarked.

"Yes." She looked across the amphitheater again. "For both of us."

Tyler didn't consider himself a sentimental sort. He definitely wasn't a soft touch. But her words, her tone, made his heart constrict, and he wished he could do something to make things easier for her and Emma.

July 5, 1932
Tuesday

Yesterday was Independence Day, and Harry took us into Thunder Creek for the festivities. There was a parade (short but fun) and games in the town park. The men played baseball. Freddie Jr. hit a home run, and all of the girls around his age were making eyes at him. Dottie and Gladys ran around with other children. There was so much food, no one who attended had any excuse to go home hungry. And the fireworks were beautiful, although they didn't last long enough for me. Fireworks, Fred reminded us, don't come cheap (he was on the committee, so I guess he knows).

We came home with the girls fast asleep in the back of the car. After putting them to bed, Harry and I sat on the porch and looked at the stars, enjoying the cooling air and holding hands. For that little bit it was easy to feel like things were just as they are supposed to be. As if money isn't a worry. As if Dottie is as healthy as any other little girl her age.

It was a good night.

I forgot to write in this diary about our anniversary. It was on the first of July. We don't have money to spare, and we both understood we couldn't do anything foolish to celebrate the occasion. I don't have luxurious long hair to cut and sell, and he doesn't have a fancy gold watch to barter either. (Oh, how I love that O. Henry story.) But Harry brought me a bouquet of the prettiest wildflowers, and I made him his favorite supper. It was enough.

Four years already. So much has happened since the day we married. We've moved twice. I've given birth twice. We owned our own land, and we lost our own land.

I love Harry more today than ever. My sister thought Harry was too old for me. He was twenty-five on our wedding day to my sixteen years. But it felt right to me then, and it feels right to me now. I feel safe with him.

If only I knew how to lift his burdens, to lighten the load on his shoulders.

God, is there a way for me to do that?

July 11, 1932
Monday

I am so excited. A package came from Iowa, and Fred delivered it to our farm this afternoon. It was addressed to both Harry and me, an anniversary gift from his parents and mine.

"It's really for you," Harry said when he saw what it was. Oh, he knows me well. As do those who love us.

It is a book. A book of poetry by Elizabeth Barrett Browning. It is beautifully bound. It is not new, of course, but it has been well cared for. I wonder if it had to be sold for lack of money. It could not have brought the price it was worth, or our parents could not have afforded to buy it. I will treasure it always.

Harry said maybe I could memorize some of the poems too. I think he may be secretly proud of me for my accomplishment in memorizing the O. Henry short story. He's never said as much, but Harry is not effusive with his praise.

Perhaps I will try to memorize some of it. Perhaps something from the **Sonnets from the Portuguese.** I'm not sure I understand everything Miss Browning writes, but I do understand this:

If thou must love me, let it be
   for nought
Except for love's sake only.
   Do not say
"I love her for her smile—her
   look—her way
Of speaking gently,—for a trick

of thought
That falls in well with mine,
    and certes brought
A sense of pleasant ease on
    such a day"—
For these things in themselves,
    Belovèd, may
Be changed, or change for
    thee,—and love, so wrought,
May be unwrought so. Neither
    love me for
Thine own dear pity's wiping
    my cheeks dry,—
A creature might forget to weep,
    who bore
Thy comfort long, and lose thy
    love thereby!
But love me for love's sake,
    that evermore
Thou mayst love on, through
    love's eternity.

Chapter 7

During the performance that night, Olivia paid far more attention to Emma than to the play. The lights from the stage illuminated her daughter's face, letting her see the joy on it.

If only I'd known she'd love it this much.

Was it a sign that she was a bad mother, this ignorance? Yes, she'd known Emma liked her drama classes and had performed in a number of school productions at Blakely Academy. She'd known Emma's latest instructor thought Emma talented. But she hadn't known a night at the theater would bring

her out of her dour mood so completely. Did the distance between Idaho and
Florida excuse Olivia for her lack of
understanding?

No. I should have known.

On the stage the character of Algernon Moncrieff said, "I haven't quite finished my tea yet! And there is still one
muffin left."

The other character groaned dramatically and sank onto a chair while Algernon continued eating.

The stage lights slowly dimmed on
the Manor House garden setting. To the
sounds of applause, the lights went up
on the amphitheater grounds, announc-
ing the intermission.

"Isn't he wonderful?" Emma asked
as she opened the program.

"Who?"

Emma's finger pointed to the name.
"Richard Merrimack. He's the actor
playing Algernon."

Voices began to buzz all around
them as audience members stood and

stretched.

"Yes. He's very good." Olivia was glad she'd watched enough of the play to reply with confidence.

"His timing is perfect." Emma rose from her chair and turned to face Kathy and her husband. "Mrs. Dover, has Richard Merrimack been with the company long?"

"A few years."

"Does he live in Bethlehem Springs?"

Kathy's smile grew. "He moved here last year. He works for a cattle ranch."

"A cattle ranch?" Olivia rose from her chair too.

"There's a large valley to the east of us, the other side of the river. That's where the Bedford ranch is."

"How did I not know that?"

Emma cast an irritated look in Olivia's direction, apparently not liking the interruption. "So Richard isn't an actor full-time?"

"No. He isn't."

"Does he want to be?"

Kathy shook her head. "I really don't know. I suppose if he did, he wouldn't have moved to Bethlehem Springs. He would have moved to Los Angeles instead."

"Maybe I could talk to him later," Emma said, hope in her voice. "He could tell me what it's like, acting with this company. He might have some advice for me. He's so good."

Olivia hated to put a damper on her daughter's excitement, but she also didn't want to take advantage of Kathy or Mr. Merrimack. "We know it can't be tonight," she said. "I'm sure the cast members are tired and busy once a performance is over. But perhaps you could introduce Emma to him another time?"

"Sure. Victor, the director, said Emma could audition next week for a role in the September play. I can ask for Richard to be present, if possible. Maybe to audition with her. I don't know if it'll happen, but I can ask."

Olivia couldn't quite read Emma's expression. Was it a mixture of excitement and impatience? Or maybe those were Olivia's own emotions.

Tyler Murphy spoke for the first time since the intermission began. "I'm getting one of those desserts they advertised on that sign on the way in. Anybody else interested?"

In unison Kathy and Greg said, "Yes."

Tyler looked at Olivia. "How about you two?"

"Oh, I wouldn't want you to—"

"Okay, five desserts it is." He stepped into the aisle and left before she had a chance to say more.

Olivia followed him with her eyes as he made his way out of the amphitheater to where the concession stand stood. She hadn't given him another thought after their brief encounter at the grocery store last week. She'd been focused on other matters. But seeing him tonight...Something about him made her feel...strange? Nervous?

Attracted to him?

The last possibility caused a quaver of alarm. She didn't want to be attracted to a man. Not any man. That was a prescription for disaster as far as she was concerned. Daniel had taught her that.

The sound of her daughter's voice broke through her thoughts, drawing her attention back to Emma and Kathy. They were talking about the performance and analyzing different scenes. Emma obviously knew this play well and was able to quote a number of its lines. Was this one of the plays she'd performed in at school?

Another wave of guilt washed through Olivia. She should know the names of every play Emma had been in and the names of the roles she'd played. Even if she'd had to obtain all of the information through the academy's office, she should have been more informed.

Her chest hurting, she sat down again, staring toward the darkened stage.

"Then I will compensate you for the years that the swarming locust has eaten."

She couldn't be sure where she'd heard those words. Sara or Kathy, more than likely. They sounded like something her friends would say while trying to encourage her. But even God couldn't make up for the years of Emma's life that Olivia had missed, nor the mistakes everyone involved in that situation had made. The past couldn't be undone. It couldn't be changed. Better choices today might change tomorrow, but the past was what it was.

A glance to her right showed that Emma was happier talking to a woman she'd just met than when she talked to her own mom. The ache in Olivia's chest increased. Would things ever be right between them?

O God, help me.

Emma wouldn't want to admit it to her

mom, but the evening had been just about perfect so far. She'd been certain an acting company in this little town would be totally lame. She'd been prepared to be bored out of her mind. But that hadn't happened.

In addition, Kathy Dover was nice and loved everything about the theater almost as much as Emma did. Her mom couldn't possibly understand any of the things they'd talked about. Plus, Kathy had already introduced her to the director, and Emma would get to audition for a part in the final play of the season. And there was also that promised introduction to Richard Merrimack, who was way too cute.

Not that **that** was why she wanted to meet him. No, she wanted to meet him because of his performance tonight. She knew this play and his part. She'd seen it performed by professional actors a couple of times, and she'd seen the movie version with Rupert Everett in the role of Algernon. But Richard

Merrimack was the best she'd seen yet. His timing. The inflection of his voice. That look he cast toward the audience at just the right moment. As far as drama was concerned, Emma learned best when observing other actors, and she was certain she could learn a lot from watching Richard.

She simply had to be part of this theater company. She had to. If for no other reason than it would make her summer in Bethlehem Springs somewhat tolerable.

The instant Tyler stepped back into the amphitheater, the cardboard tray he carried holding five desserts, he looked through the crowd, trying to see Olivia Ward. He caught a glimpse of Emma but not of her mom. Had she stepped out, perhaps gone to the ladies' room?

Only when he reached the aisle that would take him to his row did he see that she'd sat in her chair again, apparently not interested in the animated conversation the others were having. He didn't have to see her face to sense her dejection. Sympathy rose within him. Maybe he was wrong, but he thought he understood some of what she was going through. Since his sister's passing, he'd second-guessed many of his own actions, his own choices, his own words. Would Christa be alive today if he'd said or done something else? Would her last years have been happier ones? She hadn't been a child or a teenager, like Emma, but still he had to wonder if he could've made a difference.

Stepping from the aisle onto his blanket, he held out the tray of goodies toward the Dovers and Emma. They each took one of the chocolate confections. Then Tyler moved back into the aisle and went down one row to offer one of the two remaining desserts to Olivia. She looked up at him, and for a moment he thought she would refuse it. But she didn't.

"Thank you. This is generous."

"Not at all. Friends of Greg and Kathy's are friends of mine." As he spoke the words, he realized how much he wanted them to be true. He wanted this to be about more than his job, more than digging into this woman's personal life in order to please the client and his employers.

The house lights flickered, indicating the end of the intermission. Audience members began moving back to their seats on the ground, in the chairs, on the hillside. Tyler gave Olivia a quick nod and smile before returning to his blanket. A short while later, the lights went up on the stage. The setting had been changed without him taking notice of the activity. The actresses playing Gwendolen and Cecily stood at the imaginary window, looking out at the imaginary garden.

In an aristocratic British accent Gwendolen said, "The fact that they did not follow me at once into the house, as any one else would have done, seems to me to show that they have some sense of shame left."

Tyler looked at the back of the woman in front of him. Her head was bowed, so he knew she didn't watch the actors on the stage, and once again he wished he could do something to lift her spirits. But even if there was something, he couldn't do it tonight.

He returned his attention to the play.

September 2, 1932
Friday

This baby is active, often keeping me awake at night. I am much bigger now than I was with my first two at this same stage. Rose even wonders if I might have twins. Lord, have mercy. Where would we put two infants in this small house? Dr. Redenbacher said he cannot rule out twins, but he doesn't believe it is. He only discerned one heartbeat at my last visit.

How small is this life inside of me, but it still has a heartbeat. And I wonder, what plans does the Almighty have for him? Yes, I think it is a boy. Maybe because I carry him differently. Maybe because I am bigger than with the girls. Maybe none of that is a sign of anything. Yet still I believe this child is a boy.

One of my regrets is that my children will likely never know their grandparents. I had such a sweet relationship with mine, especially Grandma Agatha. She is the one who taught me to sew and to knit, and she was always present in the kitchen when there was baking to be done. I will have to teach Gladys and Dottie everything on my own. Well, not entirely on my own. Their aunt Rose is nearby. Still, Rose and Fred will be the oldest family members the children know. Fred is in his early forties and Rose in her late thirties. They are still raising children themselves. Grandparents have white hair and soft bellies and big smiles. They are grand storytellers.

At least that was true of my grandparents.

Strange to think that I will turn twenty-one before the baby is born, and Harry will turn thirty not long after the birth.

Heavenly Father, I pray for this unborn child and ask that You would give him a spirit of wisdom and revelation in the knowledge of Jesus. Enlighten the eyes of his heart so that he would know the hope of his calling in Christ from an early age until You call him home. Cause Harry to be a good and righteous father and me to be a loving and faithful mother. To this baby and to our daughters. Always and forever, amen.

October 3, 1932
Monday

Harry and Fred are both busy with the harvest, each helping the other on their respective farms. And despite our late-spring arrival to Idaho, my kitchen garden has done well. I have put by many cans of tomatoes and pickles and other vegetables, and the cherry and apple trees on the property have produced in abundance, so there will be no shortage of canned fruit and jams.

This morning Dottie seemed listless, and I wanted to call for the doctor. She's been so much more energetic over the summer. Each month seemed to bring a little improvement. Harry says I worry about her overly much. I try not to, but we came so close to losing her last winter. I didn't go to the neighbors to use their telephone. It is hard to come up with the money to pay the doctor for his services, so I listened to Harry. And tonight Dottie seemed herself again, so it would have been a waste if I'd insisted. Still, the fear creeps in sometimes.

Please, Father, don't let me fall into worry all the time. I know that You care for us. I know that You love Dottie as much as I do. More than I do. But she isn't strong. She's just a baby. Not even three years old. She doesn't talk much yet. The doctors in California said her time in the hospital has delayed some development but that she'll catch up, so I'm not to

worry (see, worry again). Still, it's hard for her to let me know what's wrong. She hasn't the words or understanding to express it. Help me, Lord, to know what's the right thing to do. Help me to act when I should and to sit still and trust when I shouldn't try to do something on my own. In Your precious Son's name I pray, amen.

Chapter 8

Tyler leaned his backside against the kitchen counter while sipping his first cup of coffee. While the remodel on his house wasn't finished yet, it was far enough along that he'd been able to return home the previous day. To his great relief. A little of Mary Ellen Foster went a long way. A nice woman, definitely, but she didn't seem to appreciate silence. If she was in the room, someone would be talking. Usually Mary Ellen herself.

He drew a deep breath and smiled. Silence truly was golden. But he couldn't enjoy it for long. Church would start in another hour, and Tyler managed the media booth, taking care of the slides needed throughout the service as well as several other tasks.

He drank the last of his coffee and set the mug in the sink, then headed outside.

The drive from his house in the forest to Cornerstone Community Church on the south side of Bethlehem Springs took less than ten minutes. Only a couple of cars sat in the parking lot before him. Once inside the church, he went to the media booth at the back of the sanctuary. The pastor found him there a short while later.

"Morning, Tyler."

"Morning, Steve."

Steve Morgan was a rail-thin man who wore dark-rimmed glasses, jeans, and cowboy boots. Although the two men were close to the same age, Steve seemed older to Tyler, probably because he had a wife and five daughters. Or perhaps it was his rapidly thinning hair.

"Saw you at the play on Friday night," Steve said.

"You were there? I didn't see you."

"I sit up in the chairs. Was this your first time? Don't think I've seen you there before."

Tyler opened one of the laptops on the desk, bringing it to life. "First time since I moved here, but I used to drive up from Boise to attend some of their plays."

"Glad Greg and Kathy managed to drag you there, then."

"They didn't. We just happened to get seats next to each other. Made for a nice evening."

"I saw you talking to Olivia Ward too."

Tyler glanced at the pastor. "Yes. We hadn't met before. But she knows Kathy and Greg."

"She attends church here on occasion."

Raising his eyebrows, as if surprised by the news, felt dishonest, but he'd done it before he could stop himself.

"I'm hoping now that her daughter is living with her, she'll make church more of a priority."

Questions tumbled in Tyler's head. Questions he didn't let himself ask. He might have to ask them later, but secretly grilling the pastor about one of his flock, especially on a Sunday morning, felt even more wrong than pretending he'd never noticed Olivia before this. True, he hadn't known who she was, but he had caught glimpses of her.

"Well," Steve said, "I'd better be off. Thanks for helping out every week. Don't know what we'd do without you. What you've managed to accomplish with our audio and visual over the past year amazes me."

Tyler nodded before returning his attention to the laptop, but the parting praise made him smile. It felt good to belong. Really belong.

Leaving his church home in Boise had been the only thing that made the move to Bethlehem Springs difficult.

He'd come to faith in Christ because of men in that church. He'd been made welcome when he was still broken, still angry, still a hurting mess. He'd been loved and mentored and discipled. He'd discovered men who showed him what it was like to have a loving father. He'd gained friends who became like brothers to him. Because of his church family, he'd ceased to be one man against the world, as he'd long felt himself to be. He'd found peace and so much more.

His thoughts went to his sister, and he felt the familiar sorrow that she'd never accepted Christ. When she would let him, he had shared the joy and forgiveness he'd found as a believer, but she'd mocked him or reviled him, depending on her mood of the moment. Sometimes he let himself hope that the seeds he'd planted might have borne fruit at the end of her life, like the thief on the cross. In her last moments of consciousness, she could have called upon Jesus to rescue her. There was a chance, if only a small one, that he would see her again in heaven.

Members of the worship team passed in front of the booth on their way to the preservice prayer time in the chapel. A couple of them greeted him. He smiled in return, glad to be pulled from his more somber thoughts.

Thanks for giving me a new church home.

He rose and followed the worship team, ready to meet the Lord in prayer with other members of the family of God.

"I don't **want** to go to church," Emma said, arms crossed over her chest.

Must you turn everything into a battle of wills?

"Dad never made me go to church."

"Your dad didn't think faith was important."

"He didn't believe in God. Neither do I."

A memory came to Olivia. Emma standing beside her in church, the little girl's eyes closed and her arms lifted in praise as she sang a worship song. Had Emma truly stopped believing what her heart had once told her was true?

Have I stopped believing what my **heart knows is true?** Olivia winced at the silent questions.

After a moment she tried a different tack. "You might see Mrs. Dover or Mr. Benson. You might have a chance to talk to them again after the service is over."

"**They** go to your church?"

"Yes, they do."

"Both of them?" There seemed to be a little less suspicion in Emma's voice.

"Yes. Both of them."

Emma was silent a long while before saying, "I guess I can go."

It was tempting to ask who was the mom and who was the daughter. Just who, exactly, was in charge? Then again, maybe she didn't want to hear her fifteen-year-old's answer to that.

"Great," Olivia said instead. "We'll leave in twenty minutes."

"Do I have to put on a dress?"

"No, honey. What you have on is fine."

"Good." Emma turned and hurried up the stairs and into the bathroom, closing the door behind her. Undoubtedly she wanted to check her makeup.

Olivia released another sigh as she walked to the large livingroom window. From this hillside her view of Bethlehem Springs was mostly unimpaired. There were plenty of trees beside and behind her house, but only a few below. From this window she could see the municipal building, the post office, the museum, and lots of other rooftops. Morning sunlight cast a golden glow over the little town she'd grown to love. She hadn't always felt that way about it. She hadn't appreciated that it was a place of refuge, a place to heal and to begin again. It had felt forced upon her by painful circumstances. It had seemed to point out her losses, her solitude, her poverty. But it didn't feel that way now. It had become home, for all its quirks and imperfections, including the people in it. She hoped Emma might eventually feel the same way about it.

And the best way to help that transformation begin, Olivia now believed, was to be a better friend to those who had befriended her. For Olivia, that would start by making church attendance a priority. Not just going on the occasional Sunday, as had been her habit. No, she needed to be an example to her daughter. She needed to live the way she wanted Emma to live.

I'll need Your help, Lord.

The bullet prayer sounded odd in her head—she'd prayed so few of them in recent years—but it wasn't, she realized, the first one she'd sent up recently. Perhaps she believed God listened after all.

Do You hear me, Lord? I need help, and lots of it.

Twenty-five minutes later, as Olivia and Emma entered through the main doors of Cornerstone Community, those same words repeated in her head. As if in answer to the desperate prayer, Kathy Dover stepped out of a room on the right side of the narthex. Surprise flickered across her face, and then she smiled.

"Well, hello again," she said, looking at Emma as she approached them. "I'm delighted you've joined your mom today."

Emma mumbled something in reply, but Olivia didn't catch what it was.

Kathy continued, "I'm still thinking what a delightful time we had on Friday night. Meeting you made it all the better."

"The play was really good."

"Do you plan to audition for a part in the September play?"

"You bet I do." Emma's face lit with excitement.

Kathy's gaze shifted to somewhere

beyond Olivia's shoulder. "Hailey, come here, please." She motioned with her hand before looking at Emma again. "Our daughter, Hailey, got home from college yesterday. Let me introduce you."

Hailey Dover had blossomed in her first year away from Bethlehem Springs. She had always been a pretty girl, but now she looked like a model straight out of some fashion magazine. She was tall and slender with green eyes and a full mouth, but Olivia thought her most striking feature was her curly auburn hair.

"Hailey," Kathy said, "you remember Olivia Ward."

"Of course. Nice to see you again, Ms. Ward."

"And this is her daughter, Emma. Emma has come to live in Bethlehem Springs."

Hailey's smile was warm. "Hi, Emma. Would you like to sit with me and some of the others from youth group?"

"Sure." Emma glanced at Olivia as if to ask if that was okay.

Olivia nodded and watched the girls walk away. It hurt that Emma would rather join a group of strangers than stay with her. It hurt her despite the fact that one of the reasons she'd brought her daughter to church in the first place was to meet new people. She'd wanted Emma to meet others close to her own age. Her daughter needed to make friends, and that shouldn't wait for fall and the start of school. She needed things to do and people to do them with over the summer or she would learn to resent Olivia even more than she did now.

"Are you okay?" Kathy asked softly.

"Not really."

"I thought you looked a little down on Friday. If you need to talk..." Kathy let the offer drift into silence.

Olivia nodded once again. "I'll take you up on that sometime."

"Anytime."

Tyler happened to look in the direction of the open sanctuary doors at the moment Emma Ward came through them, walking beside Greg Dover's oldest girl. He'd learned at the last men's group meeting that Hailey was supposed to return from college on Saturday. Obviously she'd made the trip home without mishap. He continued to watch as Hailey introduced Emma to other kids close to their ages, both guys and girls. Then the group made their way to a section in the sanctuary where they always sat.

He smiled to himself. Good for her. Good that she was getting acquainted with the young people at Cornerstone. They were a good bunch, from what he could tell. Not that kids who went to church didn't get into their share of trouble. But in Tyler's line of work, he'd learned that kids without anchors had a harder go of it.

He glanced back toward the doors in time to see Olivia enter the sanctuary.

He'd half expected her to be with Kathy, but she wasn't. She came in by herself, and for some reason he wished he could leave the media booth, go to her, make her feel less alone. Crazy for him to feel that way, but there it was.

"Hey, Tyler."

He looked in the opposite direction.

Brad Alcorn, the worship leader, stood right outside the booth. "Any chance I can add a song to the mix? I know it's last minute."

"No problem if there's a slide for it already."

"Should be." He named the song.

Tyler did a quick search on the laptop. "Yeah. I've got it."

"Put it in the last position."

"Done." With a quick drag-and-drop, he was ready.

"Thanks."

When Tyler looked toward the entrance doors again, Olivia was gone. He might have searched out where she sat, but the worship team took their places and Tyler had to focus on his media duties once again.

It's lame. Mom made me go to church this morning.

Why didn't you refuse?

She wouldn't let me.

Sorry. Miss you. Wish you could come back.

Me 2.

Talk later. Study group.

Emma dropped her phone onto the bed before flopping back on the pillows. She knew Regina wasn't off to meet with a study group. Her friend wasn't the study-group type. She was probably going somewhere with her boyfriend.

"It isn't fair."

The words seemed to bounce around the small bedroom.

Church hadn't been all bad. She liked Hailey—Kathy's daughter—but she was a college student and only home for the summer. They weren't destined to become great friends, no matter how nice Hailey was, because they wouldn't be able to hang out all the time.

"I wanna go home," she whispered as she closed her eyes.

It wasn't the big house near the ocean with its expansive grounds, swimming pool, and tennis court that she pictured when she said those words aloud. It was Blakely Academy. She'd spent far more time there than she'd ever spent at her dad's house.

"Why didn't he leave me **something** so I could stay there?"

Her dad had been forty-five, almost forty-six, when he died. Shouldn't he have been prepared for something like this? He had to know he wouldn't live forever. He could have made a will that left her some of his money.

Pretend money. That's what someone had said to her. Her dad's wealth
had been on paper. He'd lived well.
He'd let her live well too. But when he
died, it had all vanished—**poof!**—like
pretend money.

**Dad, why didn't you love me enough
to take care of me?**

Nobody ever told the truth in this
family. Nobody.

October 15, 1932
Saturday

Scruffy found himself a new
playmate. I believe the stray
dog has come to stay. I doubt
anyone else would feed him.
The beast is as ugly as sin with
his wiry brown-and-black hair
and a ripped right ear, but when
he looked me in the eyes, it was
like I could feel his gratitude for
the food and attention the girls
and I gave him. He was fed only
table scraps, but you would think
we gave him the finest cut of
beef ever. Gladys named him
Buster. I think that's something
she heard Harry call him when
the dog first came to the door
at Scruffy's side.

They are a comical sight when you see them together. Buster lopes along, and Scruffy runs all out to keep up. As I said, Buster isn't a handsome dog by any stretch of the imagination, but there is something about him that makes me love him already.

Harry always said that dogs should earn their keep, that they weren't meant to be pets. But Harry was the first to let Scruffy sleep in the house instead of outside on the porch or in the barn. And he was the first to say the nights are too cold now, and to let Buster come in and share a bed by the fire with Scruffy.

I think that is one of the reasons I love my husband so much. His tender heart.

November 24, 1932
Thanksgiving Day

We had a lovely dinner at Fred
and Rose's farm. There were
three families around the table.
Fred's, ours, and the neighbors
across the road from Fred,
Samuel and Betty Truman. Very
nice people. I didn't know them
because they go to a different
church in Thunder Creek. But
Harry became acquainted with
Samuel when he helped Fred
with the harvest.

What food we ate! Turkey
and dressing. Potatoes and
gravy. Green beans and peas
and carrots. Rolls and butter.
Cranberry sauce. Not to mention
the pies. Mercy sakes alive. Rose

does know how to make amazing pies. Two of them were the product of the fruit trees on our property.

Our property. What strange words for me to write. Of course, that farm isn't ours. The land doesn't belong to us. The house doesn't belong to us. But at least I've stopped thinking of Riverside and the lemon orchard as home, as if we might be able to return there one day. That is a step in the right direction.

We can't go back in time. That's something I've learned at last. Even if we could go back to California, even if we could go back to the orchards and our former home, it would not be the same. We are not the same.

I took much for granted. The Lord has shown me that too. We had more than many others. Yes, Harry worked hard, and we were blessed. But the Lord giveth and the Lord taketh away. Blessed be the name of the Lord. I have learned not to take what we have for granted. Not even the breath that we breathe. Be thankful in all things. An appropriate lesson for Thanksgiving Day.

And it was a wonderful day.

I couldn't count how many times I was told to sit down and put my feet up. Both Rose and Betty fussed over me. I still have over a month to go before the baby is due, but I am as large as a barn. No wonder they didn't want me in the way in the kitchen. I take up too much space.

I get terribly tired. If I weren't already the mother to a couple of rambunctious girls, I think I would sleep away much of the day. My great-aunt had thirteen children over the course of

twenty-five years. How on earth
did she manage it? It seems to
be all I can manage to get supper
on the table each evening.

Still, I am blessed.

Thank You, Father.

Chapter 9

Living with a teenaged girl—at least,
living with Emma—was like riding the
world's fastest roller coaster. Olivia felt
whipped from side to side on a daily
basis. One minute Emma was happy.
The next Emma was angry. And sometimes she was everything in between
those two emotions. Her mood could
change from minute to minute without
warning.

All things considered, Olivia and Emma's first counseling session with Adam
Green hadn't seemed a difficult hour.
At least not in Olivia's mind. Adam's
questions hadn't been invasive or even

much of a challenge. He had an easy, engaging style. Rather like spending time with a favorite uncle. Even Emma had seemed to relax after the first fifteen or twenty minutes of the session. Hostility—what Olivia had feared the most—never made an appearance.

After leaving the counselor's office, Olivia drove them to the Gold Mountain Café for lunch. The menu was limited, and there wasn't much on it that appealed to the health-food crowd. But since that crowd didn't include Olivia, she was okay with it. She wanted the fish and chips. A personal favorite that she only allowed herself on rare occasions.

Emma frowned at the laminated single-page menu in her hands. "What are finger steaks?"

"Deep-fried battered bits of steak. They're an Idaho specialty, according to my mom."

Her daughter glanced up. "Speaking of my grandmother, doesn't she want to see me?"

"Of course she does. And your grand-father too. But I told you. They're on a Mediterranean cruise and a tour of the Holy Land. They'd already left when... when the accident happened. I told them they didn't have to change their plans and come back early. You didn't want that, did you?"

"No. It doesn't matter. I hardly re-member them anyway."

Olivia wondered if that was true. And how was she supposed to explain all the complications without constantly placing blame on Daniel? As bitter as she'd been about her former husband's actions, she knew it wouldn't be healthy to poison Emma's thoughts about him, the way he seemed to have done about her. She mustn't do that to her daugh-ter. She could be honest without being cruel.

"They remember you," she said as she reached for the glass of water. "They have photographs of you all over their house."

Emma wrinkled her brow in thought. "I guess I kind of remember the pictures."

"And your grandmother wrote you letters while you were at Blakely. Right?"

"Yeah. She did."

"Did you keep any of them?"

Color rose in Emma's cheeks. "I used to, but then I threw them away."

"Oh, Emma. Why?"

"Because I didn't want them anymore."

"But why?"

"She wrote something about Dad. Something she shouldn't have."

"What?"

Emma stuck out her chin, lips pressed together.

"Your grandmother missed you. She knew I missed you. Whatever she said, it was because of that. She doesn't have a mean bone in her body."

"She thought he was being mean not

to let me fly back to Idaho for Christmas."

"That doesn't seem too awful. Were those the words she used?"

Emma looked down at the menu and didn't answer.

The server arrived at their table, pencil and pad in hand, and Olivia was thankful for the interruption. It gave her time to bring her churning thoughts under control. She quickly told the girl what she wanted, and Emma did the same.

"Oh, look," Emma said as the server left with their orders. "There's Mr. Murphy."

Olivia looked toward the door and saw Tyler following another server toward an empty spot at the nearby counter. When he saw Olivia and Emma, he grinned.

Something odd twirled in her belly in response.

"Hey there." He stopped by their table. "How's it going?" His gaze moved from Olivia to Emma.

"Great," Emma answered. "Do you want to sit with us?" She slid over. "We just ordered."

He looked at Olivia. "I wouldn't want to intrude."

How could she refuse after he'd bought dessert the other night? And besides, Emma's mood had brightened again. Having him at the table might mean less tension. "You wouldn't be intruding."

Emma slid a little farther on the booth's bench. "I saw you at church on Sunday."

Olivia didn't know why she was surprised that he went to Cornerstone. He was friends with Greg and Kathy. Still, she'd never noticed him. Of course, she hadn't been a regular attendee. But Cornerstone wasn't a megachurch by any stretch of the imagination.

He sank onto the bench opposite her. "I help in the media booth," he said, as if in answer to her silent wondering.

"Have you been doing that long?" Olivia asked.

"I started soon after I moved to Bethlehem Springs. There was a call for help, so I volunteered. Been doing it ever since."

The server came with another menu, a water glass, and a set of utensils.

"I don't need the menu," Tyler told the young woman. "I'd like the French dip, please, and a tossed salad with ranch."

"Dressing on the side, as usual?" the server inquired with a flirtatious smile.

Olivia felt a flash of irritation.

He nodded. "Yes. Thanks, Rita."

The server—Rita—walked away.

Olivia unrolled her utensils from the paper napkin. "She knows your usual. You must eat here a lot."

"Not a lot, but often enough." With a shrug he added, "I get tired of my own cooking."

It was obvious Tyler had an easy way with women. Daniel had been the same.

And suddenly Olivia wished Emma hadn't invited Tyler to join them. Even more, she wished he hadn't accepted.

Tyler looked at Emma and, as if there'd been no break in the conversation, said, "If you ever want to volunteer at church, talk to Kathy. She usually knows where help is needed."

"I might."

How did he do that? How did he and Kathy and even Adam Green get Emma to respond in a pleasant voice and an agreeable way? Why did Emma seem to like everybody—anybody—but her own mom?

What was it about Olivia Ward that made Tyler want to know her better? It was more than her looks, although she was undoubtedly pretty. It was more than his job. He'd investigated pretty women in the past and not felt this way. Maybe it was the challenge she presented to him. That she didn't want him seated across from her was clear in her taut expression. He'd joined them at her daughter's invitation, not hers. Maybe he shouldn't have, but it was too late now. He was there.

He looked at Emma. "Do you plan to audition for a part in one of the plays?"

"Yes." The girl's face lit up from the inside. "On Friday."

"That's great. Should I say, 'Break a leg'?"

"Sure, if you want to."

"What's the part?"

"Just a walk-on. Nothing big. A maid, I think. But if I become a member of the company this season, it'll give me a better shot for something more next year. Plus I can be part of the crew right away. That's fun too."

A glance in Olivia's direction told him she was both surprised and pleased by Emma's answer. He understood why. It meant Emma had accepted that this was her home. Reluctantly, perhaps, but still accepted.

In his update to the client the previous Friday, Tyler had suggested again that Peter Ward come up to Bethlehem Springs. He thought the man might be warming to the idea. While some tension remained between mother and daughter, in Tyler's opinion the home was stable and the relationship had promise. If Peter wanted to have a role in his granddaughter's life, it shouldn't be because he had the money and power to take her away from her mother a second time.

Rita returned with tossed salads. She set bowls in front of Olivia and Emma first, then put the last one in front of Tyler. "There you go. Dressing on the side." Her smile was meant to say more.

Tyler wasn't oblivious to Rita's flirting, although she should have given up by now. He'd never been rude to her, but he'd also never given any encouragement. For one thing, she was too young for him. The last thing he wanted to do was explain to a girl in her mid-twenties what had happened in the world before Y2K. For that matter, he didn't want to have to explain what Y2K meant.

"Thanks," he said with a nod.

"The rest of your order will be out soon." With a saucy toss of her head, she walked away.

Emma laughed. "She likes you."

Tyler chuckled with her. "She doesn't know me. I'm just a customer."

"No. She **likes** you."

"Emma," her mom said softly, a warning in her voice.

He looked at Olivia, trying to say with his eyes that he didn't mind Emma's comments. But she didn't meet his gaze long enough to read his thoughts. Just as well, for maybe his eyes would have said he was more interested in her than in Rita the waitress. And not because he'd been hired to look into her life. The interest he felt was more personal than that.

He needed to wrap up this case, and wrap it up soon.

December 31, 1932
New Year's Eve

It's nearly midnight, and except for the crackle of the fire, the house is silent. Harry and the girls have been asleep for several hours while I remain sleepless. I can scarcely breathe when I lie in bed. The baby seems to press on my lungs whenever I recline, and my only relief is found in the rocking chair. Something about the rocking back and forth eases the discomfort.

Oh, how I hope my labor begins soon. And I pray to God that it will be a quick delivery without complications. I am so tired and so uncomfortable.

January 7, 1933
Saturday

I wish there was a way to put laughter on the page. I just read my last entry, and I can only say that my hope came true, and God answered my prayer. Before the stroke of midnight on New Year's Eve, my labor began. And before Dr. Redenbacher could drive from his home in Thunder Creek, even before Rose could arrive to be of any help, Harry delivered Charles Harold MacIver. We were fortunate he wasn't birthed on the kitchen floor. It all happened very quickly.

Charlie is a beautiful, strong lad. Much like his sister Gladys and quite different from his sister

Dottie. Dottie has always been small and frail, but Charlie is hale and hearty. And oh, what a voice he has. His cry is hale and hearty as well.

Harry loves his daughters passionately, but there is no doubt that he's over the moon to have a son. I believe he's already planning what they can do together as Charlie gets older. Not simply working the fields or milking the cows or harvesting, but fishing and hunting too. Perhaps going to the mountains and camping in the wilderness, just the two of them. I can picture them at it even now.

I doubt Dottie will be strong enough to do those things, but Gladys will want to go with her daddy and brother. I see that in her now, before she has even turned four. Gladys will blaze her own path. I am sure of it. She will

never want to be relegated to the
kitchen or a sewing circle. Will
the world change enough to
accommodate her? I wonder.

**God, I know You are always with
my children and that You love
them even more than I do. I ask
that they would be aware of
Your presence from an early
age. Inhabit their dreams,
Father. Draw them to Your will
with each decision they must
make. You have placed these
little ones into our care. Help us
to be good parents to them, to
raise them up as they should go
so that when they are old they
won't depart from You. In the
blessed name of Jesus I pray,
amen.**

Chapter 10

Olivia opened the cover on her e-reader and waited for the screensaver to vanish and her book to appear. But even a second or two seemed a long time to wait, and her gaze rose again to the closed swinging doors of the school auditorium. Beyond them, Emma and a few other hopefuls were set to audition for a couple of remaining parts in the final play of the season for the Bethlehem Springs Mountain Theater Company.

"Hey, Olivia."

At the familiar voice, she looked in the opposite direction. "Hi, Kathy."

Her friend glanced toward the auditorium. "Today's the day, huh?"

"Yes."

Kathy walked over and sat in the folding chair beside Olivia. "Is Emma excited?"

"Yes. And nervous. She wants this more than I'm supposed to know."

"Well, from what you've said, she's got the talent for it."

Olivia glanced down as she closed the cover on her e-reader. "That's what her teachers said. I never got to see her in person."

"Why not?"

"Money, mostly. I couldn't afford to fly across the country. My income's not high, even by Idaho standards. Coming up with an extra six or seven hundred dollars isn't easy. Besides, Daniel made it clear to the people at the academy that I wasn't to be notified about such things as plays until the last minute. Heaven knows what he said about me. Maybe he told them I was a danger to Emma. On drugs or something. Or maybe all that was needed was that he held the purse strings. He paid her tuition, so what he said went."

"I'm sorry he was like that. It didn't just hurt you. It hurt Emma too."

Olivia's throat tightened, and all she could do was nod in agreement.

Kathy touched the back of Olivia's hand. "But she's here now, and you two are building a new life together. It'll get better."

She nodded a second time.

"Hey, I heard you and Emma had lunch with Tyler a couple of days ago."

Olivia looked at her friend. "What?"

"You didn't?"

"Well, yes. Sort of. We were at the Gold Mountain, and he came in. Emma invited him to sit with us since the café was so busy." That was a slight prevarication, and she knew it. There'd been room for him at the counter.

"He's a super-nice guy," Kathy said with a smile.

"Don't try to play matchmaker. You

know I'm not interested. Especially not now."

"Have you had even **one** date since I've known you?"

"No. I haven't wanted to date."

"You need to start living again. You've been stuck in a rut for too long."

"You're starting to sound like Sara."

"She's right. No wonder I've always liked her."

"My life is fine the way it is."

Kathy's expression grew serious. "You need to set a healthy example for Emma."

Olivia had thought the same thing. It was one of the reasons she'd determined to be more faithful in church attendance. Still, she resisted Kathy's words. Olivia's small circle of friends made her feel safe. As did her work. Her contact with clients was almost exclusively via email. It, too, felt safe and controlled.

"Why not give Tyler a chance? He's interested in you."

"How do you know that?"

"Because he's asked Greg and me questions about you."

A strange feeling shot through Olivia. A combination of pleasure and irritation. "What did you tell him?"

"Only good things. I promise."

Unable to help herself, Olivia asked, "What does he do?"

"He works for a law firm in Boise."

Lawyers. Olivia didn't have much good to say or think about lawyers. If she never had to deal with another one, it would be too soon.

"He's not an attorney himself," Kathy added.

"That's something in his favor."

The doors to the auditorium opened and Emma appeared, a big smile on her face. Olivia and Kathy both stood.

"How'd it go?" Olivia knew the answer, based on her daughter's gleeful expression.

"Good, I think. Really good." Emma looked at Kathy. "Victor's a great director. He made it easy."

"I agree. Everybody in the company likes to work with him."

"When will you know if you got the part?" Olivia asked.

"Next week. There'll be a read-through sometime, and then rehearsals will begin the first week of July. Right after the Fourth."

Emma looked behind her as a couple more girls exited the auditorium. "Mom, would it be okay with you if I go get a Coke with some new friends?"

Friends. The word made Olivia smile. "I suppose that would be all right."

"I can walk home afterward."

"Are you sure? I can—"

"Mom." Emma might as well have said, **Don't embarrass me.**

Olivia pressed her lips together, hesitated, then nodded.

"Thanks."

"Home in a couple hours."

"Okay." Emma turned and walked to where the two other girls awaited her.

"Are they competing for the same part?" Olivia asked in a low voice.

"Could be. Only actors were allowed at the audition, and I don't think there were more than a couple roles to fill."

"Then at least one of them will be disappointed." **Oh please. Let Emma get a part.**

"True. But don't let it worry you. Anybody who doesn't get cast is invited to be part of the crew. Emma will be involved in some way. You'll see."

Tyler exited through the doors of the Ada County Courthouse. After moving to one side, he paused long enough to fill his lungs with fresh air. Not that it helped ease the tension inside of him. A weight of concern pressed on his chest. Concern for the two kids at the center of the legal fight between their mom and dad.

Tyler's firm represented the mom, but as far as he could tell, both of the parents had plenty of problems. Which one would make the better single parent was anybody's guess. All he could do was hope the judge's final ruling would be in the best interests of the children.

Give the judge wisdom, Lord. Protect those kids.

His gut twisted with the memory of the day he and his sister had been taken from their mom's home and placed in the first of too many different foster homes. He'd been ten at the time and Christa eight. The years that followed were filled with strife and struggles, especially for Christa. She'd fought against authority from the word go. Not long after Tyler aged out of the system, he'd been able to get a job and provide a home for her, but her feet had already been set on a path of self-destruction.

He looked up at the late-morning sun as he drew another deep breath.

Strange, wasn't it? He and Christa had grown up in the same environment, experienced the same traumas, lived through the same tough circumstances, but his childhood had made him want to fight for justice for others while his sister had wanted to escape the memories through drugs and alcohol. Worst part was she'd achieved her goal—permanently.

He gave his head a shake as he walked toward the parking lot. He had a meeting with Peter Ward in half an hour, and he didn't want to be late. He was glad they could have a face-to-face meeting this time. Reports were often better understood when they could be given in person. Not that he had a whole lot more to tell Peter than the times they'd spoken on the phone. But looking into the other man's eyes while he delivered his report might help him feel more comfortable with the situation.

The older gentleman was waiting for him at the restaurant when he arrived.

Peter stood as Tyler walked toward the table. "Good to see you." He offered his hand.

"And you." Peter shook the proffered

hand.

"I'm glad we could meet in person."

"Me too."

The server brought water to set before each man. "I'll give you a moment to decide," he said before leaving again.

Peter pointed to the menu at Tyler's right hand. "Go ahead. We can talk after we order."

Tyler perused the menu quickly, deciding on the club sandwich and a bowl of soup.

A short while later, their orders given, Peter leaned forward in his chair. "Now, then. What do you have to tell me?"

"Good news, actually. I saw Olivia and Emma at a production of the Bethlehem Springs Mountain Theater last Friday night. Emma has a keen interest in the theater. She was in several productions back at her school in Florida. A friend of Olivia's volunteers for the company, and that woman in turn introduced Emma to the director. This morning she was set to audition for a part in a play that will be produced later in the season, but since I was in court here in Boise, I don't know how that went."

Peter nodded but remained silent.

"I also saw them at church on Sunday. Emma was introduced to other young people around her age. She seemed to fit in well."

Another nod and more silence.

"Olivia and Emma met with a counselor in Bethlehem Springs a couple of days ago. I gather it's to help them adjust to the new living arrangements as well as to guide Emma through grieving for her dad."

"From what I can tell, my son didn't spend a great deal of time with the girl after taking her to Florida."

Tyler nodded. He'd learned the same information. But he knew that wouldn't negate Emma's need to grieve. A loss was still a loss, and the young didn't always process loss well. He knew that from personal as well as professional experience.

"I suppose it speaks well of the mother that she knew counseling was a good next step to take."

It bothered Tyler that Peter referred to Olivia that way, but he made sure the irritation wasn't reflected in his voice. "I have no reason to believe Olivia isn't a good mother. A concerned and dedicated one."

"Yes. Well. I hope that's true. For my granddaughter's sake."

Tyler studied the man for a moment, wondering if he spoke the truth. Did he really want Olivia to be a good mom, or did he hope she would give him a reason to try to take Emma from her? After a short while, he said, "Sir, I still believe the best option is for you to go to Bethlehem Springs and introduce yourself to both Olivia and Emma. Let your decision come from personal experience. Get to know them. See how they are together."

Peter shook his head. "Not yet. I

want to know more about both of them first."

The server returned with their lunch orders, and Tyler was thankful for the interruption. It gave him time to consider his own words. Why was he so sure that Olivia was a good mother? He'd seen more than his fair share of deception through the years. Plenty of people put on a good show for others, and most of the time Tyler leaned toward being a skeptic. He didn't trust people at first glance. Sometimes he was guilty of not trusting God completely. But for some reason, he found himself wanting to believe Olivia Ward was exactly who she appeared to be—a woman who'd received a raw deal from her ex-husband and a good mom who loved her daughter and wanted the best for her.

Is that who she is? He frowned as he picked up his sandwich, hoping he wasn't steering his client in the wrong direction.

January 20, 1933
Friday

As I write, a strong wind blows
against the house, rattling the
windows and whistling beneath
the eaves. Snow is falling again.
When we lived in California, I
missed the snowy days of my
childhood, but I forgot the cold
that came with it. Or at least
didn't remember it in the same
way.

Except for the kitchen, it is
impossible to keep this house
warm. Close to the fire it's hot,
but one doesn't have to go far to
feel the chill. Even indoors, the
girls must stay bundled up, and
they are buried beneath blankets
when in bed at night in their

upstairs room. I bring little Charlie into bed with me and Harry, sharing our warmth with him.

Harry is worried about money again. No, the truth is he never stopped worrying since long before we came to Idaho. It is turning him old before his time. I miss his laughter. I miss his smiles. They happen so rarely now.

Isaiah says, "When thou passest through the waters, I will be with thee; and through the rivers, they shall not overflow thee: when thou walkest through the fire, thou shalt not be burned, neither shall the flame kindle upon thee."

That is a beautiful promise from God's Holy Bible. But the reality is the waters are over-flowing us. I hear the wind outside. It doesn't cease. It blows and it blows, and we are battered. We are overcome. I want to encourage my husband, but I don't have the words he needs. I don't have the words I need.

At times, I feel Jesus look at me and say, "O thou of little faith, wherefore didst thou doubt?" I am ashamed. How can I raise my children to be people of faith if I cannot find enough faith myself?

January 22, 1933
Sunday

Because of the snow covering
the roads, we could not go into
town for church this morning.
We stayed home and had our
own time of worship. Harry read
aloud from the book of Matthew.
The girls sat on the kitchen floor,
enjoying the warmth of the fire in
the stove, while I rocked Charlie
in my arms. But when Harry
reached these verses of chapter
10, the words seemed to pierce
my heart.

Jesus said, "Are not two
sparrows sold for a penny? and
not one of them shall fall on the
ground without your Father: but
the very hairs of your head are all

numbered. Fear not therefore: ye are of more value than many sparrows."

I am more valuable to my Father than many sparrows. Harry is more valuable. Our children are more valuable. Fear not therefore.

Father in heaven, how do I stop being afraid? If fear is what I feel, how do I make it go away? At times I am strong. I feel Your presence. I know You watch and You care. At others, I feel alone and adrift and afraid. How do I not fear the troubles of this world?

February 1, 1933
Wednesday

The sun is out, and the snow has melted. The earth is painted in lifeless colors for now—browns and tans—but there is a promise of spring in the air. A promise that green will overtake the brown. We can all feel it. Except for Charlie, of course. At a month old, he cares for nothing except sleeping and nursing at my breast. But the girls cannot wait to get outside to run and play while their daddy does his chores.

Renewal. It is one of God's promises, isn't it? He sent His Son to give new life to those who choose to follow Him.

"And be not fashioned according to this world: but be ye transformed by the renewing of your mind, that ye may prove what is the good and acceptable and perfect will of God."

I believe that means letting God change the way I think. My faith may be small, but it is enough when I follow Him and let Him do His work in me. This is how I learn to "fear not therefore."

Chapter 11

Tyler was finishing the last of his duties on Sunday when Kathy Dover appeared in the entrance to the media booth.

"Morning, Tyler."

"Hey, Kathy."

"I'm here to twist your arm."

He grinned at the warning. "Oh?"

"Will it work, or will I have to send for Greg to help me?"

"Ask first and we'll see."

"The theater company desperately needs someone to take over the sound and lights for the remainder of the season. Our current engineer has a family emergency. He's leaving Idaho tomorrow afternoon, and it's doubtful he'll be back before the end of the year."

"Are you talking about Jack Edwards?"

She nodded.

"I heard his mom has cancer. That's rough."

Kathy nodded again.

"Not sure I qualify as an engineer."

"How about 'operator'? Does that sound less intimidating? From what I understand, you know how to do it all." She motioned with her hand to take in all of the equipment in the booth.

He knew in that moment he might as well admit defeat. "What's my time commitment?"

"Four nights a week through the rest of the season. Arrive about five thirty and done by ten thirty or so. Wednesdays are run-throughs and system checks. They don't last as long. Performances are Thursdays, Fridays, and Saturdays."

"Duties?"

"Let's see." She glanced at a note-pad in her hand. "Oversee both sound and lights, but there'll be a second volunteer in the booth during performances to handle the light board. You'd perform a channel check each night before the opening to be sure the equipment is working properly. Operate the soundboard during the performances. Attend all tech rehearsals throughout the season. That's pretty much it."

"Will Jack have time to give me a run-through before he goes?"

This time she shook her head. "No, but he's left written instructions. You won't have any trouble."

He could have pointed out she didn't know that for sure. But why bother? He'd already committed himself. Besides, the truth was he **did** know his way around a soundboard and a light board, and he liked the idea of volunteering with the theater company. He'd never had the urge to go on the stage himself, but he enjoyed being around creative people. This was also another way of integrating himself into his new hometown. He liked the sense of belonging that volunteering gave him.

It didn't occur to Tyler until he walked toward his car in the almost deserted parking lot that becoming the sound operator for the Bethlehem Springs Mountain Theater might also put him in more contact with Emma Ward and her mom. As he pressed the key fob to unlock the door of his vehicle, he cast a glance skyward. "Did You set this up, Lord?"

An hour after washing the last dish from their Sunday dinner, Olivia was drifting off to sleep on the sofa, a book lying on her chest, when Emma's excited squeal brought her fully awake.

"Mom! Mom! I got the part!"

She sat up and looked toward the second-floor landing. "You did? That's great." She set her book on the coffee table. "Come and tell me about it." Relief rushed through her when her daughter didn't argue.

"Victor Benson called to let me know himself." Emma came down the stairs, her gaze locked on the mobile phone still in her hand.

"Do you have a lot of lines?"

Arriving at the bottom of the stairs, Emma glanced up from the phone at last. "No lines. I'm just a maid in a few scenes. Sort of in the background."

Olivia forced down the smile that wanted to play on her lips. All of this excitement over a bit part with no lines? She didn't understand, but she was determined not to let her daughter know that. Not when Emma wanted to share her excitement. "Oh, honey. I'm happy for you." She frowned in thought. "I've forgotten what the play is."

"**An Ideal Husband**."

"Oh, that's right. You told me it was another Oscar Wilde play. When do rehearsals start?"

"Next month." Emma sank onto the

chair opposite Olivia. "But I can begin volunteering with the crew for the other plays now. Is that all right? I told Victor I could."

"Shouldn't you call him Mr. Benson?"

"Everybody calls him Victor."

"Are you sure that—"

"He told me so himself."

While it was tempting to launch into a lecture about showing respect for adults, even Olivia realized this wasn't a battle she wanted to fight with Emma. If Victor Benson had given the cast and crew members permission to use his first name, who was Olivia to argue?

"They're already discussing what plays they'll produce next year. **Peter Pan**'s one they're considering. What if I could play Peter or Wendy? Wouldn't that be amazing?"

Something inside Olivia eased at the mention of next year. "Amazing," she answered softly.

It had been less than three weeks since Emma—unhappy, miserable, sullen, angry—had returned to Idaho with Olivia. She remembered fearing she would never see her daughter smile again. But maybe she'd been wrong not to trust that time and love could change their situation.

Perhaps she was wrong not to trust that God could change things too.

"If I'm part of the crew for the current shows," Emma said, "it'll mean I'll have to be at the amphitheater several nights a week. Maybe I could get a bike for going there and back."

"No. I'm not having you riding a bike home at that time of night. Not alone."

"But—"

"No. I'll pick you up. Maybe I can carpool with other moms and dads with kids in the company."

The look on Emma's face said, **I'm not a baby**.

Olivia ignored it. "It'll work out. You'll see."

Emma murmured something that sounded like, "All right." Then she got up from the chair and headed up the stairs to her room.

The brief time of celebration was over. So was the ability to drift off to sleep. With a sigh, Olivia rose from the sofa and went to her studio. If she couldn't take a nap, she could at least clear a few things off her schedule.

Seated on her bed, Emma opened her phone's messaging app and typed in Regina's name with her thumbs.

I got the part.

Which one?

Just a walk-on. I'll be the maid.

Doesn't sound like much fun.

Why couldn't Regina be glad for her? Then again, her friend couldn't have a clue what it was like to live in Bethlehem Springs. B-o-r-i-n-g! Playing a maid in the play **was** a big deal.

**The director's cool. I'll get a
better part next season.**

She stared at the screen of the phone, waiting for a reply. None came. After a minute, she set it aside and reached for a copy of the script. Even though she didn't have a speaking part, she still wanted to know the play from cover to cover, if for no other reason than to impress the director. She might as well start learning it now.

When Olivia turned away from her computer screen a couple of hours later, she was surprised to discover how dark the studio had become. She checked the clock on the wall. It was still afternoon. She rose and went into the living room. Outside, she saw that black clouds now obscured the sky. No wonder the house had grown so gloomy.

She hugged herself as she moved

closer to the window. In the distance thunder rolled, and the nearby trees, as if in response, began to dance before the rising wind. Her own response was to turn on all three lamps in the living room before sitting on the couch and covering herself with the throw.

The lightning drew closer, the thunder louder, and the wind began to whistle and wail. The log house was sturdy, yet even it shook before the gusts that slammed into its sides. Oh, how she hated storms like this one. The wind that could level trees, tearing them up by their roots. The lightning that could set a forest ablaze.

Thunder rolled again, even closer than seconds before. The lights flickered and died.

"Mom."

She took a deep breath. "Yes?"

"The power's out."

"I know."

"I don't have any internet on my phone."

This almost made Olivia laugh as she looked toward the stairs. "Not without power."

"Oh. Right." Emma moved down the stairs and walked to the living-room window. "Looks nasty out there."

Lightning flashed, and the clap of thunder followed a second later. Olivia gasped, one hand going to her heart, as if she could slow its rapid pulse with a touch.

"Are you scared?" Emma's tone sounded incredulous.

"I'm not a fan of wind and lightning."

"You should've seen the storms we got in Florida. They were really something. Tons of lightning and thunder and wind. They'd have to shut down the airports because of it. And that was just normal summer stuff. Then there were the hurricanes. I went through a couple of those. The school wasn't on the coast, but still." She whistled. "You'd really hate those."

Lightning flashed again, followed by

a rumble that shook the house. Olivia didn't have to look outside to know the dance of the trees had become frenetic, whipping the tops of the pines back and forth.

"Hey, Mom." Emma sat on the sofa next to her. "I'm sorry. You really are scared, aren't you?"

She released a nervous laugh. "It started when I was a little girl. A storm brought a tree down on the neighbor's house. It crushed their car too. I can still see that smushed car top in my mind. Even as a child, I knew if anybody'd been inside, they would have died. I've been afraid of windstorms ever since." She shook her head. "When I was still little, I'd hide under the bed."

Emma put an arm around Olivia's shoulders and drew her close. "It's okay, Mom. I'm here. You don't have to be afraid."

It would have surprised Emma to know how much the words comforted Olivia.

February 6, 1933
Monday

Harry is keeping something from me. I feel it in my heart. I see it whenever I look at him.

Mr. Overton, the owner of the farm, came to see Harry on Saturday. Until then, I'd never met him before. He lives in Caldwell and doesn't come out this way often. Harry wanted to talk about his plans to grow a different crop. They didn't talk in the house but went out to the fields and the barn. Mr. Overton stayed for about half an hour, and it was a long time after he left before Harry returned to the house.

I asked him if Mr. Overton was

agreeable to the change. Harry
said he was, but I could tell even
then that something wasn't right.

Harry has never lied to me
before. I'm sure of it. But by his
silence, he is lying to me now.

I think the silence must be
worse than anything he could tell
me.

February 7, 1933
Tuesday

What a failure I am. Only a week ago, I wrote in this diary how I was to "fear not therefore." And here I am, fearing whatever it is that Harry isn't telling me.

At supper tonight I asked him what was wrong. He answered with a shake of his head. "Nothing for you to worry about."

Does he see me as weak? I am not. I have given birth to three children. Doesn't that show strength?

Ecclesiastes says, "And if a man prevail against him that is alone, two shall withstand him; and a threefold cord is not quickly broken."

Together we prevail. We do not do well when we are alone. And with God, Harry and I make a threefold cord that cannot easily be broken.

Whatever is to come, Father, let Harry and me walk it together so that we prevail and are not broken. Amen.

Chapter 12

Olivia barely had time to come to a halt in the amphitheater parking lot before Emma opened the car door and got out. "Hey!" she called. But her daughter was already on her way to the entrance.

Laughing to herself, Olivia opened her own door. As her foot touched the ground, a black SUV pulled into a space to her left. She gave it only a glance as she stood and pressed the key fob to lock her car. But before she could move on, she saw Tyler Murphy step into view near the front of the other vehicle. He waved when he saw her.

Strange how she'd never met Tyler

in the year he'd lived in Bethlehem Springs, and now it seemed she saw him everywhere. Here. The school. Church. The café.

"Does this mean Emma got a part?" He approached her. "Yes.

The cast begins read-throughs tonight. What about you?"

"I've been roped into doing the sound for the rest of the season."

"Kathy can be persuasive, can't she?"

"Yes." He laughed. "That she can."

They fell into step with each other, walking toward the entrance of the amphitheater.

"Emma must be excited."

"She is. It's given her something to look forward to. She hasn't been very happy since—" She broke off her words.

"Don't worry. She'll settle in. It'll get easier."

Olivia glanced at him. Why was she tempted to be candid with him? She was normally guarded in her speech, especially with men, even friends. Tyler Murphy wasn't a friend. He was an acquaintance at best. Three weeks ago he'd been a complete stranger to her.

"Well," he said, breaking into her thoughts, "have a good evening. I've got to head up there." He pointed to a raised booth at the back of the amphitheater. Then he walked away.

She released a breath, both relieved and sorry to see him go. A confusing reality. She stiffened her spine as she looked toward the stage in search of her daughter. She found Emma chatting with several others from the cast or crew. After a moment, Emma laughed, and the sound reached Olivia's ears. Joy fluttered in her chest as she settled onto a nearby chair.

"Hey, Olivia."

She looked around to see Kathy and Greg walking toward her.

Greg greeted Olivia before kissing his wife on the cheek and heading off in another direction. When he was gone,

Kathy sat in the empty chair next to Olivia. "Do you plan to be here the rest of the evening? Because if you do, I can put you to work."

"The same way you put Tyler to work?"

Surprise flickered across Kathy's face. "How'd you know that?"

"We arrived at the same time, and he told me."

"Oh." Kathy glanced toward the booth. "Well, if you get bored, check with Tyler. Maybe he could use your help. You never know."

"Don't do that."

"Don't do what?" Her friend's expression was all innocence now.

"Just don't. I'm not interested."

With a smile, Kathy turned and walked away.

"I'm **not** interested," Olivia repeated.

Only she had to wonder: How could she convince her friends if she couldn't convince herself?

It didn't take Tyler long to feel at home in the theater's control booth. The instructions left for him by Jack Edwards were clear. Maybe he would feel nervous tomorrow night during the performance—his first time to be in charge —but he doubted it.

He leaned forward on the chair, far enough that he could see Olivia. He wondered if she planned to come and watch the rehearsals every week. Was she that interested in Emma's activities? Or was she a bit of a control freak?

Tyler had seen all kinds of parents, first as a kid in the system, then as an investigator. He'd seen the good and the horrible. He was acquainted with martyrs and narcissists and everything in between. Experience had taught him that even a great parent wasn't seen in the best light when faced with a custody battle.

Would Peter Ward try to take Emma from Olivia? He'd never liked the idea. Even less so now that he was coming to know her. She'd lost her daughter once. It shouldn't happen again. There was no reason for it.

But what if he was wrong about Olivia? What was best for Emma? That's what was important. She was the innocent here. She might look almost grown up, but she was still a child in many ways. A girl who deserved a loving, stable home.

In his memory he heard Christa weeping into her pillow in the middle of the night. Back then he'd done what he could to comfort her, but he'd been a kid himself. He hadn't known what to do or say. Not really. Especially after she started sneaking out at night, hanging with a bad crowd, using drugs and drinking. First he hadn't been able to protect her from bad foster parents. Then he hadn't been able to protect her from herself.

He leaned back again and rubbed a hand over his face, as if the action could erase the bad memories. It didn't. They were always there, ready to rise up and accuse him.

"Therefore there is now no condemnation for those who are in Christ Jesus."

On his last trip down to Boise, he'd heard a song on the radio based on that verse of Scripture. Again and again, the singer had told him he'd been set free from the law of sin and death. That Christ Jesus had redeemed him and changed him. He knew that. He believed that. He wasn't supposed to live with the shame of his past failures. His sins had been covered by the blood of Jesus. Nothing he did could separate him from the Father's love. He knew it all in his heart. So why didn't he live like it? Why did he continue to beat himself up because of the ways he'd failed himself, the ways he'd failed Christa?

A rap on the doorjamb brought him out of his troubled thoughts.

"Am I intruding?" Greg asked.

"Nope. Not much for me to do at the

moment." He looked down at the stage to be certain he hadn't missed a cue of some kind. A few actors were moving across the boards, but no one wore a mic. No one was staring up at the booth in accusation.

Greg took the empty chair near the soundboard. "Kathy and I are about to head home. Just thought I'd check to see how this is going." He waved a hand toward the controls.

"Nothing too complicated."

"Kathy appreciates how you stepped in. Took a load off her shoulders, I can tell you."

"No problem."

"I know better. You're as busy as anybody else with work and church and life in general. It's a lot to give up four evenings a week for this."

Tyler shrugged, not denying his friend's words but not confirming them either.

"We're gonna have a barbecue on the Fourth. Have a bunch of friends over.

No agenda. Just time to fellowship and eat ribs. Maybe play some games. Think you could come?"

"Are you kidding? No way I'm turning down an invitation for your ribs."

"Good." Greg stood. "We'll get more information to you when Kathy decides about the time."

"And tell me what I should bring. Make it something easy. I'm not great in the kitchen."

Greg laughed. "I'll tell Kathy to take pity on you." He left the booth.

Thanks, God.

Tyler didn't have everything figured out. He definitely hadn't nailed down the no-condemnation aspect yet. But he'd been blessed with good friends since moving to Bethlehem Springs, and he knew it. God had brought him to this mountain town, and little by little, living here was changing him for the better.

Emma stood in the wings, listening as

other cast members read their parts.
Then she moved to one side to look
toward the seating. Her mom was still
there, but her attention was directed
toward something in her hand. No doubt
she was reading a book or maybe
checking her phone. Cell service had
gotten better in the center of town in the
last week or two because of the new
tower.

"Emma," Victor Benson called.

Her attention shot to the director.

"Could you grab one of those props
on the cart there? Anything. Doesn't
matter what."

She turned and picked up a vase and
moved onto the stage.

"Thanks. Give it to Michael, please."

After doing as directed, she slipped
into the wings again, her gaze going to
the other props on the rolling cart. There
was a feather duster, a book with a faded orange cover, two ashtrays, a shepherd figurine, and a delicate teacup
and saucer on the top tier of the cart.

She let her fingertips slide over the cup and the figurine and finally the book. There was nothing on the cover to indicate what sort of book it was, so she opened to its center. Instead of a printed story of some kind, she found words written in ink.

Curious now, she picked up the book and returned to the first page.

December 10, 1931
Thursday

I'm twenty years old today. Isn't that something to write?

Was this for real? Was it someone's diary from almost a hundred years ago? Or was it a prop made to look like a real diary?

She glanced around, but no one watched her.

Her attention returned to the book in her hands, and she flipped quickly through the pages. The handwriting was the same throughout—small and neat. Every page had been filled. Not a single line had been wasted. New entries began on the line directly beneath the end of the previous entry rather than skipping to the top of a new page.

She returned to the first page and kept reading. There wasn't much to it, really. The writer was a girl of twenty, married and already a mother of two. The littlest was sick a lot, it seemed. The husband worried about money. Oh yeah. It was the Great Depression. Emma had studied that in school.

But then she came to the second entry, and her interest grew.

A new year. 1932. What will it bring?

When I was a girl, I thought I wanted to be an actress. I told Mother I wanted to go to New York City and appear on the Broadway stage. That was the same year a company performed

H.M.S. Pinafore at the theater in town. Afterward I got to talk to the actress who played Little Buttercup. Oh, how I longed to be like her. To get to perform. To get to travel the country. I was determined to leave home as soon as I finished school.

"Find something that interests you?" a voice said behind her.

Emma sucked in a guilty breath as she turned to face Timothy Simpson, one of the older volunteers in the crew. "I was looking at the props. I was...I wondered how they'll be used in the play."

"Those things?" He shook his head. "No use that I know of. Victor likes to have lots of options backstage, just in case. I brought all that from a box in my mom's basement."

"Your mom?" Emma did a quick calculation in her head. Timothy was probably a bit older than her mom, which meant his mom would be in her sixties, most likely. Her seventies at most. Too young for the diary to be hers.

"Yeah."

"She didn't want any of this? You're sure?"

"I guess not. She told me to help myself to whatever might be of use to the company, so I brought the lot of it."

Emma glanced toward the stage. For some reason she didn't quite understand, she wanted to keep reading about this girl. Maybe it was because she'd wanted to be an actress. Maybe it was to discover more about life back in the thirties. Maybe it was just boredom. Whatever the reason, she looked back at Timothy and held the book a little higher, showing it to him without really showing it to him. "Since this isn't part of the play, do you think it would be okay if I borrow it? I'd like to read it."

He shrugged. "Sure. No worries. You can have it. I can always find old books to put out. Any house in Bethlehem Springs probably has one to donate if I asked."

"Thanks." She hugged it to her chest. Timothy wouldn't care that this was somebody's personal diary. And if his own mother didn't want it, that was the same as tossing it out. Right?

February 14, 1933
Tuesday

Charlie is such a good baby.
He sleeps through the night now,
although he is an early riser.
Even before his father. He is
plump too. No surprise there.
Sometimes it feels as if I do
nothing but nurse him. But when
he smiles up at me, I am happy.

Dottie is particularly fond of
her baby brother. She loves it
when I let her hold him. She
coos and jabbers to him, and
I sometimes think they understand each other. I know it isn't
possible, but it does seem that
way. She will make a fine mother
one day.

Gladys would rather be outside

with her father than holding the
baby.

Whatever is worrying Harry,
he continues to try to hide it
from me.

February 16, 1933
Thursday

A letter came today. Aunt Tess passed away in her sleep over a week ago. She wasn't that old, and she wasn't sick, according to Mama. The doctor said that her heart failed.

I haven't been able to stop crying. I loved Aunt Tess so much. She was such an encourager. I see her in Gladys's smile. I hear her in Dottie's laugh.

It is possible we never would have had the money to visit Iowa. It is possible Aunt Tess never would have had the money to come to Idaho for a visit. But as long as she lived, I could imagine getting to see her again.

Aunt Tess loved Jesus, and I know that I will see her again in heaven. Perhaps we will sit in a beautiful meadow and recite **The Gift of the Magi** together.

Chapter 13

The following Monday, Tyler sat in the living room of Ian and Judy Applegate's Boise home. Judy's eyes were reddened by tears. Ian wore a tense expression.

"Has Lily run away before?" Tyler asked.

The parents glanced at each other before Judy Applegate answered. "No. But recently she's stayed out when she wasn't supposed to. We've had to ground her, take away privileges. But she's always come home. Late, but home. She's never been gone like this."

"And the last time you saw her was

when she left the house late on Friday morning to meet a friend?" He wrote the date and time on his notepad. Three days. Close to seventy-two hours. "There's been no other contact since then?"

"Not with us. But she called a friend on Saturday. Didn't let on that she wasn't in Boise or that we were looking for her."

"I'll want to talk to that friend."

Ian Applegate said, "We think Lily's in Seattle. Did Marshal tell you that?"

"Yes, he told me." Tyler studied the clients again.

"We appreciate that he asked you to help us." Ian reached out and took hold of his wife's hand.

Marshal Kent, one of the partners at the law firm, had told Tyler the Applegates were good people. Still, there had to be a reason why Lily, a fifteen-year-old, had run away from home. He wanted to know what that was. Was she a willful teen, trying to break free of parental authority? Or was there something more behind it? Was there trouble at home that he couldn't perceive? He always looked for answers to such questions in this kind of case, but he'd had to learn to accept when reasons couldn't be found.

He thought of his sister. No matter the reason Lily had run away, too many bad things could happen to a kid out there. He'd seen them happen to Christa.

Next he thought of Emma Ward. She was the same age as Lily, and for some reason, that made finding this girl all the more important to him.

Judy lifted some papers from the coffee table and held them toward Tyler. "We found charges on our credit-card statement online. They appear to be gas purchases and meal purchases in Ontario, Oregon, and Tacoma, Washington. Those were posted on Friday and Saturday."

"And your credit card?"

"Mine is missing from my wallet," she answered, again glancing toward her husband.

"Any charges for a motel?"

Ian shook his head. "We suspect she didn't try because ID would be required and then the card might be confiscated."

"Did you consider canceling the card or reporting it stolen?"

All color seemed to drain from Judy's face. "But charges to the card might be our best lead."

"I agree." Tyler paused long enough to look around the spacious living room, letting his gaze linger on a table that held a large grouping of photographs. By all appearances a happy family. He looked back at the couple on the sofa. "What about Lily's sister? Mr. Kent said you have another daughter."

"April," Ian answered.

"How old is she?"

"Seventeen."

"And she doesn't know where Lily is?"

"She says she doesn't."

Tyler nodded, making another note on his pad. "Would it be possible for me to talk to her?"

"I'll get her for you." Judy rose.

Tyler stood too. "It might be best if I talked to her alone." Again, there was a silent exchange between the couple, but Tyler didn't get the impression they were trying to hide anything from him. All he picked up on was anxiety over their missing child. "Sometimes a sibling will say something to a stranger that they won't say to their parents."

"Come with me. She's in the family room."

Tyler nodded toward Ian, then followed Judy out of the living room. A short hallway bypassed the kitchen and led to the family room, where a large TV with a curved screen was the main focus. However, the girl in an oversized leather chair wasn't looking at it. Her face was turned down as she swept her thumb across the screen of the phone in her hand.

"April?"

At the sound of her mom's voice, she looked up, at the same time turning her phone facedown on her thigh. To hide something?

"This is Mr. Murphy. He's going to help us find Lily. He'd like to talk to you."

The girl looked at her overturned phone before getting up from the chair, leaving no doubt in Tyler's mind that Lily's big sister did, indeed, know something about her sister's whereabouts.

Emma closed the cover on the diary, but her thoughts remained on the entries she'd read and even reread over the past five days. She felt a connection with the author. Perhaps it was the unnamed girl's onetime dream of performing on the New York stage. So similar to Emma's own dreams. Perhaps it was trying to imagine getting married when only a year older than Emma was right now or being a mother of three by the time she was barely twenty-one. Perhaps it was the hardships the family had gone through—losing a home and moving far away.

Sounds like me.

She'd flipped through the diary but hadn't let herself read ahead. Nor had she allowed herself to read it fast, like a novel she might rush through to discover the ending. If asked, she wouldn't have been able to say why she approached the diary this way.

It seemed strange that she knew the girl's husband's name—Harry—and their children's names—Gladys and Dottie and Charlie—but still didn't know the author's name. Was it the mystery that drew her close? Or was it something else?

She opened the diary and looked for one of the written prayers.

**God, I know You are always
with my children and that You
love them even more than I do.
I ask that they would be aware
of Your presence from an early
age. Inhabit their dreams,
Father. Draw them to Your will
with each decision they must
make. You have placed these
little ones into our care. Help us
to be good parents to them, to
raise them up as they should go
so that when they are old they
won't depart from You. In the
blessed name of Jesus I pray,
amen.**

The words stirred something in Emma's chest. A warm feeling. A feeling of...hope.

"God," she whispered, "are You up there? Did You listen to her prayers? Are You listening to mine?"

She didn't know why, but she thought maybe she heard God say, **Yes.**

Olivia gazed at her computer screen, but her thoughts weren't on her work. They were on Tyler Murphy, a place her thoughts wandered all too often as of late.

She'd seen him, if only for a moment, at the amphitheater on Wednesday night. Then again on Thursday, Friday, and Saturday nights. She'd seen him at church yesterday morning. And those glimpses of him lingered in her mind, unwelcome but ever so persistent.

Closing her eyes, she muttered, "Go away."

If she wasn't mistaken, Tyler's image —the one in her imagination—grinned in response.

"I've got too much work to do for this nonsense."

Despite the self-scolding, she didn't stop imagining him. He lingered there with his dark, friendly eyes and his easy smile. But why? Oh, he was good looking. No question. But she'd met plenty of good-looking guys. Tyler was little more than an acquaintance. There was no reason he should fill her thoughts the way he had in recent days. No reason at all.

"Mom?"

Thankful for the interruption, Olivia swiveled her chair toward the door to her studio. "Yes?"

Emma stepped into the room, holding an old book in one hand, her thumb holding a place between the pages. "I was wondering..." She let the words hang in the air.

Finally, Olivia prompted, "Wondering what?"

"Do you think it's okay to read the diary of somebody who's probably dead?"

The question, so unexpected, left Olivia uncertain what to say.

"I mean, if the diary was given to you—something somebody was just gonna throw out—it would be okay to read it. Right?"

"Well, yes. I suppose so." She

frowned. "Why do you ask?"

Emma sank onto the extra chair in the studio. "Mr. Simpson. Timothy Simpson. He volunteers for the theater company. Handles the props. You met him, I think. He brought a bunch of old stuff from his mom's house for the actors to use during a performance." She looked down at the book in her hand. "This diary was there, and he said I could take it. So I've been reading it. This woman —I don't know her name yet—she was a wife and a mom back during the nineteen thirties. It doesn't seem to be private stuff. Just things that happened day to day. Still, all of a sudden I wasn't sure it was okay to look through it."

"The nineteen thirties. During the Great Depression."

"Yeah, so she'd be like a hundred and ten or something if she was still alive. And that's not likely."

"Then I don't suppose there's any harm in you reading it. People publish old diaries all the time." Olivia paused. Was it possible there was a way that diary could draw Emma into the community even more? Make her feel more at home here? Leaning forward, she added, "But maybe you should go see Mrs. Simpson. Maybe the diary was taken to the theater by accident."

Disappointment—along with a trace of stubbornness—crossed Emma's face.

"I doubt that's the case," Olivia added quickly. "But if you knew more about the author, it might make the diary even more interesting."

"I suppose." Emma drew out the two words with reluctance.

"Mrs. Simpson's a very nice woman. I can get her address for you."

Emma shrugged. "Sure. Why not?"

Feeling as if she'd achieved something monumental, Olivia swiveled the chair toward the desk and opened the contacts app on her computer. A few moments later, she wrote Phoebe

Simpson's name and address on a slip of notepaper, then handed it to Emma.

Her daughter glanced at the paper before looking up in surprise. "Phoebe Simpson. You mean like the high school?"

"Yes, the school was named for her. Mrs. Simpson was a history teacher in Bethlehem Springs. Pretty much all her life, I understand. She retired three years ago, just before they opened the new high school that was named in her honor." Afraid she was losing Emma's attention, she added, "She'll probably have an interesting story or two to tell you about that diary and the woman who kept it."

Emma rose. "Yeah. Maybe. Thanks."

The phone rang, keeping Olivia from saying more. Probably a good thing. "Olivia Designs."

"Hi, Olivia. It's Kathy."

"Hi, Kathy."

"Listen, I won't keep you. I know you're working. But I forgot to tell you yesterday that Greg and I are hosting a barbecue on the Fourth, and we want you and Emma to come. Greg's making his ribs. No fireworks allowed this year because of the fire danger, but we thought we'd put up a badminton net or set up a croquet course. Maybe both. Can you come, or do you already have plans?"

"We can come. No other plans."

"Great." Kathy gave more details and, as promised, hung up without keeping Olivia on the phone long.

As she clicked to open another app on her computer, she couldn't help thinking how much her life had changed in a short amount of time. In just a matter of weeks. Somehow, having Emma living with her again had made Olivia more a part of the community too. Her few friendships in Bethlehem Springs seemed to have deepened, and she no longer spent the bulk of her time in her studio. She felt more...more alive. For years she'd merely existed, and now she was living life again. She was a participant.

"Thank You," she whispered. And as the words left her mouth, she felt another chunk of ice break away from her heart.

July 1, 1933
Saturday

It has been months since I opened this diary. So much has happened that it was difficult to find the time. That is what I tell myself. The truth is that I didn't want to write it down because it would become more real if I set it on this page.

We were forced to move again at the end of February. (That's what worried Harry back then, what he tried to keep from me for as long as he could.) The farm was sold, and the new owner wanted to live and work the property himself. I cannot blame him. And I cannot blame Mr. Overton for selling either. It is the

fate of more than one tenant
farmer to be forced from the land
they have worked. So many find
themselves adrift today.

But Harry was able to find
another piece of land, another
farm where we could have a
home. The house is even smaller
than the other, but Charlie sleeps
in our room downstairs, and the
girls share the loft above us. The
table in the kitchen is big enough
for our little family to sit around,
but no more. I miss having a
large kitchen, one where women
could gather and talk as we all
worked. Those days are gone.

Today is our anniversary.
Five years ago, Harry and I
exchanged vows in the church in
Iowa, and before the month was
over, we left everyone behind to
begin our new lives as owners of
a lemon grove in California. We
had such high hopes. So many

dreams. Who could have known the financial troubles that would overtake the country and, it seems, the world? I did not, but then, I am not as well educated as some.

I wonder if Harry will even remember what today is. He works hard from dawn to dusk. He is focused on providing for his family, not on the calendar. In the summer, one day is much the same as the one before.

When we married, the nine years that separate us in age did not seem so very much. Harry was still young, and he was exciting to be with. He worked hard and had saved up enough to buy his own land in the West.

But now it seems I see him becoming an old man right before my eyes. Do I look the same to him? I have lost weight. Not just the weight I gained while carrying Charlie. Much more than that. My dresses hang on me. And when I look at my hands— red and rough—I see my mother's hands. Old hands.

O God, I do not mean to complain. You have blessed us. You care for us. We are not starving. Harry is not riding the rails, looking for work, leaving us behind, as many men have had to do. We have not needed to send our children to other members of our families to raise. I don't mean to be ungrateful. There are more important matters than my hands that are rough or the dresses that are too big for me.

Help me to be like David in the Psalms. Help me to be honest before You, to bring You my needs and my concerns, but to always return to a place

of praise before my writing is
over. Increase my love for You.
Even more, increase my trust
in You. Amen.

July 2, 1933
Sunday

Harry remembered our
anniversary, and I blush even
as I write this. I am oh, so loved.

Chapter 14

The old bike from her mom's shed gave Emma a sense of freedom. While she wasn't allowed to ride it to the theater because of how late the shows finished, she could ride around Bethlehem Springs, and she did so most days of the week.

Not that there was a whole lot to see. The town wasn't big. The four-year high school had about 160 students, she'd been told, and that included the kids bused in from who knew how many miles away. Not that she'd met many of them, since it was the summer break. But she knew the ones who attended the same church her mom took her to on Sundays and a few who were part of the theater company. She'd gone for a Coke with Izzy Rath and her sister Ava after the auditions. They were both nice. But most of the time Emma felt like a fish out of water. She didn't really belong in Bethlehem Springs, but she doubted she would belong in Florida either if she could go back. Regina rarely texted her anymore. Life had gone on the same for her.

Not for Emma.

On this warm Tuesday morning, she turned north onto Lincoln and followed the road until she saw a black mailbox with **Phoebe Simpson** written on the side in distinct white letters. The numbers seemed to have been added as an afterthought. She rolled to a stop and stared at the small house.

"I should've gotten her phone number."

The front door opened, and a woman stepped onto the front porch. Could that be Mrs. Simpson? Emma had expected someone with white hair and stooped shoulders. That was not the woman on the steps. The same woman who'd noticed Emma and was now waving to her.

As if she'd expected a visitor, the woman came down the walk. "Good morning. Lovely day for a bike ride."

"Yeah."

"I don't believe we've met. I'm Mrs. Simpson." She smiled, and her look was warm and welcoming.

"Emma Ward."

"Olivia's daughter? My goodness, yes. I can see the resemblance now."

"Really?" Crazy, but the words made Emma feel good.

"Yes." Mrs. Simpson stepped to the side of the mailbox, opened the front, and put in an envelope before closing the front again and standing the flag on end.

"I…uh…I met Timothy…your son…at the theater. He does the props there."

"Yes, I know." The smile blossomed.

Emma wished she hadn't come. She wished she'd never told her mom about the diary. What did it matter anyway? It was something thrown away. Sure, she liked reading it. Which was funny because it wasn't exciting or anything. It was kind of sad at times too. Emma couldn't explain why it interested her. It just did.

Stupid. She should go home. She put her right foot on the raised pedal.

"Was there something you wanted to ask me, Emma?"

Her breath caught. How did she know?

"We could sit on the porch if you like?" Mrs. Simpson motioned with her hand.

"Well..."

The woman offered another smile.

"If you don't mind." Emma pulled her leg over the crossbar and stood beside the bike. "I guess I could sit for a while."

"Not only don't I mind, but I would rather enjoy the company. Come on. Let's get acquainted."

"Thanks, Marshal," Tyler said as he leaned back in his desk chair. "That's great news. I wish every case could be resolved this fast and with the same result."

"I know what you mean. Ian wanted you to know they appreciated the work you did trying to locate her." The next words from Marshal were muffled, and Tyler knew the lawyer had covered the mouthpiece with his hand while he spoke to someone in the office. A few moments later, Marshal said, "I've got to take another call. Let's schedule a lunch sometime soon."

"Will do."

They said their goodbyes, and Tyler placed the handset in its cradle. Then he let himself feel good about Lily Applegate being safe and coming home. From what Marshal said, the girl had

had a bad scare on Sunday night when someone tried to break into the car where she'd slept. Frightened, she'd called her parents the next day. Tyler was thankful she'd had the good sense to want to come home. If the break-in had been successful...He shook his head, driving away the images that came to mind.

He opened his message app and notified his contact in the Seattle area that all was well. Afterward he entered some notes in the client file.

His stomach growled, reminding him he hadn't eaten breakfast. A glance at his watch told him it was almost noon. He rose and went to the kitchen, where he made a tuna salad sandwich and ate it while standing at the counter. Having his most immediate case solved meant he wouldn't have to fly to Seattle this afternoon as planned. That was good, since he'd dreaded letting down Kathy and the theater company if he couldn't get back in time.

As he washed his lunch dishes, he thanked God again that Lily Applegate would return home without coming to any harm. But he also knew this wasn't a problem that had been solved by a single phone call home. From April Applegate he'd learned Lily had been following a boyfriend who'd moved to Washington. A boyfriend who, according to Marshal, hadn't wanted anything more to do with her. He had a new girlfriend, which was why Lily had ended up sleeping in the car.

"Help the family get back on track, Lord. Put Lily on a better path."

His thoughts turned to Emma Ward. Not because it was his job either. He thought of Emma because she was the same age as Lily, because she'd been miserable when she first came to Bethlehem Springs. Her unhappiness wasn't yet a thing of the past, but from what Tyler had observed, progress had been made. She didn't seem as angry with the world or with her mom. He was glad of that.

As for Olivia...

Thinking her name made him smile. More than that, it made him want to see her. Not just a glimpse of her. Not just a minute or two to say hello as they passed each other in the amphitheater parking lot. Something more...substantial. He wished he had a reason to call her, to see her. A reason that had nothing to do with Emma or the client who had him looking into their lives. More like a...a date.

You can forget it, Murphy. No getting involved with a subject.

He knew better. He knew not to let his emotions get tangled with his investigations. He could care, but from a distance.

"This is what happens when I've got spare time on my hands," he said aloud as he headed for the back door. "I need some manual labor."

Olivia paced to the living-room window

that looked out over the town. Where was Emma? She'd been gone several hours and had missed lunch.

"I should've asked where she was going," Olivia whispered as she picked up her car keys. But she put them down again. Driving around, looking for Emma, wasn't the right thing to do. She had to trust her, give her a little freedom. She hadn't allowed Emma to come home on her own from the theater late at night, but this was daytime in Bethlehem Springs. There was no reason to panic.

Have a little faith.

She was about to turn away from the window when she caught sight of some motion at the end of the road. A second later, she knew it was Emma, riding the bike toward home. Relief flooded through her, but she was determined not to let on how worried she'd been. She hurried to the kitchen and began wiping the already clean counters with a damp dishcloth.

"Hey, Mom."

Olivia turned off the running water. "I'm in the kitchen."

Emma appeared in the doorway. "Sorry I'm late."

"You missed lunch."

"I forgot the time."

Olivia drew a slow breath as she draped the dishcloth over the faucet to dry. "Where did you go?"

"I met Mrs. Simpson, and we got to talking."

Surprise shot through Olivia. She'd encouraged Emma to meet Phoebe Simpson, but she hadn't thought she would do it. At least not this soon.

"She's kind of a cool old lady." Emma sat on a chair at the kitchen table. "I told her about how I found the diary."

"Did you take it with you?"

"No."

"What if she'd wanted it back?"

"Well, she does. Sort of. I mean, she said I could read it. But she'd like it when I'm ready to give it back. But no hurry."

Olivia sat opposite Emma. "I see. So she didn't mean to throw it out or give it away."

"No. It must've been in the box by accident. She said it was her grandmother's diary. Millie was her name. Millie MacIver."

"And she doesn't mind you reading it?"

Emma shook her head. "I think she was glad I wanted to read it. Like it was nice to have somebody else interested. Is that weird?"

Olivia smiled. "I don't know Mrs. Simpson well, but she strikes me as anything but weird."

"I suppose."

"But now you've made me even more curious. What is it you find so interesting about an old diary?"

Emma got up and walked across the kitchen. "I wondered that myself before I talked to Mrs. Simpson." She opened the refrigerator door, her head disappearing from view as she looked inside. A moment later, she straightened, an apple in hand. "Maybe it's because Millie wanted to be an actress before she got married. I guess she ended up doing what they called professional readings, like her aunt did. Mrs. Simpson said when Millie was older she did quite a bit of that. Or maybe it's because Millie was only a year older than me when she got married. Sixteen and a half. She had her first baby not quite ten months later. A mom at seventeen. No way would I want to have a baby at that age."

Olivia was grateful for that but said nothing.

"Anyway, Mrs. Simpson said I should come talk to her again when I finish reading it. I think I'll do that. She really is nice."

There were moments when Olivia believed the bad times were behind them, that Emma had settled into Bethlehem Springs and was happy. That she didn't miss the trappings of wealth or her fancy boarding school. That she liked living with her mom again.

This was one of those moments.

July 16, 1933
Sunday

When we arrived home from church today, Harry and the girls discovered a litter of puppies and their mother in one of the stalls in the barn. We have seen the mother on the edges of this land over the past couple of months. Perhaps she has stayed in our barn at night, but we haven't fed her or tried to make her ours.

However, it will not surprise me if Scruffy turns out to be the proud papa. The puppies are hairless and without much in the way of markings, so it is too soon to tell. But I think I see something of Scruffy in them. Gladys and Dottie are charmed by the little creatures, and Charlie giggled when Harry held one of the pups up close to his face. I suspect we shall not easily get rid of these puppies as they grow. The children will want to keep them all.

The mother must have a name if she is to remain with us.

Scruffy, what shall your missus be called?

July 20, 1933
Thursday

As I weeded the garden in the
cool of the morning (the days
have been very hot this week),
I looked up to see the girls
playing with Charlie on a blanket
I spread on the ground. He
wanted desperately to crawl
away, so Gladys brought over
some sticks and rocks and made
up a story about them. At least
I think it was a story. Sometimes
I swear she speaks two
languages. One moment it is
English and very understandable,
and then it is something else
entirely. A language I do not
comprehend, even as her mother.
   Dottie and Charlie listened to

her, as if enchanted. They understood their big sister without a problem.

I thought of how they are growing up right before my eyes, like the vegetables in my garden rising in rows. As their mother, I must be wise enough and attentive enough to get rid of the weeds in their lives. I must tend and water them and nurture them with the truth of Christ so that they grow straight and strong, reaching for the sun. Only not the sun that vegetables reach toward. My children must reach toward the Son.

The weight of responsibility fell on me, pressing on my shoulders. Am I wise enough? Am I good enough?

In the very instant those worries flooded my mind, I felt these words in my heart: "But thanks be unto God, who always leadeth us in triumph in Christ, and maketh manifest through us the savor of his knowledge in every place."

I do not know how else to write it except to say I felt God smile upon me.

These children, Gladys and Dottie and Charlie, are His before they are mine. I can trust them into His care. He will help me and Harry to raise them to follow Jesus. He will lead us all to triumph in Christ.

Amen.

Chapter 15

No amount of chopping firewood or clearing brush on his property, and no amount of reading case files or doing research or preparing for a future court appearance, was able to keep Tyler's thoughts from drifting time and again to Olivia Ward. He wanted to know her better. Not as an investigator but as a man. The logical side of his brain said that wasn't smart. What would Peter Ward have to say about that? But he didn't care. It had been years—too many years—since he'd met a woman who made him feel like this. Eager to see her. Impatient when he couldn't.

And so he called her.

She answered on the third ring. "Olivia Designs."

"Hi, Olivia. It's Tyler. Tyler Murphy." He sounded like a nervous high-school kid, his voice quavering. Not the best way to start.

"Oh. Hi, Tyler."

He cleared his throat. "I was wondering if you'd like to go to dinner with me?"

"Dinner?" Surprise laced the lone word.

"Yes. In Boise. Would be a nice change from the Gold Mountain Café, don't you think?"

She laughed softly before answering, "But you have the performances."

He'd forgotten. Despite going to the theater last night for the system checks, thoughts of Olivia had driven the obligation out of his head. "That's right. I thought maybe Monday or Tuesday next week. I'm free on those nights."

"Monday's Independence Day. Emma

and I already have plans."

He winced as he closed his eyes. "The Fourth. I forgot." He sounded worse than a nervous kid. Would he completely bungle this? "Tuesday night, then. A nice drive. A nice meal. I'd have you home by nine. Ten at the latest."

"I don't know."

He sensed her pulling back from the idea. He even understood. From what he'd learned, she hadn't dated anybody in the years since her divorce. And he even understood why she'd soured on men. Her ex had handed her a raw deal. Still, since Emma's return, Olivia had taken a few steps outside of the sheltered life she'd built for herself. Dinner with a guy—dinner with **him**— might be a good next step.

Before she could flat-out refuse his invitation, he asked, "Do I need to get Emma's permission?"

There was a hesitation, then another soft laugh. "No. I don't think so. But would you let me think about it? I'll let you know when I drop Emma off at the theater tonight. I'll come to the control booth."

"All right. Sounds good." That wasn't the truth. It didn't sound good. Not to him. But at least it meant he would see her tonight for a few minutes. "Talk to you then."

After ending the call, Tyler opened his laptop and entered some case notes in a new file. But it wasn't long before he opened the Ward file. As he scrolled through the photographs in one of the folders—a lot of them photos of Olivia—he realized that if she accepted his invitation to dinner, he would have to remove himself as the investigator. Maybe he needed to do that anyway. At the moment, everything about Olivia Ward seemed perfect to him. He knew she wasn't perfect. No one was. Everybody had flaws. Everyone made mistakes.

But he couldn't see what those mistakes or flaws might be in Olivia.

Tyler Murphy wanted to take her out to dinner.

It wasn't as if Olivia hadn't been asked out in the years since she'd moved to Bethlehem Springs. Not often, but a time or two. So it wasn't the invitation that had taken her off guard. It was the response she'd wanted to give him. She'd been tempted to say yes, and that hadn't happened before. Actually she'd been more than tempted. She'd **wanted** to go out with him. She still wanted to go out with him. Which made no rational sense whatsoever.

It wasn't a good time to rock the Ward boat—an unsteady boat that had started taking on water as soon as Olivia flew to Florida to get Emma. To continue the analogy, the storm that had engulfed mother and daughter seemed to have quieted somewhat, and it was better not to let anyone else join them until they were safely into port. If ever.

There. She'd decided. She would tell

Tyler no. She would let him know she wasn't interested in a relationship. She must focus on Emma. She and Tyler had mutual friends. They attended the same church. They would undoubtedly see each other and speak on occasion. But that was enough. A polite friendship was all she could handle. It was all she needed.

She checked the clock on the wall and decided to prepare lunch before returning to her latest design project.

"Emma, are you hungry?" she called on her way to the kitchen. Silence was her only response. "Emma?" When there was still no answer, she climbed the stairs and rapped softly on her daughter's door. "Emma?"

"Go away."

She drew back from the door. Only a few minutes ago, she'd thought they were doing better, that the storm had quieted. What had gone wrong? Drawing a breath, she rapped again before opening the door. "Honey?"

Emma lay on her side on the bed, her eyes red from crying.

"Sweetheart? What is it?"

"Just leave me alone." Emma rolled to her other side, her back toward the door.

"Won't you—"

"Please go away." Emma's voice broke on the words.

"Sometimes it helps to talk."

Emma rolled back and sat up. Despair had been replaced with anger. "Why couldn't you leave me where I was? I was happy at my school. My **life** is there."

Wordlessly, Olivia sank onto the chair near the door. What was there to say? Emma knew the reasons.

"Regina and some of our friends from school went to Italy."

It took Olivia a few moments to recall who Regina was.

"She doesn't want us to be friends anymore. I'm in Idaho, too far away. And besides, I couldn't afford to go to

Italy. She said my dad didn't care what would happen to me if he died."

A sick knot formed in Olivia's stomach, and an anger to match her daughter's expression flared in her chest. She'd like to throttle Daniel for his thoughtlessness, his carelessness, for the hurt he'd caused his own daughter. And if she could, she would give the cruel Regina a piece of her mind, a setdown that the girl would never forget.

Tears welled again in Emma's eyes, and she fell back on the bed. "I hate it here. I hate it."

"Not everything, surely."

"Everything. Everybody."

Olivia drew a slow breath and released it. "Even the theater company? Even Kathy and Hailey? Even Izzy and Ava?"

Emma huffed but didn't answer.

Yesterday, at their counseling appointment, Emma had told Adam Green how much fun she was having working with the other members of the Bethlehem

Springs Mountain Theater Company. She'd explained about the part she would have in the final play of the season and even mentioned the diary she'd found. She hadn't sounded like a girl who hated Bethlehem Springs and everything and everyone in it. She'd sounded...almost happy.

Did every mother get whiplash living with a fifteen-year-old? Or was their situation more difficult than most?

"Emma." She rose from the chair. "I would change things if I could, but I can't. I'm sure your father didn't mean to leave you with nothing." **Was** she sure of that? She wanted to believe her own words, but did she? "Most people don't consider that they could die before they are old. I'm sure he believed he had a lot more time to put his affairs in order."

Emotion thickened her throat. No, she wasn't sure. She didn't believe her own words. Daniel's financial affairs had not been an accident. Whether his choices had been punitive in nature or forced upon him by others, she didn't know. But he had to have known what would happen to Emma if he were to die. He'd known and had done nothing to prepare her or help her.

How could he do that to her? His own daughter. How could he?

Olivia left Emma's room, closing the door softly behind her, tears blurring the way before her.

July 31, 1933
Monday

Charlie woke up long before dawn, and after I changed his diaper, I took him out to sit on the front porch to watch the sunrise. The air was sweet with the smell of dew-covered alfalfa. The half-moon lingered on the western horizon as the sky lightened from pewter to a pale blue. In the quiet of the morning, I could hear the whimper of the puppies in the barn. They remain in the stall for now, but before long they will venture beyond those boundaries.

Eventually we all venture beyond our boundaries, don't we? We begin our lives nestled in the protection of our family. But one day we grow up, and we discover there is a larger world, and off we go. If I hadn't met Harry, I never would have seen California. If we hadn't lost our orchard, I never would have seen Idaho. I would have missed the beauty of this area with its rivers and creeks, with its rich farmland reclaimed from the desert, with rugged mountains to the north and to the south.

Sometimes I have felt lost, and then I have wished for the security of my girlhood home. I miss my parents. I miss someone else providing the comfort, someone else being brave in the face of trials. But we cannot go back in time. Time only goes in one direction, and I am the mother now. The mother of three at the age of twenty-one, and living in Idaho. How could I ever have imagined that?

August 15, 1933
Tuesday

For many days a hot wind has
blown through this valley. A layer
of dust covers everything in the
house. I clean, and before the
day is over, all my cleaning has
been undone. I should not
complain. I have read of the
terrible dust storms that have
happened from Nebraska to
Texas. We met a family at church
who came here from Oklahoma
earlier this month, and the
woman said it seems like the
earth just rose up and blew away,
headed for the Atlantic Ocean.
They lost everything to the
Depression, drought, and dust.
Far worse, I think, than the

troubles that befell my family, although our losses were bad enough.

The book of Ephesians instructs us to give thanks for all things. God knows I struggle with that. It is easy to be thankful for the good things in my life. For my husband. For our children. For this home, dusty though it is. For good health. For good friends.

But for the trials and troubles? That is much more difficult. Thanksgiving, our pastor says, should permeate the life of a believer. A true Christian will not withhold thanks for some things, for the hard things, but will always be thankful for every-thing, in every circumstance. I have asked God to make that true of me, but I fear He has a difficult student in me. I do not learn as quickly as I would like.

Dear heavenly Father, take Your
wind and blow away the stubbornness in me. Blow away my
complaints. Make me thankful
in and for all things, as Your
Holy Word tells me I should be.
Perfect in me the good work
You began, until the day of Jesus Christ. Only You can do it,
Lord.

Chapter 16

An overcast sky that afternoon matched
Emma's mood. As soon as the car
came to a stop in the amphitheater
parking lot, she released her seat belt
and got out.

"Emma!"

She ignored her mom and hurried
toward the entrance. She didn't want
to answer any more questions, and she
didn't want to be told things would get
better. Nothing would get better. Not as
long as she had to live in Bethlehem
Springs.

"I hate it here. I hate it."

Her mom could bring up the theater

or Kathy Dover or Hailey or Izzy or anybody else, and it wouldn't make a bit of difference. Her old friends didn't even stay in touch unless she texted them first. It hadn't been even two months since her dad died, and Emma was forgotten by everybody who used to care. She was a thing of the past to all the girls at Blakely Academy.

It stunk. It really stunk.

Backstage, Emma joined the rest of the crew and the cast just as the director began telling them about a few last-minute changes.

"Emma." Victor Benson's gaze found her. "We'll need you to serve as a stagehand for the next three nights. Richard, will you fill her in?"

"Sure."

She looked to her right and found Richard Merrimack leaning against the back of the stage. He gave her a nod and one of his slow grins, and her heart skipped a beat or two in response. He was so cute. Not that he'd given her much notice since she'd joined the company. He probably thought she was still a kid. She wasn't sixteen yet, and somebody had told her Richard was about twenty or twenty-one.

Wouldn't it just frost Regina if a hunk like Richard Merrimack took an interest in her? The thought made her want to smile for the first time since getting that awful text from Regina.

The pre-performance meeting broke up, and Richard pushed off the stage and walked to where Emma stood. "First time as a stagehand?"

"No." She shook her head, moistening her lips with her tongue at the same time. "I've done it for plays at my old school."

"Where was that?"

"Blakely Academy. It's a girls' school in Florida."

Once again, he grinned that special grin of his. "We probably do things different here."

Was he putting her down? Mocking

her?

"Come on. We'll do a quick walk-through. Luckily, there aren't a lot of changes from one act to another. And you probably know what to do. You pay attention to details. I've seen you. I'll bet you know this production forward and back."

Not mocking. He'd noticed her. Maybe he thought she was a kid, but he **had** noticed her.

Olivia stood just inside the entrance to the theater. Was she waiting for a glimpse of Emma? Or was it talking to Tyler she dreaded? Both, she supposed.

Emma appeared out of a wing and walked to the center of the stage. Beside her was a young man who looked familiar. It took a few moments for her to remember that he played Algernon in the current production. As she recalled, Emma thought him wonderful in the role. And whatever he was saying to her now, she paid close attention. Better yet, she didn't look as sullen as she had upon arrival. Thank goodness.

Then again, was she paying him **too** much attention? He was too old for her. He was a handsome young man, but definitely a man. Emma was an impressionable girl—one at a dangerous age.

Oh, please don't let her get her heart broken by a guy in addition to everything else.

Drawing a breath, Olivia headed in the direction of the control booth. As she climbed the steps, she reminded herself that she didn't need to get her heart broken by a guy either. And even if that wasn't likely to happen, she hadn't the time or the energy for a real relationship. Emma needed her to focus on her alone. Ever since the divorce, all that Olivia had wanted was for her daughter to come home. Now Emma was here. She must be Olivia's priority.

She rapped lightly on the door to the

control booth.

"Come in." Tyler swiveled his chair toward her as she entered. "Hey there."

"I shouldn't stay. I can see you're busy."

"Not at the moment. Not for another hour or so." He motioned to the other chair in the small room. "Have a seat."

Heat rose in her cheeks. She didn't know why. She wasn't embarrassed. Yet she found it difficult to meet his gaze. Even harder to tell him what she'd come to say. That she wasn't interested in going out with him. That this wasn't a good time for her. That she couldn't handle any further complications—and she was certain that's what he would be. A complication.

"Please," he said, intruding on her thoughts. "Sit for a minute or two."

Almost against her will, she did his bidding.

Tyler looked through the glass toward the stage. "Emma's fitting in with the rest of the crew. She works hard. Everybody can see that."

Olivia followed his gaze in time to see Emma and Richard disappear once again into the wings. "She's still struggling, though."

What was wrong with her? Why did she say that aloud? It wasn't any of his business.

"I'm not surprised," he said. "Her world's been turned upside down."

"Yes."

"Change is hard for everybody. Even in the best of circumstances." He was silent for a short while, then added, "I was ten when the state took me and my younger sister from our home."

Olivia turned to look at him.

"We didn't have any other family to take us in. Our dad was dead, and our mom...Well, she just wasn't able to take care of us. So we grew up in foster care. Some of it was good, some not so good." His expression suggested his last words had been an understatement. He drew a breath, then continued,

"But Emma's got a mom who loves her and a real home, even if she doesn't feel like it yet. It won't be easy, but I believe she's got a lot going for her. She's gonna be okay."

"A friend in Florida sent an unkind text message to her today. It threw her."

"Kids can be mean."

Olivia's throat thickened, making it impossible to respond.

"You two are seeing a counselor. Right?"

"How did you know that?" she asked softly.

He gave a slight shrug. "Small town. You have to want to keep something a secret and never tell anybody."

"Was it Kathy who told you?"

"No, and it wasn't Greg either. Just so you know." A frown furrowed his brow. "Anyway, wherever I heard it, it's a good idea. The counseling, I mean. I wish my sister had—" He broke off suddenly, and a pained expression crossed his face before he turned away, his attention now focused on the sound-board.

What had he been about to share about his sister? There was grief involved. That was obvious. There was a wound in him that hadn't yet healed. Empathy rose within her, and she wished she could comfort him.

Tyler cleared his throat. "Sorry." He met her gaze again, and there was no sign of the unhappy emotions that had filled his eyes moments before. "I'd better let you give me your answer about dinner next Tuesday before I have to pay attention to my job here." The smallest of smiles tugged at the corners of his mouth. "I hope you came here to say yes."

"Yes." Which, of course, was not what she'd meant to say. She'd planned a polite but firm refusal. She'd planned to make it clear that it wasn't a good idea, that she was better off without romantic entanglements, that her focus must remain on Emma. She'd made up her mind. Except it seemed her heart wanted something else.

A grin took over his entire face. "Great."

Before Olivia could correct herself, the door to the booth opened with a creak, and a male voice said, "Hey, Tyler, we've gotta—" Whoever it was stopped abruptly.

Tyler looked away from Olivia. "What is it, Drew?"

"I'd better go." She rose from the chair. "Like you said, you have a job to do."

"I'll call you."

"Yes, call me." And when he called, she would tell him she'd been mistaken, that she couldn't go out with him. That's what she would do. She wouldn't make the same mistake next time.

Drew waited until Olivia left the control booth before explaining what had brought him there. Fortunately, Tyler had a quick and easy fix, and before long he was alone in the booth again. In the amphitheater below, attendees were beginning to find seats or assigned places to spread blankets. Picnic baskets were opened, takeout containers were lifted from sacks, short-legged lawn chairs were unfolded, sweaters and jackets were tucked away until the cool evening air replaced the heat of the day.

Watching the scene unfold, Tyler released a relieved breath. Somehow he'd dodged a bullet. Olivia had come to the control booth to turn him down. He'd felt that in his gut the moment she'd stepped through the doorway. But at the last moment she'd given a different answer, and before she could change her mind again, Drew had interrupted them.

He didn't know if what transpired had been divine intervention, but he thanked God anyway. He wanted this chance with Olivia. He wanted it more with each passing day. She was special. She was...What? The one?

He chuckled softly as he made some adjustments to the controls. He was staring forty in the face, and this was the first time in his life that he'd seriously thought a woman might be the one and only for him. He wasn't sure he'd even believed in two people meant for each other. Sure, he'd been attracted to women. He'd even toyed with the idea of marriage about a decade earlier. But in the end, he'd known they weren't suited for the long term. And if he got married, it would be for the long term.

Sometimes he'd wondered if his experiences—in his youth, in his work—had soured him on the idea that relationships could last. Maybe he'd passed on relationships that could have become more, but he'd never been sure enough to stick around.

Olivia made him want to stick around.

Olivia stared at the ground as she walked

to her car. **I should go back. I should tell him that wasn't what I meant.** She pressed the button on her car fob. The lights blinked and the horn beeped. **I should do it now.**

But instead she opened the door and got in. Her gaze went to the entrance of the amphitheater. Above the wall she saw the roof of the control booth.

Go back and tell him no.

Her mobile phone rang, and she pulled it from her purse. Sara's photo filled the screen. "Hi, Sara."

"Hey, Olivia. I wasn't sure I'd catch you."

"The new cell tower is up. I can get service nearly anywhere in town, but I don't have to go far outside of Bethlehem Springs to lose it again. Why don't you come up to visit me and see for yourself?"

Sara chuckled. "Why don't you come down to Boise? We both know why. Life is nuts."

Olivia nodded. "Yes."

"Got a moment to talk?"

"Sure." She put the key in the ignition, turning it so she could lower the windows. "What's up?"

"That's my question. I wanted to know how you're doing. We haven't talked in a couple of weeks, and even if we don't have time to see each other, I still want to know how you're doing."

"I'm doing okay. Mostly."

"Honest?"

"Honest."

"How about Emma?"

Olivia sighed, her gaze returning to the theater entrance. "One day I'd tell you she's fine. The next she's not so good."

"It'll get better."

"That's what people keep telling me, including the counselor."

"I wish there was more I could do than just talk to you on the phone."

"There isn't. But I love you for wanting to help."

"Okay, then. Tell me what else is happening. Are your parents back from their big trip yet?"

"The week after next."

"When your mom's rested, let's have lunch so I can see her pictures and hear her stories. They must have seen some fabulous things in all these weeks they've been away."

Olivia nodded, even though Sara couldn't see her. "They have. She's updated me every week. And yes, we'll do lunch for sure."

"Are you doing anything for the Fourth? You and Emma could come down and go to the fireworks with us. Surely you could spare a few hours for that."

"Actually we have plans. We're going over to Greg and Kathy's for a barbecue and some games."

"Well, good. You won't be alone. That should be fun."

Olivia drew a deep breath. "There's something else. Believe it or not, I've got a dinner date on Tuesday." She squeezed her eyes closed. Why had she said that? Just minutes ago she'd meant to go back to the control booth and cancel the date. She'd been so sure she wouldn't keep it.

"Would you mind repeating that?" Sara said in a hushed voice.

"You heard me."

"I heard you. I just don't believe you."

"Thanks."

"Who is he? Do I know him?"

"His name's Tyler. You haven't met him. He moved to Bethlehem Springs from Boise about a year ago. We were introduced the night I took Emma to see her first play at the Mountain Theater. He's friends with the Dovers."

"Small world." Sara laughed softly. "That's especially true in Bethlehem Springs."

"He attends Cornerstone."

"That's good to know."

"I don't know why I'm telling you any of this. It's only one dinner, and I have no intention of it leading to another. It isn't a good time for me to try to have a relationship. I've got way too much on my plate."

"I wish we were doing FaceTime right now. I'd love to see your face."

"You know what, Sara, I've got to go. I'm at the amphitheater."

"Okay. But you'll owe me details come Wednesday."

"Talk to you later." She pulled the phone from her ear and hit the End button, tempted to curse the new cell tower that had made her mobile phone more reachable.

August 29, 1933
Tuesday

Harvesttime is here again. The kitchen garden has provided wonderful food for our supper table. Harry works from dawn to dusk, and he falls into bed at night and sleeps like the dead.

Lately I have found myself thinking about city life. Maybe because I once thought I wanted to go to New York City. What must it be like to live surrounded by tall buildings, living in rooms three, four, or five or more stories above the ground? To never hear the crickets as night falls over the earth? To never smell the air at harvesttime? (There is something about the evening air in late

August that I can't describe
but that is so distinct.)

How could I have imagined I
would want a life lived among
bricks and stone?

I look at Harry with the children
and the puppies running around
in the yard on a Sunday afternoon, and I know that God gave
me the life He intended for me.

"And he that supplieth seed to
the sower and bread for food,
shall supply and multiply your
seed for sowing, and increase
the fruits of your righteousness."

I read that today in 2 Corinthians,
and the words tugged at my heart.
It is about harvest. It is about this
life that is so precious to me.

I am not sure what God wants
to say to me through that verse. I
just know He is speaking to me
and wants me to understand
something. And so I will listen
until I understand.

September 9, 1933
Saturday

A hobo came to our door around noon today. Harry was at Fred's farm, helping with the bailing of hay. Gladys and Dottie went with Harry to play with their cousins. I was home alone with Charlie, enjoying the cooling temperature and the quiet of the day.

When I opened the door in answer to the knock, the man (he appeared to be about the age of my father) stepped back. He held the brim of his battered hat with the fingers of both hands, and his head was bowed, as if in apology. His face and hands were grimy, his hair long and untidy, his clothes tattered and in need of a good wash. The sunkenness of his grizzled cheeks told me he had not eaten in a while. At least not eaten enough.

"Is there any work about, madam?" he asked me. "I could use a meal, if you'd let me work for it."

This man was no tramp. I saw that in his eyes when he finally looked up. He did not want a handout. He had fallen on hard times, but he held on to his pride as best he could.

Harry might have had something more substantial for him to do, but I only knew that we could use firewood chopped and stacked. But I insisted that he eat first. How can a man work hard when his stomach is gnawing with hunger?

When he left late in the afternoon, he said, "God bless

you, madam," and walked away with his bindle bouncing against his back.

And I thought to myself, **God has blessed me**, and a feeling that I can't describe welled up inside of me. It was almost as if I could feel the hand of God stroking my hair and feel the warmth of His smile upon my head. His smile wasn't because I helped a man in need, although I think that pleases the Lord. No, it wasn't because of anything I did to earn His pleasure. It was simply because He loves me.

I don't think I have ever known that so surely as I knew it today.

Chapter 17

An hour before the rest of the guests were expected, Tyler arrived at the Dover home to help Greg set up the croquet course and the badminton net in the oversized backyard. He found the kitchen a hive of activity, Kathy putting something in the oven while Hailey took something out of the fridge. After a quick hello, he was glad to get out of their way.

"Hey, Tyler." Greg stood near the door to the shed by the back fence. "Thanks for coming early."

"Glad to." He went down the steps and crossed the lawn.

"I should've looked for the games before now. The shed's a disaster." Greg pulled the door open wide, revealing stacks and piles of various shapes and sizes.

Tyler laughed. "You weren't kidding."

"Last time I saw the croquet set, it was in that corner. The badminton net and rackets should be in one of those boxes."

"I'll look for the croquet set," Tyler volunteered.

"Great." Greg moved inside the shed and began opening boxes. "So what's new with you?"

"Nothing much. Work's kept me busy. Lots of online work as of late, so that's made life easier." He stopped on his way to the corner and looked behind him. "I guess the one new thing is I'm taking Olivia Ward to dinner tomorrow in Boise."

Greg met his gaze. "Really?" He grinned. "Now, that is something. Last I knew, Olivia doesn't date. Not anybody."

"Mmm."

"Come to think of it, when was the last time you were on a date? You're not exactly a Casanova."

Tyler ignored the question and replied to the comment. "I'll take that as a compliment." He turned toward the corner again and began moving items to the right and the left. Part of him wished he hadn't told Greg about his plans with Olivia. After all, it might not turn out the way he wanted.

"Found it!" Greg cried.

A moment later, Tyler spied the top of the croquet set. "Me too."

"All right. Let's get these set up before Kathy reminds me I should have done it last night or first thing this morning."

Tyler laughed again as he followed his friend out of the shed.

General conversation was forgotten as they set up the badminton net on west side of the back lawn and the croquet court on the east side. The net took no time at all, but the croquet court was a different story as they stepped off the distance between wickets and drove stakes into the ground at both ends. Tyler had to stifle the urge to make sure everything was precise, that the distance between wickets was exactly the same throughout the course. He knew good and well that his perfection-ist tendencies weren't appreciated in every circumstance. The setup of a croquet court was one of those. At least for amateurs at a Fourth of July get-together.

"Good job, guys," Kathy called from the back deck.

Tyler shaded his eyes against the sun as he looked up. "Thanks."

As the word left his mouth, he saw that Olivia stood next to their hostess, and he felt a quickening of his pulse. He hadn't known she would be at the barbecue. He should have guessed, of course. She was friends with Kathy and Greg. But for some reason he hadn't expected to see her today. And there was a part of him that wished she hadn't come. Or that he hadn't come. Because what if she chose today to tell him she'd made a mistake and wouldn't go out with him tomorrow?

"She **is** pretty," Greg said as he stepped to Tyler's side.

"Yeah, she is."

"A good person."

"I've noticed that too."

Greg put a hand on Tyler's shoulder. "But she's still...I don't know. **Fragile** is the word Kathy used. Anyway, be careful with her."

Tyler gave his friend a look.

"I'm serious. Her divorce was brutal, and her ex was a class A jerk from what I can tell. She was financially in the hole for a long time. Years. And she had to go without seeing her daughter for years too. Not sure of all the reasons for that. Only know that between lack of money and the ex, that's what happened. It was rough."

Tyler knew all of that and a lot more besides, but he couldn't say so. Not to Greg. The information was confidential. He'd worked that way for years, gathering intelligence that he then passed on to a client. Why did it suddenly feel...wrong? No, not exactly wrong. In most instances what he did was important. But when it came to Olivia...

He cleared his throat, then said, "I'll be careful."

"I know you will." Greg gave him an encouraging smile. "Never doubted it."

Tyler wondered if that was true, given he'd felt the need to give a warning.

"Now I'd better tend to those ribs before Kathy accuses me of shirking my duties."

Olivia watched as Tyler followed Greg across the yard to the gas grill on the patio below the deck.

I'm going out to dinner with him tomorrow.

The thought made her stomach churn, but not with dread. It was more like nervous excitement. An unexpected reaction after spending the last four days thinking she should call and cancel the date.

Kathy leaned forward over the deck railing. "Do you boys need anything to drink after all that hard work?"

"I'd take a Diet Coke," Greg called back to her. "If it isn't too much trouble."

"Same for me," Tyler added. "Thanks, Kathy."

"No trouble." Kathy straightened and turned, her gaze on Olivia. "Would you mind taking the drinks down to the guys while I tend to things in the kitchen?" She pointed to a large cooler on the opposite side of the deck. "You'll find them in there."

With a nod, Olivia went to the cooler and pulled two cold, dripping bottles of Diet Coke from the ice-filled interior. As she went down the steps to the patio, she heard girlish laughter behind her and was relieved when she recognized the sound of Emma's voice in the mix. She wanted to turn. She wanted to look up and see her daughter smiling, but she didn't allow herself to give in to the desire.

"Here you go." She held out the drinks, one in each hand.

Tyler took them both since Greg was turning meat on the grill. "Thanks."

Her stomach skittered in response to the smile he gave her. She felt the warmth of it from the inside out.

"Dad, where are the rackets and birdies?"

Olivia turned as Hailey, Emma, and the Rath sisters, Izzy and Ava, reached the bottom of the deck steps.

Without turning from the grill, Greg answered, "On the tree stump near the end of the badminton net."

"Oh. I see them now. Thanks."

The four girls hurried on.

Now it was Olivia's heart that skittered. The four days since Regina's text had wounded Emma's spirit had been difficult for the most part. But it seemed this would be a good afternoon and evening for Emma. Which meant it would be good for Olivia too.

"She's made some friends," Tyler said in a low voice.

She looked at him and nodded, her heart warmed by the care and concern he showed—for Emma, for her. And she realized she wasn't sorry she'd accepted his invitation to dinner. She didn't want to cancel their date. She wanted to get to know him better, and he seemed to want to know her better too. That was a good thing. They didn't have to become anything more than friends. But who could have too many friends?

"Hey, Tyler. Grab that platter, will you? The ribs are ready to come off."

Tyler gave Olivia another quick smile before turning to do Greg's bidding.

Rather than stand there with nothing to do, she hurried up the steps and went into the kitchen. "How can I help?"

"Would you get the salads out of the fridge and take them to the food table on the deck?" Kathy opened the oven door, mitts on her hands. "They're in blue containers on the middle shelf."

"Sure." Olivia found the items and carried them outside.

Kathy was right behind her, carrying a hot dish of baked beans. "Okay, what am I missing?"

"It doesn't look like you **could** be missing anything. There's enough food here to feed an army."

Before Kathy could reply, a voice from inside the house called, "Ding-dong. Anybody home?"

"That'll be Chip and Wendy." Kathy moved to the open sliding door. "We're out here. You're just in time."

Moments later, Izzy and Ava's parents stepped onto the deck, a covered dish in Wendy's hands. Greetings were exchanged all around before Kathy summoned everyone to gather in a circle, holding hands. Greg said a blessing, and then thick paper plates began to pile high with ribs and coleslaw, baked beans and chips, and more. The four girls, who'd given up their badminton game to eat, settled together on the ground in the shade from the deck. Greg and Kathy's younger children, Ethan and Sophie, sat at the picnic table under the deck. The adults chose to remain on the deck itself.

Olivia observed the others as she settled on a chair. It occurred to her how many invitations she'd received through the years that she'd declined. How sad it seemed to her now. What had been accomplished by closing herself away? Nothing except increasing her sense of loneliness.

"Penny for your thoughts." Kathy settled on a nearby chair.

"Inflation makes that pretty worthless."

Her friend chuckled in reply.

"Actually, I was thinking how glad I

am we came today."

"Me too."

Olivia looked down at the food on her plate. "But if I eat all of this, I'm going to need a nap, not a game of croquet."

"Too bad. It's either badminton or croquet. Nobody gets to leave without playing one or the other."

"Well, I'll do my best. I promise."

September 18, 1933
Monday

Dottie began running a fever this afternoon. I should have noticed something was amiss right away. Perhaps I didn't because she has seemed ever so much better than she was when we first arrived in Thunder Creek. And she doesn't seem to be terribly ill. The fever isn't high. She seems a little listless. That is all.

I am borrowing trouble again, I suppose. I really must break that habit.

November 1, 1933
Wednesday

How many weeks have passed? It's hard to remember without staring at a calendar. The sun rises and it sets. Days go by. Everything is the same, and yet everything is changed. The hollowness of my heart leaves me numb. I go about my chores. I nurse Charlie, and I read to Gladys. I prepare the meals. I wash the clothes. And yet I am not there. Not really there.

I haven't picked up this diary since Dottie's illness began. After I read one of my last entries, I wept again. Where is God's smile now? Does He see me? Does He care?

Dottie began running a fever on a lovely afternoon. The blue sky was dotted with puffs of clouds. Strange how I remember that so very clearly. It was still September. The weather was warm beneath the sun. It was later in the night that I heard coughing and went to check on the girls. Gladys slept peacefully, but Dottie was tangled in the sheets. Her face was flush and damp, and she couldn't seem to draw a good breath. She cried out when I touched her, as if it caused her pain. Cool cloths turned hot almost as soon as they were laid upon her forehead. She moaned and whimpered, but she rarely opened her eyes. Harry went for the doctor, but there was nothing he could do. Nothing any of us could do but watch and wait and pray. Oh, how we prayed.

Our precious Dottie went home to heaven two days later. We buried her on a Saturday. Her cemetery plot rests near the edge of a gentle hill overlooking the creek. The water plays a pretty melody as it tumbles over rocks and stones. I know that she can no longer hear it, but she would love it all the same.

Three years and six months. That was all the time she had with us. It was not enough. Not nearly enough.

I am shattered.

God, do You care?

Chapter 18

Emma closed the diary and set it on the nightstand. Tears pooled in her eyes, and it made her feel stupid. It wasn't as if she actually **knew** Millie. She could only catch glimpses of who the author had been and what she'd felt.

All the same, she did know what it was like to lose somebody she loved. Not just her dad either. She'd lost her mom too. Just in a different way—and not forever.

She remembered when Dad had moved them to Florida. Emma had cried and cried. She'd missed home. She'd missed Mom. She'd missed Grandpa and Grandma. The missing had been even worse after her dad put her into Blakely Academy. She'd been a scared and lonely little girl for a long time.

Strange. She'd sort of forgotten all of those feelings, how sad she'd been and how long she'd felt that way.

She glanced at the closed diary and wondered if her mom had felt like Millie MacIver. After Emma was taken away, had Mom felt shattered too?

Olivia sighed as she turned off the computer. She'd spent hours working on a design for a client but hadn't been happy with anything she'd come up with. She would end up trashing them all in the morning, more than likely. But for now she needed to get ready for her date.

Her stomach somersaulted at the thought—and not for the first time that day.

"Hey, Mom."

She looked toward the door where Emma stood. "Yes?"

"I wanted to ask something. Is now a good time?"

"Of course. Come on in." She waited until her daughter was seated in the other office chair, then asked, "Is something wrong?"

Emma shook her head. "Not wrong." She frowned. "But I haven't been very nice to you lately."

Olivia kept silent, refusing to confirm or deny the comment.

"I'm sorry. It wasn't your fault what Regina said to me. It isn't your fault she doesn't want to be my friend anymore. But I took it out on you."

Now she had to answer. "It's okay. I understand, and I forgive you."

"I'm reading Millie's diary. You know. The one I found. Her little girl died. She was only three years old."

"Oh, that's sad."

"Yeah. It is." An embarrassed smile tipped the corners of her mouth. "It made me cry when I read it."

Sensing there was more to come, Olivia resisted the urge to rise and go to her daughter.

"Mom, she wrote afterward—a lot of weeks after Dottie died—that she was shattered. That's the word she used: **shattered**. And it made me wonder something. Is that...Is that how you felt when Dad took me away?"

The breath caught in Olivia's chest, and tears sprang to her eyes. The remembered pain was surprisingly sharp. "Yes," she whispered. "**Shattered** is the perfect word to describe how I felt."

"You really wanted me."

The lump in her throat kept Olivia from answering aloud. All she could do was nod, happy that it seemed Emma had begun to understand, that she'd begun to see through some of her dad's half-truths and outright lies about Olivia.

Emma worried her lower lip between her teeth for a short while. "And did you...Did you wonder if God cared?"

Yes. She mouthed the word, still unable to speak.

"Why don't You care?"

She remembered the words—or had it been an accusation?—as they'd been torn from her heart.

"So...you still believed in God? Despite what happened?"

"Yes."

"But you didn't think He cared about you?"

Olivia hooked a shank of hair behind her ear. "I didn't. Not for a long while. I didn't stop believing in God. It just felt as if He'd moved very far away from me." She drew a breath and released it. "But I'm beginning to understand that it was me who moved away. Not Him from me. He stayed close, even when I couldn't feel Him or hear Him. He was there."

"I didn't go to church when I lived in Florida."

"I know."

"Dad wasn't religious. He thought it was all...stupid."

Olivia nodded—and in her memory heard her own mom's warnings about being yoked with an unbeliever.

Emma frowned. "I guess I don't think it's stupid, exactly. I mean, Hailey Dover believes in Jesus, and she's smart. She talks about God and Jesus a lot. I don't understand a lot. Millie writes that way too."

O God, help Emma find her way to You. Help me find my way too. I believe. Help my unbelief.

Emma's shoulders rose and fell on a sigh. Then she shook her head and smiled. "You'd better get ready. You don't want to keep Mr. Murphy waiting."

"Emma, it is okay with you that I go out with Tyler, isn't it?"

"Yeah. Why not? I think he's nice."

"I suppose I should have asked before I accepted his offer."

"Mom, it's okay if you like him. I'm good with it."

"Then you're right. I'd better get ready." She stood. "Are you sure you don't mind staying home alone?"

"I'm almost sixteen, Mom. I'm not a baby. I can be on my own for a while."

"I know that. But—"

"It won't even be dark before you're back. You said so yourself." She flicked her fingers in a shooing motion. "Go have a good time."

Shouldn't this be the sort of conversation that happened in reverse? Shouldn't **she** be the one telling her daughter not to be nervous before a date? Not that she was ready for Emma to have a boyfriend. She would just as soon put off that complication and worry for a while.

With a quick nod, she left the studio and went to her bedroom. Fifteen minutes later she walked out to the living room, wearing a pair of white jeans and a yellow summer top. She carried a sweater in one hand in case air-conditioning made the restaurant cold. She'd put her long hair up and had even made use of some makeup.

Seated on the couch with her phone, Emma glanced up from the screen. "Wow. You look nice."

"Thanks."

Her daughter couldn't know, of course, how nervous she was.

"He's here, Mom."

It's only one dinner. It's only a few hours. It's good for you to do this. It's good to make a new friend. Nothing's at risk. It's only a dinner.

Tyler released a breath when he turned his SUV onto the highway about ten minutes later. Every moment they'd been in Olivia's house—him exchanging a few words with Emma, then listening as Olivia gave some last-minute instructions to her daughter—he'd feared she might still change her mind. But somehow they'd managed to get out the door and into his vehicle, and now they were on their way to Boise.

As they left all signs of Bethlehem Springs in the rearview mirror, he glanced at his passenger. Did she know how pretty she looked in that yellow top, her dark hair pulled up on her head?

"That was great fun at Kathy and Greg's yesterday," he said into the silence, his gaze back on the road before him.

"Yes."

"My favorite part was when your team beat Greg's in the croquet match."

That got the hint of a smile out of her.

"I liked that myself," she answered.

Okay. This drive might not be so bad after all. "I hadn't met the Raths before. They seem like a nice couple."

"Yes. Emma's become friends with Ava and Izzy because of the acting company, so I knew them a little already."

"I've probably said this to you, but it's good to see Emma settling in. She starts rehearsals for her play this week, doesn't she?"

"Yes, she does. How did you know?"

He kept his eyes on the winding highway. Making it sound dramatic, he said, "The guy in the control booth knows everything." Then he laughed. "No, seriously, I get the schedule every week. I know what's being rehearsed and what's in production and who all the players are, including the crew. I pretty much see all the comings and goings. I've only been at it a couple of weeks, but I was thrown right into the action. I'm a fast learner and really good with names and faces." She didn't need to know that the last trait was handy for the work he did.

"You make friends easily too. Don't you?"

That drew his gaze for a moment. "Yeah, I suppose I do."

"You're comfortable with people. I've noticed that. Even strangers."

"I suppose that's true too." Again, a handy attribute for an investigator.

She spoke softly this time. "I envy you."

"I guess it's my personality type."

"What type are you?"

"You mean like Enneagram or Myers-Briggs? Don't know. Never bothered to test."

She chuckled. "And yet you know what they are."

"I'm a fount of useless—and sometimes useful—information." This time when he glanced over at her he saw a full-fledged smile.

"I take it you like to read."

"That I do." True enough, although most of the information he had stored in his head was because of his job, not because of the books he read.

"Fiction or nonfiction?" she asked.

"Both." He felt her looking at him, as if trying to figure him out. Good. That might mean he had a chance at a second date, even if it was only out of curiosity. "What about you?"

"I read both, too, but I prefer novels."

Now here was information he didn't have about her. "What genre?"

"Historical fiction, mostly. All different settings and times. I like a variety. The past couple of years, I've developed a love for audiobooks so I can listen when I'm doing other things."

"I'll have to get some recommendations from you. I spend a lot of time in the car, driving back and forth between home and the valley."

"Kathy told me you work for a Boise law firm."

"Yeah." He braced for some questions he didn't want to answer. Hopefully he'd be able to change topics without it being awkward.

"But you're not an attorney."

"No, I'm not." He drew a breath and exhaled. "I'm something of a researcher. I look for information the attorneys need." All true, if somewhat evasive. "Meaning I'm on the computer a lot."

"I'm glad you're not an attorney." There was a coolness in her words that hadn't been there before.

"Me too," he said, hoping to lighten the mood. "I'd rather tell lawyer jokes than be one."

She didn't respond, and that chilled feeling remained in the air.

"Santa Claus, the tooth fairy, an honest lawyer, and an old drunk are walking down the street together when they all spot a hundred-dollar bill. Who gets it?"

Again, he was met with silence. When he glanced her way, he found her staring out the window at the passing hillside.

He drew a breath and answered his own question. "The old drunk. The other three are fantasy creatures." He waited a few heartbeats, then asked, "How many lawyer jokes are in existence?"

From the corner of his eye, he saw her turn to look his way.

"Only three. All the rest are true stories."

"Not funny," she said, despite the mirth in her voice.

"Okay. I'll see if I can come up with some better ones for...for later." He'd wanted to say "for next time," but he figured he'd better not push his luck. There were still a few hours to go on this date.

November 30, 1933
Thanksgiving Day

But there is no thanksgiving in my heart. I went with Harry to Fred and Rose's. I watched as the younger children played together. I helped Rose in the kitchen. I bowed my head when Fred said the blessing.

But I wasn't there. Not really.

December 1, 1933
Friday

Mark 4: "And on that day, when even was come, he saith unto them, Let us go over unto the other side. And leaving the multitude, they take him with them, even as he was, in the boat. And other boats were with him. And there ariseth a great storm of wind, and the waves beat into the boat, insomuch that the boat was now filling. And he himself was in the stern, asleep on the cushion: and they awake him, and say unto him, Teacher, carest thou not that we perish?"

Carest thou not that we perish?
Carest thou not that I perish?

Jesus, why do You sleep?
Jesus, do You care?

Chapter 19

By the time Tyler pulled into the restaurant parking lot, the last of Olivia's nerves were forgotten. Those awful lawyer jokes he'd told had helped, and she'd enjoyed the rest of the hour-long drive. It surprised her how much they'd found to talk about. Usually she kept her thoughts to herself. "My business is my business" had become her motto soon after her separation from Daniel. But it hadn't been that way this evening. She hadn't been reluctant to answer Tyler's questions or to ask questions of her own. Unusual...and quite nice.

Once in a parking space, Tyler turned off the engine. "Hope you like churrasco."

"I don't know what that is." She wondered if she should be nervous again.

He motioned toward the restaurant. "It's Portuguese...or maybe it's Spanish...for grilled meat. You'll see." His face took on an odd expression. "Please tell me you aren't vegan."

"You can relax, Tyler. I eat meat and other animal products without regret."

"Whew. I never thought to ask before I made reservations. Shows you how out of practice I am at this sort of thing." He got out, then rounded the front of the vehicle and opened her door.

"Thanks."

"This is my favorite Brazilian restaurant in Boise. I think you'll like it. Great salad bar. But I come here for the entrées. Different kinds of beef, pork, and chicken. All you can eat. Some of it's got barbecue sauce. Some's wrapped in bacon."

They were almost to the door by this time.

"You know," Olivia said, "you don't have to convince me to like it."

He grimaced as he reached for the door handle. "Sorry. Like I said, I'm out of practice."

She was definitely going to ask him about that, as soon as the right moment arrived.

"Welcome to the Brazilian Grill," the hostess greeted them.

Tyler gave his name and the reservation time.

The hostess checked the schedule on the desk, smiled at Tyler, and said, "If you'll follow me."

With his hand lightly cupping Olivia's elbow, they made their way to a table for two by a window with a view of the mountains. The restaurant's interior was open and spacious. Judging by the full tables, the place was popular.

They hadn't been seated long when

their server came. After getting their drink orders, the young man explained that they would be served **rodízio** style, with the meat brought to the table on long skewers. "You'll choose what you want, and the servers will slice the meat from the skewer onto your plate."

Olivia leaned toward Tyler after the server left. "This is different."

"A word of advice. Take small portions the first time around. They've got all different kinds of meats and preparations. You'll want to sample them all."

"Noted."

"Want to start with the salad bar?"

At least she didn't need him to explain what that meant. "Sure."

It really had been too long since she'd done something like this, Olivia thought as they wended their way to the salad bar. Forget that she hadn't been on a date since before she and Daniel got married. After they'd married, her husband had been too busy to go out.

At least that had been his excuse. He hadn't failed to wine and dine other businessmen when it served his purpose, but those dinners had been at the Ward home with Olivia working hard to impress. Not exactly fun. And since the divorce? Her idea of a treat was something from the deli in the local grocery store.

"You're lost in thought," Tyler said after they were both back at their table.

She shook her head. "Not really."

His eyebrows lifted.

"Well, maybe a little. I'm even more out of practice than you are."

He laughed softly, nodding.

"So why is that for you? Why no special someone in your life?"

He shrugged. "Nothing major. Moving up to Bethlehem Springs played a part in it, of course. Small town. Fewer single women. But mostly it was a series of...mmm...disappointments while I was living in Boise. It was just easier to keep to myself."

Olivia speared some lettuce with her fork. "I understand."

"But meeting you made me want to change that. Made me want to make an effort."

She set down the fork without taking a bite. "Tyler, I don't want…I don't want to give you false hope about…about where this might lead. I'm not…I'm not sure my life has room for more complications. You know Emma came back to live with me recently. She and I are still getting reacquainted. I'm not sure I have—"

He put up a hand to stop her from saying more. "Let's not overthink this. We found enough to like about each other to agree to go out to dinner together. Here we are. Maybe all this evening means is that we'll become friends. Maybe it'll be something more. But let's not take on the pressure of wondering what might be. Let's just continue to get to know each other."

The tension left her as quickly as it

had come. "Okay." She picked up her fork again. "I'm good with that."

Tyler lowered his gaze to his salad plate, wanting to give her time to collect her thoughts, to calm her nerves. She was skittish, that was for certain, and he understood the reasons. Hopefully this evening would make her more trusting around him.

Of course, he had an unfair advantage. He'd looked into her life for his work. He knew more about her than she knew about him. Maybe more than she would ever know about him. Maybe more than she knew about herself. He knew to steer clear of certain topics. He could guess what caused that deer-in-the-headlights look in her eyes when they moved onto dangerous ground. Maybe that was more than an unfair advantage. Maybe it was wrong.

He glanced up at the same time the first of their servers arrived, this one with a skewer of bacon-wrapped sirloin.

He wasn't sure what he might have said without the interruption. By the time the young man moved to the next table, Tyler had turned his thoughts in a safer direction.

"What's the difference between a lawyer and a jellyfish?" he asked as he pushed his salad plate to one side.

Olivia gave him an amused look. "Another one?" She shook her head. "I haven't a clue."

"One is a spineless, poisonous blob. The other is a form of sea life."

"Oh, that's bad. Does your employer know you tell these jokes?"

"Where do you think I learned them? Seems like I hear at least one every time I go into the office in Boise."

Her smile made something warm curl in his belly. He'd like to make her smile like that all the time. He'd like to ease her worries—about Emma, about money, about home repairs, whatever. He'd like to replace all of her bad memories with good ones. He'd like to make her trust him.

He lifted both hands in a gesture of surrender. "Okay. No more lawyer jokes for the rest of the evening."

On the drive down from Bethlehem Springs, they'd covered books and music and even a few movies. Tyler was trying to decide what to bring up next when Olivia asked, "Are you originally from Boise?"

"No. I was born in Wyoming. My mom moved to Boise after my dad left us. I have a vague memory of the move. I'd just turned five. I only know my age because of the apartment where we lived. We weren't there long, but long enough for me to start kindergarten."

"You've mentioned a younger sister. Does she still live in Boise?"

He'd rather talk about books, music, or films again. "No. Christa...died."

"Oh, Tyler. I'm sorry." She set her fork on her plate. "I didn't know."

"It's been three years." As if time made it easier to think or talk about.

Empathy filled her eyes, along with unspoken questions.

He drew a breath and released it. "Christa got off track as a teenager. Made a lot of bad decisions. She felt rejected. Unloved. She tried everything to dull the pain she felt. Boys. Sex. Drugs. Booze. Anything and everything. I wasn't much help. I tried, but I made plenty of mistakes myself, especially when we were younger. I tried to make a home for her once I was legally an adult, but that didn't go well. Later, she cut me off for long stretches of time. Sometimes for years. She didn't like it when I meddled in her life."

"I'm sorry," she said again.

"It isn't easy to watch someone you love self-destruct." He closed his eyes for a moment. "She died from an overdose."

"Oh, Tyler," Olivia whispered.

He steadied his breathing. "I know you don't care for lawyers, but most of the work I do for the firm is about protecting at-risk kids. I like when I can make a difference. Maybe save one from going down that same troubled path as my sister."

"Of course you do."

"Something else I've learned is I need other people. For way too long I thought it was up to me and only me to help Christa. To save her from herself. I thought I needed to do it all on my own, under my own steam. But God helped me see, finally, that I needed other people in my life. I didn't have much in the way of a birth family, but I've been grafted into the family of God, and His family is big and varied. I began to find there were lots of good people who would come alongside me, in both my personal and professional lives. Without some of them, I don't know how I would have survived Christa's death." He stopped, looked down at the table, cleared his throat. "Sorry." He looked up again. "Didn't mean to preach at you."

"You weren't preaching." It was her

turn to look down at the table. "There's a lot of…wisdom in what you said."

Another server came, this time with brown sugar–glazed ham, followed by another with grilled pineapple. By the time both were gone, Tyler was ready to change the subject.

Olivia beat him to it. "Your work sounds very different from manning a control booth for a theater troupe and whatever you do at church. How'd you get interested in that?"

"I sort of fell into it." He chuckled. "It started at the church I attended in Boise. It was a small congregation, sort of like Cornerstone but even smaller, and so it was all-hands-on-deck. When they needed a volunteer, they would take anybody willing to work, then train them. No previous experience required. So one day I volunteered, and before I knew it, I was working in the media booth. I know my way around computers, so that part was easy." He gave a slight shrug. "When I moved to Bethlehem Springs, I was glad when they needed the same kind of help. Made it easy to get involved, to become a part of this corner of God's family."

He didn't say that he liked to observe people as they came and went, although that was true. It was surprising how much a guy could learn about his friends and neighbors that way.

Olivia tilted her head slightly to one side as she looked at him. "I wish I was more like you."

"Meaning?"

"It's always been hard for me to get involved. I'd feel more like I belonged. I know I would. But I usually hang back."

"Well, if you feel like joining me in the media booth at church, I'll find something for you to do. I promise."

Was that trust he saw in her eyes as she smiled? "I may just do that," she said softly.

He hoped it was trust. And he hoped he would never disappoint.

February 12, 1934
Monday

We will be moving again. I feel as if someone hit me, knocking the air from me. It is the way I felt when I was a girl and a group of kids piled on top of one another and I was on the bottom. I was terrified, and I screamed and screamed for the others to get off, to let me go. But they were laughing and talking and no one knew my panic was real. It was real. So very real.

I am buried, God. I am at the bottom, and I am in a panic. I am crushed. Make it stop. Make the others move. Get off me. Get off me. Get off me.

February 13, 1934
Tuesday

I feel like I am able to breathe a little better today. The initial shock about another move is over. We learned yesterday morning that the farm where we have been tenant farming has been taken by the bank, and we are to be evicted. In some ways this feels worse than when the other farm was purchased and the buyer planned to live there and work the land. This time, the house will stand empty. This time, the land will not be tended. A cold-hearted bank has taken it.

Banks do not have hearts. A bank is a business. It does not see us. It does not see my children in need of a home.

We have no choice but to move. But where? Where will we go this time?

Harry says that he cannot continue this way, that he must find another kind of work. But what? With millions of men unemployed, riding the rails, looking for work, what will he do? Will we become like the hobo I fed months ago? Will we stand at someone's back door, hoping for a handout?

I look through the pages of this diary, and I wonder what happened to my faith. I feel lost at sea. At least what I think it would feel like for that to happen. Afraid because I am tossed to and fro and I cannot see land, and I seem to have lost my anchor.

God, don't You care?

Chapter 20

Olivia came awake slowly. Without opening her eyes, she knew daylight had crept into her bedroom. Not crept. Taken over. It was well past time she was up and about. Work awaited her, but she decided to linger in the pleasant feelings of a good night's sleep and sweet dreams.

Sweet dreams that had included Tyler Murphy.

A sigh escaped her parted lips. Foolish, foolish, foolish to let herself give in to his charms. She knew it was idiotic, but she couldn't seem to stop it from happening. He'd charmed her. Completely.

Opening her eyes, she stared at the ceiling. **I've only known him a month, and we didn't really talk until last night. So basically, we just became acquainted. How can I feel this way?**

The room remained silent, providing no answers.

He is nice.

But was he nice enough to risk liking him, to risk getting closer, perhaps more than liking him? She closed her eyes, this time covering them with the crook of her right arm.

He's cute too. That smile. Those eyes.

That wasn't helping.

Get up. Get to work. Think about something that matters. Like paying the mortgage and utility bills.

Emma's voice from the previous night whispered in her memory. **"You look like you had a good time, Mom."**

"I did." The answer she'd given her daughter last night had surprised her then, and it surprised her as she repeated it now. And it brought a smile to her face. After all, she hadn't had a first date in close to two decades. Last night could have been a complete disaster. **But it wasn't. It was...wonderful.**

Oh, for pity's sake! Had she completely lost her senses? There she was, lying in bed, having a conversation with herself like some dotty old woman. She tossed aside the sheet and sat up on the side of the bed, ready at last to face the day—and determined not to give Tyler another thought.

Half an hour later, showered and dressed, her hair caught back in a ponytail, she headed for the kitchen and her first cup of coffee. She popped a pod into the coffeemaker and waited nearby as the hot brew slowly filled the waiting mug.

"Morning, Mom."

She glanced over her shoulder. "Morning."

"You slept late." Emma padded on

bare feet across the kitchen to the toaster.

"I know."

"I've got rehearsal tonight."

"I remembered."

Emma dropped two slices of bread into the toaster and pushed the lever down. "Starting next week, we'll rehearse Mondays and Tuesdays."

"It's on my calendar."

"Mom, why don't you let me ride the bike so you don't have to take me and pick me up every night? It's not that far, and the bike's got lights and reflectors."

"I know it isn't far. But—"

"Please. I'll wear the helmet. I can even get one of those reflective windbreakers if you want me to. And this is Bethlehem Springs. It isn't a big city."

Olivia turned from the coffeemaker with mug in hand to look at her daughter. Was she being overprotective? It wasn't even a mile to the amphitheater. Once off of Elkhorn Road and onto Skyview Street, the way was well lit.

"And I'll be home no later than eleven," Emma added, her voice verging on a whine.

Olivia released a breath. "Let me think about it."

"I promise I'll—"

She gave her daughter a look that stopped any additional wheedling.

As she watched Emma butter the toast, lips pressed tightly together, it occurred to Olivia that the scene was similar to ones played out in countless homes around the world every day. It was normal. The realization made her smile as she left the kitchen. Without looking behind her, she said, "Find out what one of those windbreakers would cost."

"Okay!"

In her studio she opened her window blinds before sitting in front of her computer. Then she checked her calendar app. There was one project she simply had to finish today, and a list of several small tasks she would love to check off as well.

"Mom."

She looked toward the studio doorway.

"Between thirty and fifty dollars. For the windbreaker." Emma held out her phone. "Wanna see?"

"Sure." She took the phone from her daughter's hand and studied the first picture before scrolling down to read the particulars and then move to the next…and the next. When she was done, she offered the device back to Emma. "Thanks."

"Can we order one of them?"

"I've got to get some work done first. And remember, I'm still thinking about whether or not to let you do it. We'll talk about it more at lunch. Okay?"

The war of words playing in Emma's head was plain on her face, but she had the good sense not to speak any of it out loud.

We're both learning.

Olivia turned back to the computer screen, opened her favorite design application, and before long was deeply engaged in her work.

"Thanks for meeting with me, Mr. Ward." Tyler slid his phone, screen down, to the corner of the table before picking up his glass of Diet Coke. "I didn't feel like this could wait for our Friday phone call." A few other customers talked softly behind him, but Tyler kept his attention focused on the older man opposite him.

"I was glad to come. Do you have something new to report? It sounded important."

"Not something new, but I do think it's important."

Peter Ward raised his eyebrows in question.

Tyler took a sip of his beverage, thankful that the Boise restaurant was mostly quiet at this hour of the afternoon. "Sir, I think it's time to end this investigation. It's wasting your money and my time to continue with it. Your granddaughter is in good hands with her mother. I thought so early on, and nothing I've uncovered has done anything to change my opinion."

"I see."

"Do you?" Tyler took a breath and plowed forward. "I hope so. Because it seems to me that you would benefit from having those two in your life, and they would benefit from having you in theirs. I don't know what caused the rift between you and your son. I don't know why he cut you off from knowing your former daughter-in-law or your only grandchild. I don't need to know. I've seen way too many fractured families, and it can happen for all kinds of reasons. But this I can tell you: the people who make an effort to heal their families are never sorry they tried, even if their efforts fail. And I know Olivia and Emma Ward well enough now that I believe your efforts to reach out won't fail."

Peter leaned against the back of the booth and looked long and hard at Tyler. "According to the court papers, Daniel didn't think Olivia was a fit mother."

"Excuse me, sir, but from where I sit, your son did what he could to take everything away from Olivia, including their daughter, just because he could. He had the money and the power to do it, and so he did. He didn't do it because he thought he was the better parent or because he wanted to be the better parent. It didn't take much investigating to discover that."

"You seem very passionate about this."

Tyler nodded. "Yes, I guess I am. Your son wanted to hurt Olivia, and that's what he did. Again, it doesn't matter why." He looked down at the table for a few moments. When he raised his eyes again, he added, "Mr. Ward, from what I can tell, you're a good man with good intentions. But if you try to take Emma from her mother, I'll help them fight you, not work for you."

"I see," Peter said again, his eyes narrowing.

"The firm wouldn't have to fire me because of it. I would quit first."

The hint of a smile tugged at the corners of Peter's mouth as he raised his hands in a gesture of surrender. "You won't have to quit your job, son. I understand."

Tyler reached into his pocket and withdrew a slip of paper. "Here are Olivia's phone numbers. The top one is her business, the bottom one her cell." He slid the paper across the table. "And if you'd rather write to her first, her address is there too."

"You're a persuasive young man."

"I hope so."

Peter held out his right hand, and Tyler took hold of it. Peter said, "It's been a privilege to get to know you, Mr.

Murphy."

"Thank you, sir. Same is true for me."

A short while later, they parted ways outside the restaurant entrance. Tyler watched as the older man walked to his car and got behind the wheel. Then he headed in the opposite direction, hoping that when he told his immediate supervisor the Ward case was closed, his boss would be as understanding as Peter Ward himself—and wouldn't guess that the reason for the closure had become more personal than it should be.

February 20, 1934
Tuesday

Today felt warm. A break in winter, although I know the cold will return. I walked out into the barren fields, all alone, without a coat even, turned my face to the sun, and allowed myself to pretend that all is well.

No, not pretend. I allowed myself to pray for renewal.

When I am weak, He is strong. The Bible tells me it is so.

How does that work? What is my part? I am already weak. Be strong in me, Jesus.

Last night I read this in John 6: "Upon this many of his disciples went back, and walked no more with him. Jesus said therefore

unto the twelve, Would ye also
go away? Simon Peter answered
him, Lord, to whom shall we go?
thou hast the words of eternal
life."

To whom shall I go? I can only
go to Jesus.

**Here I am, Lord. Weak and
weary. Afraid of what lies ahead.
But only You have the words of
eternal life. Speak. I am trying
to hear.**

March 8, 1934
Thursday

I am pregnant. And just as when
I realized I was pregnant with
Charlie, we have lost our home.
If we cannot find another farm
for Harry to work, if he cannot
find another job, we will have to
move in with Fred and Rose.
There are already six of them in
that house. How will there be
room for four more, one of them
a rambunctious toddler who gets
into everything? And another
baby on the way. Another mouth
to feed. Another body that needs
clothes and shelter.

I sound ungrateful. We will
not be homeless. We will not live
in a tent under a bridge as some

are forced to do. We will not go hungry. We have family. A generous family who will give us shelter and love us.

We have lost so much already. When will the losses stop? I am weary.

Isaiah 40: "Hast thou not known? hast thou not heard? The everlasting God, Jehovah, the Creator of the ends of the earth, fainteth not, neither is weary; there is no searching of his understanding. He giveth power to the faint; and to him that hath no might he increaseth strength. Even the youths shall faint and be weary, and the young men shall utterly fall: but they that wait for Jehovah shall renew their strength; they shall mount up with wings as eagles; they shall run, and not be weary; they shall walk, and not faint."

I am waiting, Father. Renew my strength. You give power to the faint. That is me. I want to run and not be weary. Help me, God, I pray. Help my family.

Chapter 21

Nerves tumbled in Emma's stomach as she entered the amphitheater that evening. Tonight the cast for the last play of the season—the September play—would do a walk-through, reading their lines, the director helping them catch his vision for the production.

Not that Emma had to worry about catching a vision. Not when it came to her part as a maid, at least. She would be dusting in the background, maybe bringing tea and biscuits. She had no lines to learn. Of course, she knew a lot of the other characters' lines by heart. She'd read the script multiple times since being cast in the play.

From the far side of the theater, Izzy saw Emma and waved in greeting. She waved back before starting toward her friend.

"Are you excited?" Izzy asked as Emma got closer.

She shrugged, indicating it wasn't a big deal. But in truth, she **was** excited. It didn't matter that she didn't have any lines or that it was only a bit part. This was a first step to an acting role next season. She was sure of it.

"Did your mom bring you?"

Emma glanced over her shoulder toward the entrance, half expecting to see her mom standing there. "Yes. But she's agreed to let me ride my bike some nights. She had to order some things first, including a reflective jacket."

"Mothers." Izzy rolled her eyes.

"I know."

"Victor made me your understudy. Did you know that?"

"An understudy? I don't have any lines."

"Doesn't matter. Everybody has to have one in case they get sick. But they'd better have a shorter skirt for me to wear or I'll trip over it. You're taller than I am." Izzy leaned closer, as if sharing a secret. "Just don't get sick. Then I won't have to worry about it."

"They probably have a maid's costume in lots of sizes."

"Probably." Izzy's eyes widened as her attention went beyond Emma's left shoulder. "Look who's here."

Emma obeyed—and felt her breath catch again. But this time it came with a rapid pulse.

The boy was definitely cute. Probably a year or two older than Emma and Izzy. Dark hair and eyes, and a smile that lingered on his mouth, as if to say he knew he'd drawn their attention even though he wasn't looking back at them.

"Who's he?" Emma whispered.

"Nate Jensen."

"Does he live in Bethlehem Springs?"

"Yes."

"I haven't seen him before. Is he part of the troupe?"

"Nate? No way. He makes fun of stuff like this. He'd never be in a play."

"So why's he here?"

"Exactly my question. He's up to something, I'll bet. He's trouble."

As if ready to acknowledge the two girls were talking about him, Nate turned his dark eyes in their direction.

Uneasiness swirled in Emma's stomach. Or maybe the feeling was something else. It was hard to tell. She'd spent years at an all-girls school and had never had a boyfriend. Not an actual, real-life boyfriend. Not like Regina, who'd been a boy magnet.

"All right, everyone," a voice called from the stage.

Emma turned to see Victor Benson standing front and center.

"Let's get started. If I could get my

cast to join me up here."

Emma took two steps forward, then glanced over her shoulder. Nate Jensen was nowhere to be seen. Soon enough, he was forgotten.

"Am I intruding?"

Tyler grinned at Olivia. "Not at all."

She stepped into the control booth. "Emma starts rehearsals tonight."

"I know. Want to watch from up here?"

"Yes, if you don't mind."

"I don't." He rolled the second chair back from the boards and watched as she sat on it. "I was hoping I'd see you."

She gave him a questioning glance.

"I really enjoyed last night."

"I did too."

Was that hesitancy he heard in her reply? He'd hoped they'd gotten past that.

"Will you be here for the whole walk-through?" she asked as she looked down at the stage.

He decided not to tell her that Wednesdays were the nights he did quick system checks and then went home. "Yes. I'll be here."

"Emma's excited to be part of this cast." She leaned toward the window. "I just want her to do well. To fit in."

Tyler wished he could encourage her somehow. No, what he wished he could do was hug her, hold her. They weren't at that place yet in their relationship, but he hoped it would happen soon. "She'll be fine. From the times we've talked, she seems like a smart kid." He was skirting the full truth there. His opinion was based on more than a few brief conversations with Emma, and he felt a twinge of guilt over that. Never, in all of his years working as an investigator, had his work spilled into his personal life. He'd never had to worry about it. He'd had his clients. He'd had the subjects of his investigations. He'd had his personal life. And there'd never been any overlap. Until now.

"You're frowning," Olivia said. "Is something wrong?"

He blinked and met her gaze. "Lost in thought, I guess. Nothing's wrong."

Her responding smile was tentative, as if she wasn't sure he'd told her the truth. Which had a way of increasing his guilt.

Olivia looked out the booth window again, watching as the actors moved around the stage. Emma exited one of the wings, pretending to carry a tray or something like it. She went to a table, one of the few props on the stage, and set the imaginary item in its center.

"See," Tyler said. "She's a pro."

"She's done theater before, but I've never seen her in a play." Sadness laced her words.

Again, he wished he could offer real comfort. Again, he resisted the urge to hold her.

"What on earth?" Olivia shot up from the chair.

Tyler's gaze returned to the stage in time to see a bookcase, upstage right, come crashing to the stage floor, narrowly missing both the table and Emma. He also caught a glimpse of a boy running from the back of the amphitheater. Within a heartbeat, Tyler was out of the booth and running himself. Gut instinct told him the bookcase had been pushed. It hadn't been an accident. But whoever the boy was, he'd disappeared by the time Tyler made it through the house seats to the exit the boy had used behind the stage.

When he turned around, he saw the director standing in the wing, looking in his direction.

"Is Emma okay?" Tyler asked.

Victor nodded. "She's okay."

"That wasn't an accident."

"No, I don't think it was."

"Has anything like this happened before?"

This time Victor shook his head.

"Do we know who it was?"

Another shake of the head.

A girl's voice intruded. "I know."

Tyler turned to see Izzy Rath coming from the opposite side of the crossover.

"It was Nate Jensen. I saw him earlier, before rehearsal started. He isn't part of the cast or crew. No reason for him to be here."

Tyler asked, "Did you see him push the bookcase?"

"Well...no. But he's not here now." Her shoulders stiffened and her chin tilted up, even as tears filled her eyes. "Emma could've been hurt."

"Thank you, Izzy," Victor said. "Maybe you should go sit with your friend. She's kind of shaken."

The girl did as told, leaving the two men staring at each other.

Tyler wished he'd had a chance to ask Izzy a few questions about Nate Jensen, but that would have to wait. "Do you want to call the police, Victor?"

"What could they do? No one saw what actually happened or who did it.

It's only a suspicion that it was intentional and who was behind it."

"Then let me do some investigating. See what I can come up with."

"I'm okay with that. If it's not asking too much."

"It's not." He gave a firm nod to Victor before walking around to the front of the stage.

Emma now sat on the ground, her mom on one side and Izzy on the other.

Behind Tyler, the director said, "Everyone, given what's happened, let's call it a night. We'll regroup and begin rehearsals again on Monday."

Voices buzzed as Tyler walked the remainder of the way to Emma. "Are you sure you're all right?"

She nodded.

Olivia said, "The bookcase scraped her arm as it went down."

"It doesn't hurt. It just scared me."

"It was too close," Olivia added, her voice rising with anxiety.

"Mom," Emma said softly, "I'm okay.

Stop worrying."

Tyler squatted in front of both of them and waited until Emma met his gaze. "Did you see or hear anything?"

"No. Just all of a sudden, the case fell. I was paying attention to what the other players were doing and saying, not to what was going on behind me."

"Of course you were." He shifted his eyes to Izzy. "Do you mind if I come over to see you tomorrow, ask you about what you saw and heard?"

"No. That's okay."

He nodded. "Good. Then let's get out of here." He stood, then offered a hand to Olivia.

"Thanks," she said as he drew her to her feet.

He leaned closer. "Are **you** okay?"

She blinked, then answered, "Yes. I think it scared me more than it did her."

"I think so too." He offered a quick smile. "I'll call you tomorrow."

Something in her eyes told him she appreciated his concern.

He watched as they walked to the exit, and only when they were out of sight did he return to the control booth to lock it up for the night. Tomorrow, he meant to find out more about Nate Jensen.

March 18, 1934
Sunday

A man at church told Harry that
he thinks he can help him get a
job in a place called Bethlehem
Springs. He is a cousin of the
man who would hire him.

All my life I have lived on the
land. My grandfathers were
farmers. My father is a farmer.
My husband has been a farmer.
We have grown lemon trees
and corn and alfalfa hay. We
have kept horses and cows and
chickens and dogs and cats.
I have never lived in a city or a
town where one house is right
next to another. And I have never
lived in the mountains either.
I am used to seeing mountains in

the distance, but the land where I have lived is flat. This place we may go is in the mountains. How different will that feel?

Leaving this farm, leaving Thunder Creek, will mean leaving Fred and Rose and their children. It will mean I can't visit the cemetery and tell Dottie how much she is missed and how much I love her. My heart hurts when I think of it.

Change is hard.
Life is hard.
God is good.
I will remember that.

May 6, 1934
Sunday

How long it's been since I wrote
in this diary. For a few weeks,
after our move to Bethlehem
Springs, I couldn't find it. I
thought it was lost. But now
it is found, and there are words
to write.

We have begun a new life.
A new life in a new place. And
oh, how very different it is from
what we knew before. Harry got
the job in a lumber mill outside
of this mountain town. The work
is hard, but he seems to like it.
He seems to walk a little taller
these days. My heart is glad for
him. Very glad.

We are more than two hours

away from Fred and Rose, and our old Ford cannot be depended upon for lengthy distances. We miss seeing them every Sunday, and it will be hard when it comes time to have the baby and Rose is not with me. She made such a difference when Charlie was born.

We have rented a house on Jefferson Street. There is a hill right across the street from us, and beyond it is the road that leads south to Boise City. The river is beyond the road. To the north, we are told, is a spa with natural hot springs. Perhaps someday we will get to see it for ourselves.

My morning sickness is over at last. I am thankful for that. I suffered worse this time than for any of the other three pregnancies.

Three. That makes my heart

hurt to write it. There were three other pregnancies, but there are no longer three children left on this earth. Only two.

I miss Dottie. We all do. She would have loved living in the mountains. She would have loved the pine trees and river. She would have loved the horses. There were still horses and buggies in Thunder Creek, of course. But it is different here. There are more men on horseback at all times of the day. There is a large cattle ranch in the valley to the east of Bethlehem Springs, and many of those men come into town to drink as well as to cause trouble. At least that is what our neighbor has told me. She wishes Prohibition never ended. I don't know if it is true about the troublemaking. I haven't seen it for myself. I hope I won't.

There is a beauty in this place that touches my heart. The tall pines reach for the sunlight, which starts later and ends sooner because of the mountains to the east and the west. They are like the masts of the tall ships I've seen in books. One morning, after it rained in the night, the clouds seemed to come all the way to the ground, blanketing us in a silvery mist. I could see it moving, as clouds do. Different from a fog that settles. I'd never seen anything like it before. It felt mysterious, and I wonder how long it will be before I see it again.

Chapter 22

As Olivia reached for a can of green beans, she heard someone call her name. Glancing to her left, she saw Kathy Dover approach, pushing a shopping cart.

"Olivia," Kathy repeated, "I heard what happened at the theater last night. Is Emma okay?"

"She's fine. It scared me lots more than it did her."

"Victor says Tyler's looking into it."

Olivia nodded.

"Well, if there's anything to be found, he's the man who can find it. It's his job after all. Investigating."

Again, she nodded, but this time she found herself wondering what being an investigator actually meant. She hadn't asked Tyler any questions about his work. Not really. It had been enough to know he wasn't an attorney.

And at that thought, one of his lawyer jokes repeated in her mind, making her smile.

"I saw that," Kathy said.

"What?" She reached a second time for the can of beans and put it in her cart.

"That look on your face. Does it have anything to do with your dinner with Tyler?"

"How did you know about that?"

"At the barbecue Tyler told Greg he had a date with you. Greg told me."

"Nothing's private around here." Olivia gave her cart a little push forward, looking for the canned corn.

Kathy kept pace.

"Okay. Yes. It does have something to do with Tyler. He likes to tell lawyer jokes."

Her friend's expression changed to one of bemusement.

"I think they're funny." She tilted her chin up, waiting for Kathy to tease her.

Instead, Kathy laughed. "I like Tyler's sense of humor too. Although now I feel left out. He's never told me one of his lawyer jokes." She swirled her cart in the opposite direction. "I'd better get my own shopping done. Will I see you at the theater tonight?"

"I'll drop Emma off. I won't be coming in. She wants a little more freedom. To not always look like she needs her mom there." Olivia frowned. "Do you think it would be all right for her to ride her bike to and from the theater? I mean, did you let Hailey go out alone at night when she was Emma's age?"

"Almost sixteen? Sometimes. From one friend's house to another. I know it's a scary world, but Bethlehem Springs still feels safe to me. As for Emma, it isn't that far between your house and the theater. You could make her promise to call you when she gets there and then again before she starts back home."

"It was easier when she was little." Olivia released a sigh.

Kathy smiled in understanding. "I came to believe that God made the teen years hard so that moms will be ready to send their kids out into the world. Otherwise we would want to keep them at home with us forever."

"You may be right about that."

"The wonderful thing, Olivia, is that on the other side of those hard years there can be a great friendship with your adult child. Do you remember those rough years for me and Hailey?"

She did remember, if only in part.

"And now we're becoming the best of friends. Yes, I'm still her mom, but it's more than that between us now. For Hailey and Greg too." She shook her head, a wry expression replacing the smile. "It's a good thing, because we're reaching that phase with Ethan."

"You make parenting look easy."

"Do I?"

"Yes."

"Well, I'll attribute that to lots of prayer. For my kids and for me." Kathy glanced at her watch. "Now I have to get going. If I don't see you at the theater, I'll see you Sunday." She rolled the cart down the aisle and disappeared around the end of it.

Olivia didn't move in the opposite direction. Not right away. Instead, she let her friend's parting words about prayer repeat in her mind. How much had she prayed for Emma? How much had she prayed for herself? Not much. Not often. Even now, with her trust in God returning, she remained silent most of the time. She didn't pray. Not really.

You don't have because you don't ask.

She frowned. Were those words from the Bible? They seemed familiar. They felt like words that had once been a comfort to her.

God, help me be a good mother. Please.

It was a start.

After rapping on the door of the Jensen home, Tyler took a step back and waited. He was about to give up when he heard a sound coming from the back side of the log house. He moved to the far edge of the deck and called out, "Hello?"

He didn't have to wait long before a man—tall, broad, grizzled, and holding an ax—stepped into view.

"What d'you want?" he asked, his tone less than welcoming.

"I was hoping I could talk to Nate."

"He ain't here."

"Are you his father?"

"No business of yours, but I am."

Tyler left the deck and walked toward Will Jensen. He'd learned the names of Nate's parents and younger brother—along with a few other pertinent details—before driving to this remote cabin in the forest to the southwest of Bethlehem Springs.

"I'm Tyler Murphy." He offered a hand.

Will Jensen looked at it but didn't take it. "What d'you want?" he repeated.

"There was an incident at the amphitheater in town last night. Nate was seen there, and I was hoping he could help me find out what happened."

"Are you sayin' he's in trouble?"

"No, sir. I'm saying I'd like his help in piecing together what occurred last night."

Will turned his head and spit into a bush beside the cabin. "You a cop?"

"No."

"Then my kid don't have to talk t'you."

"No, he doesn't. But I would appreciate it if he did. Would you tell him I was here?" He withdrew a card from his shirt pocket. "There are the numbers where I can be reached."

Will Jensen took the card with obvious reluctance and put it in his pocket without a glance.

"If you'd ask him to call me," Tyler added.

The man grunted as he turned and strode beyond the back of the cabin. A few moments later, Tyler heard the sounds of firewood being split.

He released a breath, feeling lucky that Will Jensen hadn't used the ax on him. He'd been told Nate's father wasn't a friendly sort. From what he'd just seen, that was an understatement. Not to mention that he'd smelled whiskey on the man's breath at ten o'clock in the morning. That didn't bode well. Especially for Nate, his younger brother, and their mother. Tyler had seen too much to believe otherwise.

He turned and walked to his vehicle, his eyes taking in the forested mountainside. As far as he knew, the Jensens didn't have any neighbors for a good mile or two. The dirt road that had brought him to the cabin was narrow—no room for two vehicles going in opposite directions—and rutted by weather and time. From all appearances it didn't get much traffic. He assumed Nate and his brother had to walk over a mile to where they could catch the school bus.

Tyler liked living in Bethlehem Springs, but he wouldn't care to be this cut off from civilization. There wasn't phone service, from what he'd learned, although the Jensens did have power, judging by the wires running from a pole to the log house. He could only guess whether or not they had indoor plumbing.

He started the engine and backed out of the long drive, then followed the road north again toward town, all the while mulling over what he'd learned that morning about Nate.

It seemed likely that Izzy's suspicions were correct. Who else besides Nate would have pushed the bookcase over, disrupting the rehearsal? The boy had been at the amphitheater without good reason. He wasn't a friend of anyone in either the cast or crew. He wasn't an aspiring actor. Add to that, he'd been in frequent trouble from an early age, both in school and with the local police. To Tyler, it was also telling that he'd acted alone—still assuming it was Nate who'd pushed the bookcase. He hadn't done it to show off for others. He'd done it for the thrill alone.

When Tyler reached Bethlehem Springs, his intent was to drive to his house. But somehow his SUV made a right off of Main onto Elkhorn Road. There was only one reason for that. It took him to Olivia's house. Within a few minutes, he pulled into her drive.

Emma stepped onto the deck as Tyler got out of his vehicle. "Mom's not home," she called to him. "She went to get groceries."

"That's okay. I came to see you." That was mostly true. "How're you doing?"

"Wish everybody'd quit asking me that. It isn't like I was hurt."

"No. But you could've been." He climbed the steps to the deck. "May I ask you a few questions?"

"Sure."

He motioned to the chairs off to one side. "Shall we?"

She shrugged before walking to one of them. As she sat, she tucked a bare foot underneath her bottom. She looked relaxed and unconcerned as she twirled her long hair around an index finger.

Tyler saw through the act. Emma had been more shaken by the near miss than she wanted to let on.

He sat opposite her. "Tell me about Nate Jensen. Did you know him before last night?"

"I don't know him at all. Last night was the only time I've seen him, and that was from a distance. We weren't introduced or anything. Izzy noticed him first, and she told me who he was. She wondered why he was there."

"And where, exactly, was he?"

"On the walkway in front of the chairs. Over on the right side of the house."

"Was he alone?"

"Yes, and Izzy said the only reason he'd be there was because he was up to something." She frowned. "But I didn't see him after we started to rehearse. Maybe he went home. Maybe he wasn't there when the bookcase fell."

"Maybe. Guess we won't know for sure until I talk to him, and that hasn't happened yet."

"Mr. Murphy, don't make a big deal of this. Please. I don't want to be the girl who causes trouble for other kids in town. Nobody'll like me."

"All I'm after is the truth, Emma. Nothing more."

The crunch of tires on gravel drew their gazes to the driveway. Olivia's

Outback pulled around Tyler's car and parked near the steps. The interruption was fortuitous as far as Tyler was concerned. Emma wasn't up to more questions.

"I'll give your mom a hand," he said as he stood. "We'll talk again another time."

Emma watched as Tyler went down the steps and opened her mom's car door. Then she went inside and up the stairs to her room.

People needed to stop freaking out about what had happened at the theater. It wasn't a big deal. It could've been an accident. Maybe nobody pushed the stupid bookcase. Maybe it tipped over on its own. Maybe the boards were uneven or something.

She flopped onto the bed, remembering that moment Nate Jensen had looked at her before the rehearsal started. She remembered the uneasy feeling in her stomach. It was almost like she'd wanted something she shouldn't have. Even from a distance, he'd seemed dangerously handsome.

Was there such a thing? Could being handsome also be dangerous?

Well, maybe. But everybody seemed to think Nate had pushed the bookcase. If so, had he wanted to hurt her or to get her attention? Seemed he'd failed either way. He couldn't have her attention if all he'd done was run off.

Unlike Tyler Murphy with her mom. He wasn't running off. Even Emma could see that he wanted to be around plenty. Maybe for good. Did her mom want that?

It didn't matter anyway. People met, fell in love, sometimes got married, and then they moved on. She'd seen it happen to her own parents. She'd seen it happen to the parents of her friends at Blakely Academy. Love didn't seem to last. Not like romantic movies wanted a person to believe.

Of course, there were couples like

Kathy and Greg Dover. Love had seemed to last for them. And Izzy's parents. They were still together. So maybe it was possible to have a happily ever after.

Maybe...

June 1, 1934
Friday

I wish we could go back. Not
back to Thunder Creek, although
we had happy moments there.
No, I want to go back to
Riverside. Back to the lemon
groves. Back to the life we once
knew. Back before Dottie got
sick. I thought I was past this
longing for what used to be.
I thought I had stopped thinking
of California as home. But it has
overtaken me again, and I can't
seem to be free of it. I awake in
the night, crying, missing what
is gone. Wishing for what might
have been.

Harry worries about me. I see
it on his face. I see it in his eyes.

He wants to comfort me and
doesn't know how. What could
I tell him? What would comfort
me? I don't know. I feel so lost.
I can't even feel joy about the
baby that grows inside me. I am
so caught up in my own pain.
It isn't right. It isn't the way I
want it to be.

God, do You see me?
Do You hear me?

June 15, 1934
Friday

A doe and twin fawns visited our little yard this morning, nibbling at the grass and the shrubbery that grows near the house. When I noticed them, I held my breath, hoping the children wouldn't make noise that would startle them away.

There is something special about new life. All new life. Human babies. Fawns. Puppies. Ducklings. Colts. Calves. Kittens.

I feel the baby move inside of me. Another new life is coming to this house. I wrote that I was unable to feel joy about the new baby. Maybe it isn't joy just yet, but it will be. Perhaps this little

one is enough to make me stop
wishing for the past.

Chapter 23

Early the following morning, Olivia sat on the deck of her home, watching as daylight began to peek through the pines and spread a buttery glow across the rooftops of the town. On the table next to her chair sat a steaming mug of coffee. On her lap lay an open journal, one of many she'd been given through the years but had never used.

"It helps to write your feelings down," Sara had told her years ago, around the time that Olivia was at her lowest point.

"Journaling is good for the soul," Kathy had said a few Christmases ago.

Her present to Olivia that year had been a couple of journals with a Bible verse printed on every page.

Then, as if he knew about the journals she had collecting dust on a bookshelf, Adam Green had added his voice to the chorus. **"Putting your experiences on paper can help you understand your choices. Both why you made certain decisions in the past and why you should, perhaps, make different ones in the future. I recommend you keep a journal. Write in it every morning or before you go to bed at night. Give it a minimum of six weeks. See if you can form a habit. Perhaps you'll begin to see things more clearly."**

Six weeks seemed a ridiculous amount of time. What did Olivia have to journal about? Her life was relatively the same from one day to the next. Get up. Take a shower. Make coffee. Get to work. Even with Emma living with her, the routine remained much the same

from day to day. Her most exciting out-
ing was to the grocery store. Only that
wasn't what Adam, Kathy, and Sara
wanted her to write about. They wanted
her to explore the choices she'd made,
the feelings she'd felt.

Tyler's image intruded on that thought.
It might not hurt to write down her feelings about him.

Maybe later.

Kathy wrote prayers in her journal.
Olivia supposed she could try that to
start with. Only yesterday she'd considered how little she prayed. For herself
or for Emma. If she wasn't able to pray
silently, perhaps she could make it a
habit to do so on paper.

Another thought came to mind. Emma
remained captivated by Millie MacIver's
journal. Rather than reading it quickly
and giving the diary back to Phoebe
Simpson, Emma had limited the number of entries she allowed herself to
read at each sitting. Olivia didn't understand her daughter's interest in the old

journal. Maybe she needed to read it herself. Perhaps then she would see why others recommended she keep one of her own.

After taking a sip of her quickly cooling coffee, she took the pen from the table and wrote the date. Only then did she read the verse at the top of the page: "For I know the plans that I have for you," declares the Lord, "plans for prosperity and not for disaster, to give you a future and a hope" (Jeremiah 29:11).

She knew the verse, of course. Years ago she'd memorized it. But then had come her divorce and the loss of her daughter, and she'd stopped believing that God's plans for her came with hope. Or that He cared what happened to her at all.

"But You do care, don't You, Jesus?" she whispered.

She wanted to believe it. She mostly believed it. And yet...

She took the pen and began to write:

God, I don't know how to pray
anymore. I stopped believing
You wanted to hear from me.
I stopped believing that it made
any difference. In my heart I
know that isn't true. The Bible
tells me You love me. It says You
have good plans for me. It also
says that in this world we will
have trouble. Why did I think
I would be exempt from it? And
yet that must be the reason for
my despair and anger. Because
I thought trouble only came to
others, not to me. Why not me?

Emma is home again. Emma is
with me. It's what I've longed for,
hoped for, dreamed of. Now it
has happened, and I should be
praying for her, even if I never
pray for anyone else, not even
myself. And yet the words feel
trapped inside of me, unwilling to
form, unwilling to be spoken.

The disciples asked for Jesus

to teach them to pray, didn't they? They didn't say to teach them how to pray. They just said, "Teach us to pray." Teach me to pray, Jesus. Make me faithful once again. Help me to find my roots, my anchor.

Father, forgive me for my years of rebellion.

Olivia stared at the last word she'd written: **rebellion**. Had she thought of her silence that way before? That her lack of prayer had been an act of rebellion? That her continued silence was **still** an act of rebellion?

No. She'd justified her anger. If God wouldn't stop—hadn't stopped—Daniel from leaving with Emma, then Olivia would simply ignore Him.

"I'm sorry." She closed the journal, the pen in the gutter of the book. "I'm so, so sorry. Forgive me, Lord. Show me a better way."

She stared down at the town again.

Bethlehem Springs had begun to awaken. A car moved along Bear Run Road, passing the Baptist church. A moment later, the sheriff's vehicle pulled into the parking lot behind the municipal building.

"I love this place."

She opened the journal again and wrote:

I love living in Bethlehem
Springs. When I came here over
six years ago, I hated it because
I had nowhere else to go. I was
depending on the charity of a
friend. My parents would have let
me stay in their spare room, of
course, but I didn't want that. It
would have felt even worse than
borrowing this house from Sara.
They'd already done so much
for me. Besides, I didn't want to
be seen. I wanted to be alone.
To wallow in my grief.
Maybe God's hand was in this.

Maybe His plan included bringing me to this place, to this town, to people who would become my friends.

Like Tyler Murphy.

Tyler. What are my feelings about him? I'm not sure. I like him. But do I risk too much by liking him?

Leaving the pen in the gutter of the journal, she closed the book a second time. She needed to think before she wrote more about Tyler in her new journal.

Tyler clicked Send, and his initial findings on a new case flew through cyberspace on their way to the assigned attorney. He was glad to have that chore checked off his list. It left the rest of his Friday open to do whatever he wanted. His first choice would be to call Olivia to see if he could take her to lunch. But he was afraid he might spook her if he tried to see her every day. Slow and easy. That was the best way to win her affections. He was convinced of it.

Then again, a chance meeting might be okay. Too bad he couldn't think of a way to make a "chance meeting" happen. One thing for certain, there was no possibility of running into Olivia if he stayed at his house, so he might as well head for the Gold Mountain for lunch.

Half an hour later, he parked his vehicle on Lincoln Street near the feed store and walked the rest of the way to the restaurant. The busy lunch hour had waned, and he didn't have any trouble finding a table. He said hello to a number of people on his way to it.

Rita arrived as he slid onto the seat of the booth. "Haven't seen you in here lately." She set a glass of water and a paper-covered straw on the table. "Gone off our food?" The question sounded almost like an accusation.

"No." He offered a quick smile. "Just been busy."

"Thought you didn't like your own cooking."

Had he said that to her in the past? He didn't remember, but he might have.

"Know what you want?"

"I do." He gave her his order.

"Dressing on the side, as usual." She wrote on her pad.

"Yes. Thanks."

As she walked away, loud laughter drew his attention to the entrance in time to see two teenaged boys enter the restaurant. One of them—he knew from his research—was Nate Jensen. He watched the boys make their way to a table not too far from his own. A short while later, when Rita arrived with two glasses of water, the second boy made a vulgar comment that made Tyler's jaw clench. Rita handled it with aplomb, but that didn't lessen his irritation.

Just then, Nate looked in Tyler's direction, and his amused expression drained away. He said something to his friend before rising and walking over to

Tyler. "I don't know what you wanted, mister, but keep away from my place. My dad don't like strangers pokin' around our business. Neither do I."

"I wasn't trying to poke around. I just had a few questions."

"And I don't gotta answer them." Nate leaned down, his knuckles now resting on the table.

Tyler didn't look away from the boy's angry face, and he kept his own expression passive. He knew better than to blink when someone like Nate was being belligerent. Bullies were cowards first. That's what experience had taught him.

Nate straightened, a self-satisfied smirk curling his mouth.

"You were at the amphitheater," Tyler said. "We hoped maybe you could tell us what happened when that bookcase tipped over."

The smile faltered. "I didn't see anything."

"Think on it. Something might come

to you. It could be a little thing. Like where you were standing when it fell. Luckily, no one was hurt, but it was a close call. So everyone in the theater company would like to know why it happened."

Nate turned away. "Come on, Billy. We're outta here."

"But I—"

Nate left the Gold Mountain, not waiting for his friend.

Any doubt Tyler might have had about the boy's guilt was gone. He didn't know a motive. There might not be one in the general sense of the word. More likely, Nate had done it for excitement alone. He'd given the bookcase a push because it was there and because he could, consequences be hanged. There was a side of Tyler that wanted to catch the kid and exact justice. Another side wanted to rescue him from the circumstances that had made him who he was.

Christa entered his thoughts, as she

did at such times. He'd never been able to step in and turn the tide of trouble in his sister's life. Could he do something for Nate Jensen? At the moment, he couldn't think how, but he would pray about it.

July 4, 1934
Wednesday

I was asked to do a couple of dramatic readings at the Independence Day celebration today. I have no idea who told Pastor Reynolds that I have done them in the past. Harry said it wasn't him. It only took a little bit of practice for me to remember the words to the readings I've memorized. Afterward many people came to tell me how much they enjoyed it. And I confess, it warmed my heart to hear the praise.

Mother used to say that I loved to perform almost from the moment I could walk and talk. She may be right about that.

(I miss her. I miss her wisdom
and her laughter.)

They had a picnic and games
in the park. There were musicians
in the band shell, and Harry and I
danced. I felt awkward, what with
my growing belly. Harry said he
wished he could have taken me
dancing for our anniversary, but
there's no place in Bethlehem
Springs with dancing, especially
not on a Sunday. I told him
dancing at the town celebration
was good enough for me.

We are making friends. Maybe
we will truly belong here.

July 16, 1934
Monday

When I was a girl, I lived where
the land was flat, and I could see
for miles and miles and miles. I
read about mountains in books,
and sometimes I heard folks talk
about them. But I couldn't
imagine them. Not truly. I had to
see them to understand.

Harry and I crossed mountains
on our way west. We crossed
the Rockies, and we crossed
the Sierra Nevada. We also saw
grasslands that were unlike anything I knew, and we saw deserts
that seemed unending. But it
was the mountains that spoke
to my heart in a way I still don't
understand. They called to me.

Maybe that's why I've stopped longing for other places at last. Maybe that's why Bethlehem Springs has stopped feeling like such a foreign and lonely place to me. I am living in the mountains we only traveled through before.

On most Sundays, after church, Harry drives us up into the mountains to the north for a picnic lunch beside a creek. The water runs so clear that I can count each and every rock and pebble (or I could if I wanted), and the air smells sweet. Gladys and Charlie race around, laughing and squealing with joy.

I wonder sometimes, are there mountains in heaven? Are there clear-running streams? Is Dottie able to run and giggle and squeal as she plays? And horses. Are there horses in heaven? Dottie loved horses so.

I am able to write those words without quite as much pain as before, although the missing doesn't stop. The missing will never stop. The grief remains, but the pain feels to have lightened. Not gone. But lightened.

I have three months before our new baby arrives. I am as big as a barn.

Chapter 24

"So this is where you hide every Sunday morning."

It wasn't Olivia's comment that brought a smile to Tyler's lips as he turned toward the booth's entrance. The sound of her voice was enough to do that.

"Morning," he said.

"Good morning." She stepped into the booth.

"You're here early."

"Well…" She glanced around at the various computers and equipment. "You said if I joined you here, you'd find something for me to do. So here I am."

He remembered issuing the invitation when they were at the Brazilian Grill, but he hadn't expected her to accept. At least not this soon. "You bet." He rose from his chair and went to retrieve a second one, rolling it over to a space on the right side of the booth. "Have a seat."

She complied.

"Where's Emma?" he asked.

"Waiting for her friends in the lobby." She gave her head a slight shake. "Is it silly, how happy it makes me to say that? That she has friends to wait for?"

"No. Not silly at all."

"When we first got here, after her dad's funeral, I didn't think she would ever make friends, ever make peace with me, maybe not ever leave her room again." She smiled wryly. "Not that it's perfect, but it's better than it was at the start."

He waited to see if she would say more. When she didn't, he handed the instructions for the morning service to her. "It's just me in the booth most Sundays, but I never turn down help when it's offered. Read that over, then I'll explain your duties."

"Nothing like diving right in."

He grinned. "Nothing like it."

Tyler wasn't surprised, of course, that Olivia was a quick learner. It took almost no time for her to know what was expected of her, and she performed her tasks with ease throughout the service. Having her there in the booth made him want to be with her all the more. He didn't want to go slow. He didn't want to be careful. He wanted her in his life. He wanted to share moments like this with her again and again. He wanted to share Sunday mornings and date nights and evenings at the amphitheater. He wanted her to tell him her worries about Emma and he wanted her to listen as he shared about his work. He wanted the exciting and the mundane, as long as it happened with her.

At the end of the service, he leaned toward Olivia and said, "Why don't you and Emma come to my place for lunch?"

He saw surprise in her eyes. A second later, he saw something more. Pleasure?

"Nothing fancy. I'll grill burgers."

She was silent a short while before answering, "What can I bring?"

"Just yourself. I shopped yesterday and have all the fixings."

"Okay. We'd be delighted."

"Emma's welcome to bring a friend or two. Like I said, I stocked up."

"You're very sweet," Olivia said. "Do you know that?"

If they hadn't been in the media booth on a Sunday morning, he would have leaned forward and kissed her right then and there.

Emma saw her mom come out of the sanctuary wearing a dreamy kind of smile. No one needed to explain that look to her. Maybe she'd never had a boyfriend, but she'd felt her heart go flip-flop a time or two. Less than a minute later, Tyler Murphy came through the same doors, and Emma knew for certain the cause of her mom's smile. He wore one that looked very much the same.

The realization made Emma feel a little strange on the inside. Happy and upset with her mom at the same time. The second part didn't make a lot of sense. She had no reason to be upset. She liked Tyler and had been glad when he'd asked her mom to go out. He was nice. And he was good to them, Emma as much as her mom.

Her dad had dated lots of women in the years they were in Florida. She hadn't met a single one of them in person, but she'd seen the photographs, both online and in magazines. None of his dates had been more than twenty-five. Only ten years older than she was. The last one she remembered reading about had been twenty. Chances were good Emma wouldn't have liked her. She probably wouldn't have liked any of them.

"Hey, honey." Her mom stopped in front of her. "Tyler's invited us to lunch at his place. He's going to grill hamburgers. He says it's okay if you ask your friends to go with us." Her gaze flicked to Hailey and Izzy, who stood nearby.

Again, she had conflicted feelings. Part of her wanted to see Tyler's house without anyone else along. Another part preferred to hang with friends.

Friends won out.

"Izzy. Hailey. You want to have hamburgers at Mr. Murphy's house?"

"Sure," Izzy answered. "I'll go ask Mom."

Hailey said, "I wish I could, but I've got plans this afternoon. A friend of mine's having a baby, and I promised to help with planning a shower. I'd better get going. Have a good time." She gave a little wave and walked toward the exit.

Emma turned to face her mom and Tyler. "I guess it's me and Izzy, if her mom says it's okay."

"Great." Tyler glanced at her mom. "You'd better follow me in your car. My place can be a little hard to see from the road."

"Whoa!" Emma leaned forward in the passenger seat. "Awesome house."

Olivia had to agree. It was an awesome house. Built against a hillside, the entire front of the second story was made of glass. A deck wrapped around the front and both sides.

"It used to belong to the Morgenshterns," Izzy said from the back seat. "Did you know them, Ms. Ward?"

"No, I didn't."

"They were really old and didn't speak English very good."

Tyler stood waiting for them at the base of the steps leading up to the deck. "Welcome," he called as Olivia and her passengers got out of the Outback.

"We were admiring your house." Olivia looked up at the peaked roof and the tall pines that towered above it.

"I was lucky. It came on the market at the right moment, and I was able to snap it up before someone else could. It needed a lot of work. A crew finished putting on the new roof last month, along with a remodel of the kitchen." He motioned with his head. "Come on. I'll show you around."

Olivia glanced over her shoulder to be sure Emma and Izzy were behind her, then followed Tyler up the steps.

The deck was about five times the size of the one on her home. It seemed made for outdoor parties, especially with the lovely view it had of the forest and mountains, along with a glimpse of a wide valley far to the west.

"Come on inside." Tyler pulled open the glass door on the left side of the deck.

The living area had a rustic appeal, beginning with a stone fireplace. The room wasn't huge, but the floor-to-ceiling windows across the front made it feel that way.

"You must do a lot of entertaining." Olivia's gaze rose with the cathedral ceiling.

"Afraid not. In fact, you'll be my first."

She looked at him in surprise. He seemed like the kind of guy who liked to be around people. Why own a house like this and never invite anyone over?

His answer came as if he'd heard the silent question. "Like I said, it needed a lot of work. I've done most of it myself in my off hours, and what I couldn't do, I've hired done." He grinned. "But I guess I'm ready for guests now."

"Can we look around?" Emma asked.

"Sure. My bedroom and office are on this floor. A couple of guest bedrooms and a TV room are downstairs. And I turned the corner loft over the kitchen" —he pointed upward—"into a library.

The previous owners left behind a bunch of books, so I made a place for them, plus my own collection." He turned toward the kitchen. "I'll start lunch while you three look around."

The two girls rushed toward the stairs that led to the loft, but Olivia followed Tyler.

"I can see the house later," she said when he glanced behind. "I'll help with the food for now."

The sparkle in his eyes as he looked at her made something pleasant coil in her midsection. A feeling long forgotten.

He stepped toward her, his hand reaching for the door of the refrigerator. She could have stepped away. Maybe she should have stepped away. But she didn't, and he seemed to forget what he'd wanted in the fridge. Instead, his hand lightly brushed her upper arm. His gaze searched her face and must have found an answer, for he drew closer still.

Eyes closed now, Olivia caught a

quick breath in anticipation before his lips touched hers. The sensation that spiraled through her in response made her knees turn to jelly. She swayed forward, into the hard wall of his chest. His arms wrapped around her, holding her upright.

She'd forgotten what a kiss could do. Or had she ever known? Had she ever felt this way before? Yes, she thought she had, but the memory was long forgotten. Time had little meaning to her. Did they stand like that for seconds or for hours? She couldn't be sure.

At some point, Tyler drew his head back. But not far. Enough to end the kiss. Not so much she couldn't feel the warmth of his breath on her skin.

He cleared his throat and whispered, "We're supposed to be fixing lunch."

"I know."

"I wasn't planning that when I invited you to come eat with me."

"I know."

He cleared his throat again, this time

taking one step back from her, releasing her from his embrace.

Her legs felt wobbly and uncertain, and she reached for the kitchen island to steady herself. A short while later, sounds from the loft steps caused her to walk toward the windows and pretend an interest in the view. But she saw nothing.

Was it possible that a single kiss could change her world? Had the touch of his lips upon hers changed her? Then again, it could mean nothing. Or worse than nothing. It could lead to hurt and pain.

"Mom, we're gonna check the downstairs. Want to come with us?"

She didn't turn. "No, thanks. You two go ahead." Had she sounded normal? She wanted to sound normal.

After Emma and Izzy left, Tyler joined her at the window. "You okay?"

"Yes."

"Should I apologize?"

She turned to face him. "No."

"Is it okay that I wish I could do it again?"

She gave him a tremulous smile, afraid and yet still wishing for the same. "Yes. But don't." Her glance went to the stairs leading to the lower level. "Not now."

"Right. Hamburgers for hungry teens and adults. I'll go fire up the grill."

July 18, 1934
Wednesday

A terrible storm blew through
the mountains yesterday. Black
clouds roiled in the heavens,
thick and threatening, driven
before a mighty wind. The trees
bent and swirled until I thought
surely they would snap in two.
The lightning came next,
followed by booms of thunder
that shook our house.

I stepped onto the porch. My
heart hammered as I watched the
storm move across this valley.
The wind tore at my dress and
my hair. It rattled the shutters.
A large branch from a tree sailed
down the road as I watched.

Sometimes we think we have

control of life, and then God
displays His power through
nature, and we know how
insignificant we are.

July 21, 1934
Saturday

Today, Harry finally took us to
see the New Hope Health Spa.
It is ten miles to the north of
Bethlehem Springs, and it is ever
so much more than I expected.

There is a lodge. Four stories
tall and made of logs. Very fitting
for the location.

Even though we were not
guests, they allowed us a tour
of the lodge. There were thick
carpets on the floors and
beautiful artwork hanging on all
the walls. Both the large entry
hall and the dining room featured
enormous stone fireplaces. I was
even allowed a glimpse of the
kitchen. So large and gleaming

with what Harry called stainless steel. I had never seen the like.

Across from the lodge is the bathhouse and the two pools that are fed by the natural hot springs. In the bathhouse are private bathing rooms with large porcelain tubs as well as two steam rooms, one for men and another for women.

What was completely unexpected was the resort's prayer chapel. Do most resorts have prayer chapels? I know nothing about such places, so I cannot be sure. But it felt unusual, all the same.

The name above the entrance said it was the Danielle McKinley Prayer Chapel. The interior was simple. Plain even. Rugged. And yet the feeling that came over me as I stood near the altar was one of awe and beauty. I am quite certain that one can often feel

God's presence there.
    Perhaps one day I can go
back.

Chapter 25

Late on Monday morning Emma walked through the living room, her eyes on the open diary in her right hand. "Hey, Mom."

"In my studio," came the reply.

"Have you ever been up to the New Hope Health Spa?" She stopped in the studio doorway.

Her mom swiveled her chair away from the computer. "Yes, but not in years. The place closed down before my time. At least forty years ago. Maybe longer. It's all boarded up, and the last time I was there, some of the outbuildings had started to fall down. The pools were empty except for debris."

"Really? That's too bad. Millie made it sound like it was really something to see." She closed the cover of the diary as she spoke.

"I remember it made me feel sad to see it like that. From everything I've read and seen, it was an amazing place in its heyday. There are a lot of photos of it in the museum. If you're curious, you could go see them. And I'll bet Mrs. Simpson could tell you about it too. She would have been a young woman when all those visitors came to stay at the spa."

"Yeah. Hadn't thought of that." She turned to leave. "Maybe I'll call Izzy and see if she wants to go to the museum with me."

"If you want to wait until I get my work done, I could take you later this afternoon."

"Thanks, but I'll call Izzy. We can ride our bikes over."

"Okay."

She pretended she didn't hear the disappointment in her mom's voice as she headed to her bedroom. While she could finally admit she loved her mom, she still didn't want to spend every minute with her.

Determined to finish her latest design before turning off the computer for the day, Olivia didn't budge from her desk chair. She didn't sip the water in the mug on the desk to her left. She didn't stand to stretch her legs or ease the tension in her neck. She focused on nothing but the work itself. When she was able to click Save and close out of the program, she was startled to find how much time had passed.

A moment later, just as the darkness that had stolen over her studio registered in her head, a crack of thunder caused her to jump. A squeal of alarm tore from her throat. As with the last storm that had blown through Bethlehem Springs, she hurried around the house, turning on the lights. Would Emma come out of her room as long as the power stayed on, or would it take loss of the internet to make her stir?

Lightning flashed and thunder boomed again.

"Emma?"

No answer.

Wait. Emma had gone to the museum with Izzy. But that was hours ago. Surely she should be home by now. Emma might find the history of this area interesting, but not enough to keep her at the museum for several hours.

She climbed the stairs and opened the door to Emma's room. The bed was unmade, and the old diary lay open, pages turned down, on the nightstand. A pile of dirty laundry filled the corner near the closet. A couple of posters from the Bethlehem Springs Mountain Theater had been thumbtacked to the wall since the last time Olivia had checked her daughter's bedroom. If she wasn't mistaken, that cowboy actor was featured in them both.

Light flashed at the window and the boom shook the house, eliciting another gasp from Olivia. She hurried from the room and down the stairs. Just as she arrived, the heavens loosed a torrent of rain.

Was Emma out in this?

She grabbed the phone and called her daughter's cell phone. It rang until it went to voice mail. Next she looked up the Rath number and called there. She felt a moment of relief when Izzy answered.

"Hi, Izzy. It's Emma's mom. Is she there with you?"

"No, Ms. Ward. I haven't seen her."

A shiver of alarm passed through her. "You two didn't go to the museum?"

"No. She asked me to, but I couldn't go today. Mom's got me helping to paint my bedroom."

"She must have gone alone," Olivia said, more to bolster herself than for Izzy's information. "Thanks. I'll need to go get her. No way can she ride a bike out in this storm."

"It's bad out there for sure."

As soon as she put the phone down, Olivia searched for the phone number for the museum.

Please let her be there. Please let her be there.

A woman answered after a few rings, a wait that seemed interminable.

"Hi. This is Olivia Ward. My daughter planned to come to the museum. She left before the storm. I wanted to see if she's still there before I drive over to pick her up."

"Sorry, Ms. Ward. We haven't had any visitors to the museum since about eleven this morning, and that was an older couple. No one is here now but me."

"Thank you." The words came out a whisper as she lowered the phone and set it in the charger.

Where was Emma?

Lightning flashed again, and the

thunder was instantaneous. Tree limbs scraped against the house as the tall pines swirled in a crazed dance. Olivia wanted to curl into a ball beneath her studio desk and hide her head until the storm passed. But she couldn't. Emma was out in this storm some-where. She needed to go look for her. She needed to find her. But where? Where should she look?

Ask Tyler.

Was that her own thought or the voice of the Spirit? She didn't know or care. She only knew she wanted his help. She grabbed his card off her desk and dialed the first number.

"Hey, Olivia."

She wanted to return his cheerful greeting, but her hello came out as a sob.

"Olivia? What is it?"

She drew a breath, trying to control the panic she felt. "It's Emma. She's somewhere out in the storm. I don't know where." Another sob stopped her words.

"I'll be right there. Hang on. I'm coming."

Tyler was as good as his word. He was out of the door of his house and on his way in under two minutes. His heart pounded in his chest as he whispered a prayer for Olivia and Emma. He'd heard the terror in Olivia's voice. He didn't know what she thought had happened to her daughter, but he knew she was scared.

Tree branches littered the road in front of him, and he swerved to miss them before turning off of Main onto Elkhorn. Thirty seconds later, he was stopped in her driveway and racing up the steps to her deck. She opened the door before he reached it. Tears streaked her cheeks.

Without a word, he took her into his arms, holding her close against his chest. When a gust of wind struck the house, she burrowed closer, a small cry escaping her. He eased her farther into the living area and closed the door with his heel behind him.

He waited until she grew still, then said, "Tell me what happened. Did the two of you argue?"

"No." The word was muffled against his shirt. She took a step back, and reluctantly he let her go. "No, she didn't run off. We didn't fight. I thought...I thought she'd gone with a friend to the museum, but Izzy couldn't go and the museum said Emma hadn't been there."

"Any other friends besides Izzy know where she might be?"

"I don't think so."

"Did you try Hailey?"

She shook her head.

"I'll do it."

Over the next few minutes, as the lightning and thunder began to grow more distant, he called Kathy Dover's house, then Phoebe Simpson's number, and finally Victor Benson, in case the

director might know of another friendship formed within the acting company.
No one knew anything that would help.
No one had seen Emma today. But
there were plenty of volunteers ready to
go look for the girl.

"You're sure she took the bike?" Tyler
asked Olivia.

She nodded. "She leaves it beneath
the deck. It's gone. I looked after I called
you, just to be sure."

Which explained why her hair was
damp. He wished he could pull her
close again and hold her until the fear
was gone and her hair was dry. But he
couldn't.

"Let's go. I'll drive. You look. Bethlehem Springs isn't that big. We'll find
her."

"I'll grab some towels. If she's out in
it, she'll be soaked to the skin."

He gave her a smile of encouragement, glad to see that she'd calmed a
little more.

"It's the storm," she said, glancing

toward the large window in the living room. "Big winds and all that go with them scare me. They always have."

Again, he wanted to hold her. He wanted to whisper that she never needed to be frightened again. That he would be with her, if she'd let him.

She went for the towels and returned with them and an umbrella. She wore a light rain coat over her summer top and jeans. Hopefully she would have little need of the rain coat or umbrella, beyond getting to and from his car.

They were both silent as Tyler drove up and down the streets of Bethlehem Springs, accompanied by the steady sound of the windshield wipers. There was no sign of the bicycle, no sign of Emma. He wouldn't have admitted it to Olivia, but Tyler had begun to feel some anxiety.

Then, on his second time driving down Washington Street, just as they were passing the museum, Olivia sucked in a quick breath. She turned to look at him.

"I think I might know where she went."

"Where?"

"Up to the site of the old spa."

"That's ten miles from here."

"I know. But it wasn't stormy when she left. And maybe she didn't know how far it was."

Tyler came to a halt at the stop sign at Main. "Why do you think she went there?"

"She read about it in an old diary. It's why I suggested she visit the museum. To see photographs of what it looked like in its prime."

"But she didn't go to the museum."

"No. After Izzy couldn't go with her, she may have decided to just go see for herself."

Tyler turned right onto Main Street. "Okay. Let's see if you're right."

Emma huddled beneath a fir tree, the branches offering little protection from the rain. Out near the road lay the bike, its front wheel separated from the fork or whatever it was called. The accident had happened so fast, she wasn't even sure what caused it. Just suddenly the bike had crashed down, minus the wheel, and she'd been sent flying and skidding along the gravel on the side of the road.

At least the thunder and lightning had moved on, and now there was only an occasional rumble in the distance. That part had been extra scary. She knew it wasn't good to be out in the middle of a storm like that. But where could she have gone except to hide under a tree and hope lightning, if it struck, would pick a taller tree?

Wait! That sounded like someone calling her name. Was she hearing things? She got to her feet, bent over to avoid the lowest branches, and stepped toward the road. Squinting against the rain, she saw the approach of a familiar SUV. Tyler's car. And it was her mom calling her name.

Limping, she hurried to the road and waved both arms in the air. The SUV stopped before it reached her, and her mom was out in a flash.

"Emma!"

"Mom!"

Nothing in her life had ever felt as good as that second her mom wrapped her in a tight embrace.

"I was so scared," her mom said.

"I wrecked the bike."

"It doesn't matter. Are you all right?"

"I think so. Just some scrapes and bruises."

"I couldn't find you. We looked everywhere."

"I should have told you where I was going. I didn't know it was gonna storm."

Rain ran down her mom's face. Or were those tears? Both, probably. Come to think of it, Emma was crying too.

She remembered then how scared of storms her mom was. But even so, she'd come out looking for Emma. She'd been more worried for Emma than for herself. Mom would sacrifice just about anything for Emma. She loved her that much.

Her mom guided her toward the SUV. "Let's get you home."

"Yeah." She looked back at the twisted bike. "I'm ready."

July 23, 1934
Monday

Another storm raged through the mountains today. Not as fierce as last week, but fierce enough. I'm told forest fires are burning far to the north. How far away? Is this little town in danger? What of Harry's employment, should the forest be destroyed?

Those thoughts frighten me.

But this is what Psalm 91 tells me: He that dwelleth in the secret place of the Most High shall abide under the shadow of the Almighty. I will say of Jehovah, He is my refuge and my fortress; my God, in whom I trust.

May I remember that when fear
and doubt find their way into my
heart once more. As they do too
often.

July 28, 1934
Saturday

"And who knoweth whether thou art not come to the kingdom for such a time as this?"

I read the book of Esther this morning, and that verse from the fourth chapter has repeated in my memory throughout the day.

I have complained a lot since our money troubles began. I have objected to the trials and questioned God's care because of my own loss and hardship. I have looked around Riverside and Thunder Creek and Bethlehem Springs and seen those who suffer even more than I, but also those who seem to have no troubles at all. I have asked if God cares. I have not found all the answers.

But what if I came to this place (to this kingdom) for such a time as this? Has God placed us here for a purpose?

I don't know the answer to that question either. But I wonder.

Chapter 26

When the office phone rang early on Tuesday morning, Olivia saw her mom's number on the caller ID and answered it with a smile. "Hi, Mom."

"Hello, darling. We're back. All safe and sound. And we can't wait to see you and Emma."

"We can't wait to see you either."

"Are things better between you two? I know when we last talked you sounded a bit stressed."

"They're better, Mom. Not perfect, but better. Emma's involvement with the theater company has made a big difference. She's made a few friends too."

"That's wonderful news."

"We did have a bit of excitement yesterday. To be honest, it wasn't excitement. It was a scare."

"What on earth happened?"

Olivia gave a quick summary of the previous day's storm, her fears when she didn't know where Emma was, and Emma's accident.

"But she's all right?" her mom asked when Olivia fell silent.

"Yes. She's fine. I was the one who was a mess."

After another moment of silence, her mom asked, "Would it be all right if we drive up today? As I said, we can't wait to see you both."

Olivia swiveled her chair toward the clock on the wall. "Of course I don't mind. What time should we expect you?"

"About noon? We can take you to lunch at the café in town."

"You don't have to do that. I'll fix sandwiches. We'll have a better visit if we stay at the house. Not as noisy."

"All right. I won't argue about that."

Her mom said something more but the sound was muffled. Olivia guessed she'd covered the mouthpiece. Then, her voice clear again, she said, "Your dad says we should be there around eleven forty-five or so."

"We'll be looking for you."

As soon as she ended the call, Olivia left her office. At the base of the stairs, she called, "Emma!"

"What?"

She waited to answer until her daughter opened the bedroom door and looked down. "Your grandparents are driving up from Boise to see you. They'll be here around lunchtime."

If Emma was eager to see her grandparents again, she didn't show it. Was it any wonder? Despite Olivia's mom writing letters to her only grandchild through the years, they'd become strangers.

That won't last long. Mom'll win her

over in no time. Dad too.

The phone in her office rang again, and Olivia—not knowing what else to say to Emma—went to answer it. She didn't recognize the number on the screen. "Olivia Designs."

A male voice said, "Is this Olivia Ward?"

"Yes."

"I'm Peter Ward."

At first, that meant nothing, and she waited for him to say more.

"Daniel's father."

She dropped onto the chair. The pleasure she'd felt, knowing she would see her parents today, vanished. Her mind went blank, her lungs starved for air.

"I was hoping—" He broke off, cleared his throat, then continued. "I was hoping I could meet you."

How should she answer her former father-in-law, a man she'd never met? "Meet me?"

"Yes. And my granddaughter."

Dread iced through her. This was a complication she didn't need. Peter Ward was a complete stranger to her. She wouldn't know him if he passed her on the street. She'd never even seen a photograph of him. Daniel hadn't told his father about their wedding or about the birth of Emma. He'd explained nothing about what had caused the estrangement, other than saying his father couldn't be trusted and wasn't welcome in their lives.

"Olivia? Are you there?"

He sounded like Daniel. An older version, perhaps, but the similarity was unmistakable. Was he like Daniel in other ways?

"Olivia?"

"I'm here." She gave her head a slight shake. "I...I...Mr. Ward, you caught me by surprise."

"I'm sure I did. Listen, I don't know what my son told you about me. Whatever it was, I don't imagine it was flattering." He paused, as if waiting for her to confirm or deny his statement. When she did neither, he added, "I had only one son. I have only one grandchild. It's too late to mend bridges with Daniel, although I did try while he was alive. But it isn't too late to know Emma..." His voice trailed into silence.

"Mr. Ward."

"Peter, please."

"Mr. Ward, I'm sure you understand that these past couple of months have been difficult ones for Emma. She's had to accept the death of Daniel. She's lost her home and her school friends. She's had to move to a state she barely remembers. And she's getting to know me again after a long time apart. That hasn't been easy either." She wanted to bite her tongue. She hadn't meant to be quite that honest with this stranger.

"I understand."

"I don't want...I don't want to spring too much on her."

"I agree. But I do want to meet her. And you."

She felt some of the tension leave her shoulders. Daniel wouldn't have responded with patience. He would have applied icy pressure. "I need to meet you first. I have to be sure it's the right thing for Emma."

"You need to be sure I'm not the monster Daniel told you I was." It was a statement, not a question.

"He never called you a monster."

"Didn't he? Then I'm surprised."

Were you? Were you a monster? Are you one?

As if he'd heard the silent questions, Peter Ward said, "My son and I disagreed on many things, Olivia. But I'm not a bad man. I was never cruel to him. Critical but never cruel. I don't want anything from you other than to have the privilege of being a part of Emma's life. If only in a small way."

She rubbed her forehead with the pads of her fingers, eyes now closed.

"Would you be willing to meet with me in Boise?" he asked.

"You're in Boise?"

"I moved back to Idaho around the same time Daniel and Emma moved to Florida."

"Oh."

"We could meet in a public place. At a restaurant, perhaps."

She released a sigh. "All right. Let me check my calendar and get back to you."

"Please let me know soon."

"Yes. I promise. I'll call you back in a day or two. Should I use the number you're calling from?"

"Yes. That's the number. And thank you, Olivia. I appreciate it. More than you know."

She said goodbye and set the phone on her desk, then covered her face with both hands. Had she done the right thing, agreeing to meet Peter Ward? Was she opening a door to even more trouble and heartache? Daniel had brought so much pain into her life. She'd loved him when she married him, but his lack of respect, lack of tenderness, lack of love in return, had begun long before he left her. It had taken her several years to admit that truth.

Was Peter Ward cut from the same cloth? Had Daniel learned it all from his father? If so, she didn't want to know him, and she didn't want her daughter to know him either.

God, help me know what to do.

Tyler didn't really need an excuse to call on Olivia, but checking to see how Emma was provided him one. And he would be able to tell her that the bike wasn't beyond repair. It was being worked on right now.

A car he didn't recognize was parked in Olivia's driveway when he arrived. He'd assumed she would be on a lunch break about now. Hopefully the car didn't belong to one of her design clients. If it did, he would have to make the visit a short one.

As he got out of the car, he grabbed

a notebook off the passenger seat, another handy excuse if he needed one. Then he took the steps to the deck two at a time. Before he reached the door, he heard a burst of laughter from inside. Somebody was having a good time. Maybe he should come back later. No. He was there. He might as well stay. He knocked before he could change his mind.

The door opened moments later. "Tyler." Olivia's smile relieved his worry that he'd come at a bad time. Better yet, there was no sign of the distraught mother he'd held in his arms the previous day.

"Thought I should check in and see how Emma's feeling."

"She's no worse for wear. Come on in." The warmth in her gaze matched the warmth in his chest.

He followed as she led the way to the dining area, where an older couple sat opposite Emma. They looked at him, curiosity in their eyes. It only took a glance for him to know these had to be Olivia's parents. The resemblance was indisputable, especially to her mom.

"Mom. Dad. This is Tyler Murphy. Tyler, my parents, Faith and Olin Lewis."

Her dad rose and held out his hand. "A pleasure to meet you."

Tyler had the distinct feeling that his name had come up in conversation before this introduction.

"Mom and Dad are just back from a cruise to the Mediterranean and a tour of the Holy Land and Turkey. They were gone eight weeks."

"Must've been amazing," Tyler said.

"They started saving for it when I was a little girl." Olivia sat and reached for her mom's hand. "They could've taken the trip lots sooner if they hadn't dipped into that fund to help me out more than once."

"I'll bet waiting didn't matter to them if it meant helping you."

"You're right, Mr. Murphy." Her mom smiled—a smile very much like Olivia's.

"And the trip was worth the wait." Her gaze went to her grandchild. "But we were anxious to get home again because of Emma. It's been too long since we last saw her in person."

Tyler thought of Peter Ward, who'd never met his granddaughter. Had Peter decided what he would do next? He was no longer a client, so Tyler couldn't ask. He could only wonder and wait.

He gave his head a slight shake to clear his thoughts, then looked at Emma. "Thought you'd like to know that your bike's being repaired. You should have it back in a day or two. It'll be good as new."

"Thanks."

He looked at the notebook in his hand. "What about this? Is it yours?" He held it up. "I found it in the library at my house."

"It's Izzy's. She takes notes in it at church." Emma took it from him. "I'll let her know."

Olivia touched his arm. "Would you like to join us? We finished eating, but I can make you a sandwich."

"No. I don't want to intrude."

Olin said, "You're more than welcome to stay."

He didn't know if he should join them. He only knew that he wanted to. So he pulled out a chair and sat at the table.

It didn't take long for the conversation to return to stories about the cruise. While Tyler listened, he observed Emma. Something was different about her. A kind of lightness of being. He'd seen her happy before, and this was more than that. Maybe it was simply easy to feel good in this present company. There was an easy banter between family members. Even Emma, who hadn't seen her grandparents in many years, participated easily.

Christa would have loved this. She would have loved all the laughing, the swapping of stories, the teasing. She'd never had a chance to experience a real family. Never had a grandparent to accept her unconditionally. Never had a mom to love her the way Olivia loved Emma. By the time she was sixteen, Christa had given up on everything, including herself.

Tyler hadn't had a chance for moments like this either, but he'd wanted them. Wanted them still. It was too late for his childhood, but maybe it wasn't too late for the man he'd become. Generations seated at a table. Love enough to go around. A woman by his side.

Olivia by my side.

To belong here. Not as a guest at this table and in this house but to truly belong. That's what he wanted. Could he make Olivia fall in love with him? He hoped so, because if he wasn't mistaken, he'd already fallen in love with her.

August 5, 1934
Sunday

The reverend's sermon this
morning was on God's sovereignty. God's will be done. His
will is always done. But what
about Dottie's death? Was that in
God's will? Was it planned from
the beginning of time? Were
her days numbered from the
very start? Or did she die only
because sickness still exists
on the earth?

And what about man's free
will? How can God be in control
of my life, yet I have the choice
to do what I want? I do not
understand how the two can be
true at the same time. And yet
when I read my Bible, that is

what I see there. Both are true.

Sin and sickness and death exist in this world because of the fall. Jesus overcame sin and death, and yet they remain for a time. The end will be as God declares, even while He allows us to go our own way.

Am I too simple and uneducated to grasp how both God's sovereignty and man's free will can exist together? Or is this meant to be one of God's mysteries?

If I understood everything, I would be like God. That was what caused Eve to sin—wanting to be like God. The Serpent said if she ate from the tree she would be like God, knowing good and evil, and that the fruit would make her wise.

It isn't a sin to seek wisdom. But it is a sin to want to be like God.

Father, there are truths of the faith that You reveal, but there are other things that remain a mystery. Reveal to me what I need to know, and help me accept the mysteries that should remain so. Amen.

August 6, 1934
Monday

Harry was irritable at supper
tonight. It took a while for me
to get him to say why, but finally
he told me that a few men were
laid off today at the mill. He has
worked there only a matter of
months. Although he did not
admit it to me, he is afraid he
will be next. Then what would
we do?

   It is almost midnight as I write
in this diary. The baby is active,
and I cannot sleep. And so I sit
at the table, writing, and hoping
I can make sense of all that I feel.
But I cannot. The chance that
there could be another move
overwhelms me. I cannot handle

it. It is more than one woman
should have to handle.
   Isn't it?

Chapter 27

Heart racing, Olivia entered the upscale Boise restaurant shortly after one o'clock on Thursday. She hadn't told anyone about her plans to meet Peter Ward, but suddenly she wished she had. Sara or Kathy, mothers themselves, might have had wisdom to share. Her own mom or dad could have guided her, without doubt. Even talking to Tyler would have helped. He was a good listener, never rushing to give advice. It was just one of the things she liked about him.

She gave Peter's name to the seating hostess, who said, "Yes. Mr. Ward's waiting for you. Follow me."

Classical music played softly from speakers overhead. Pristine white cloths covered the tables. Men and women sat in twos, threes, and fours, continuing discussions that had begun over food. She didn't need to look at a menu to know a single meal here would swallow her food budget for a week. Daniel had been comfortable in settings like this one. Not so Olivia, and now she felt at a disadvantage. Had Peter Ward chosen the restaurant because he'd known that about her?

She saw him then, rising from his chair as she and the hostess approached. A man in his seventies, he was undoubtedly her former husband's father. The same narrow face. The same pointed jaw. The same sharp eyes. Even the same friendly smile—although she'd learned not to trust Daniel's. She wouldn't trust Peter's either.

"Olivia. I'm thankful you came."

With a curt nod, she sat opposite him,

glad he hadn't offered his hand. She wasn't ready for that.

He pointed to the menu on the table before her. "Whatever you choose will be delicious."

She wasn't hungry, doubted she could eat a bite. Her stomach had become a bundle of nerves. After looking through the menu—more to delay talking than because she cared what was in it—she ordered soup and salad.

"I'll have the same," Peter said to their server.

Silence fell over the table once they were alone again, but Olivia didn't try to fill it. This was **his** meeting. Let him speak first.

At last he did so. "Let me tell you a little of my story. Would that be all right?"

"Of course."

"I wasn't a very good father. I was absent more than I was present when Daniel was a boy. I was building my business, and the demands of my profession always seemed more important than the needs of my wife and son. I regret that now, of course. I wasn't harsh. I wasn't demanding. I didn't play the disciplinarian. I simply was not there."

Olivia nodded to indicate she listened.

"Daniel was away at college when his mother passed suddenly. After her funeral, he had no reason to come home again. He soon made it clear that he wanted nothing to do with me or the company I'd built. I can't say this for certain, but I believe his goal was to build something bigger than his father's. And he did exactly that. From what I ascertained through the years, he was ruthless in his ambitions and far more intelligent than I ever dreamed of being."

There was a sadness in Peter Ward's eyes that tugged at Olivia's heart. She hoped she didn't reveal her feelings.

"I learned of your marriage to my

son only after the wedding took place. When I tried to talk to Daniel about it, he made it clear that nothing had changed. I wasn't welcome in his life. Period. I wasn't to call. I wasn't to try to see him. It was then that I realized how much he despised me. It was more than him believing I'd been a poor father. So much more. Sadly, I don't know the reason why. I must have done something, but I don't know what."

She had to respond. "I'm sorry." Words that offered scant comfort.

"I complied with his desire to be left alone until I learned about Emma's birth. Then I tried again. More than once over the next years. But my efforts only seemed to make things worse. Then came the divorce, and Daniel got custody of Emma."

She winced, and her gut tightened like a rock. It was then the server arrived with their bowls of soup and plates of salad, and she was thankful for a few moments to compose herself.

Peter speared some lettuce but didn't lift it to his mouth. Instead, he put the fork on his plate. "Olivia, I made a great many mistakes in my life. I have many regrets. But my greatest regret, after failing my son, is that I don't know my granddaughter. I'm not a young man. I don't know how much time the good Lord will give me on this earth. Five years. Ten. Fifteen. I would like a chance to know Emma. That's all I'm asking for. A chance."

She stared across the table, trying to assess the man and his motives. What would be best for Emma? That had to be how she made her decision. What would be best for her daughter?

She recalled Emma with her grand-parents on Tuesday. She thought of the laughter and the almost instant connection and love that had filled the house as the two generations became reacquainted. Emma's faded memories of her Grandma Faith and Grandpa Olin had changed from black-and-white to vibrant color right before Olivia's eyes.

But Emma didn't know Peter Ward. He was a stranger to her. Was it fair of him to want to have a relationship with Emma after nearly sixteen years of silence?

Is it fair of me if I don't let him try?

She wished she could get up and leave. She wished she'd never taken his call. What if this made things worse and not better? What if Emma got hurt again?

"I don't know how much time the good Lord will give me on this earth."

She drew a breath as the words repeated in her head. "Mr. Ward, are you a man of faith?"

"Do you mean, am I a Christian?" The slightest of smiles curved his mouth. "Yes, I am. I came to know Jesus in the months after my wife passed."

"Daniel wasn't a believer."

"I know. I think it was one of the things that angered him. That I had come to believe in something beyond what was right here, beyond success and financial gain. Or maybe he hated the idea that I believed God could forgive me for the wrong things I'd done. He thought it unfair that I could be redeemed."

"He didn't like it when Emma and I went to church."

"That doesn't surprise me."

She realized then that her decision had been made. Her own faith had faltered after the divorce and losing Emma, but she'd been given another chance. Many other chances. Could she do any less for Emma's paternal grandfather?

"I'll talk to Emma. We'll figure something out."

"Thank you, Olivia. Thank you from the bottom of my heart."

As had become his habit on performance nights, Tyler parked his vehicle at the far end of the lot. He'd started his walk to the entrance when Emma and Izzy sailed by him on their bikes—Emma's newly repaired—one of them a little too close for comfort.

"Hey!" he called.

They answered with laughter, the sounds fading as they drew closer to the backstage entrance of the theater. He grinned. It was a good thing that Emma liked him. If she didn't, he wouldn't stand a chance with Olivia.

Olivia... Just the thought of her name brought a spring to his step. He was a goner, pure and simple.

"Hey, Tyler."

He stopped and turned at the sound of his name, watching Greg Dover's approach. "Hey, Greg."

"Did you hear about Will Jensen?"

The smile slipped from Tyler's face, and his gut tightened. Having met the man, he knew it wasn't a leap to expect the news to be bad. "No."

"Beat Nate so bad it put the kid in the hospital. Jensen's been arrested."

"When did it happen?"

"Last night."

"What about Mrs. Jensen and Nate's brother? Were they hurt?"

"No. They weren't home when Will went off on the boy, from what I was told. I guess they've gone down to the valley to stay with family she's got there. That way she'll be close to the hospital too."

"Anything we can do for them?"

Greg nodded as the two men started walking toward the theater entrance. "I was hoping our men's group could help with the move. Karen Jensen is adamant that she and the boys won't be coming back to Bethlehem Springs."

"Good decision on her part. Probably should've happened long before this. I had a bad feeling when I met her husband." He didn't add that he'd seen more than one case where a woman stayed one beating too long. "Is Nate going to be okay?"

"Hope so. I heard he's got a number

of broken bones. Left leg. Right arm. Maybe a concussion. Possibly some internal injuries."

"Count me in for whatever help you need. My schedule's on the lighter side right now. I should be able to make any day or time work if I have a little bit of notice."

"It probably needs to be tomorrow, but I'll let you know."

Tyler stopped walking. After one more stride, Greg did the same and turned to face him.

"Greg, you don't think this has anything to do with me looking into what happened at the rehearsal last week, do you?"

"No." His friend's hand alighted on Tyler's shoulder. "No, I don't think it did. Will has always been volatile, especially when he drinks. And from what I've heard, he drinks all the time. Hopefully he'll be kept in jail longer than in the past. Keep him away from his wife and kids until they're good and safe."

Tyler ran a hand over his face. "The evil that men do."

"Even so, Lord, come quickly."

He met Greg's gaze and nodded in agreement. "Amen."

They parted then, Greg to look for Kathy, Tyler to man the control booth.

His thoughts stayed on Nate and his father as he prepared for the night's performance. Nate carried plenty of long-term emotional wounds. Tyler had recognized them when he met the kid at the Gold Mountain. He'd sensed the hurt inside the boy, probably because he could have easily traveled a similar path. He hadn't been beaten and ended up in a hospital, but he'd seen his share of the underside of society throughout his own childhood. He could have been embittered by it. He could have caused mischief or gotten into serious trouble. Or he could have tried escaping through drugs and alcohol, the way his sister had. But he hadn't gone any of those directions.

Why? What made one person choose one path and another choose a different one, even when raised under similar circumstances?

He gave his head a slow shake. He doubted he would ever know for certain if Nate had pushed over the bookcase on the first night of rehearsals, although his gut told him he had. But it didn't matter now. Nate couldn't cause any more trouble in Bethlehem Springs because he wouldn't live here after this. But if the opportunity arose when Tyler helped with the move, he would suggest to Mrs. Jensen that the boy get some much-needed help.

"Knock, knock."

The sound of Olivia's voice chased the troubled thoughts from his head and brought the return of a smile to his mouth. "Hey there."

"Am I bothering you?"

"Never." He pointed to the extra chair. "I saw Emma arrive on her bike, so I didn't expect you to be here."

"I came to see you."

Few words could have pleased him more than those.

"I wanted to talk to you about something."

"Of course."

She sat on the other chair. "I went down to Boise today to meet someone."

He remained silent but gave her an expectant look.

"Emma's grandfather."

Why make the visit sound unusual? Olin Lewis had been in Bethlehem Springs two days ago.

"Emma's **other** grandfather. Daniel's father."

He should have known that Peter would follow through eventually. Yet the news still surprised him, and he didn't know what to say.

"He wants to meet Emma," she added.

"How do you feel about that?"

"Confused. Conflicted. Unsure how it will affect Emma. I don't know what

Daniel even told her about his father. Maybe nothing. Even when we were married, he never spoke about him."

"So what did you tell Mr. Ward?"

"That I would talk to Emma and figure something out."

Something relaxed in Tyler's chest. "Seems fair."

"But I wondered if you could do something for me first. Before I tell Emma."

"What's that?"

She looked down at her hands, now folded in her lap. After a brief silence, she looked up again. "I'd like you to investigate him."

August 18, 1934
Saturday

Harry did not come home for supper last night. He worked late, and then he spent the evening in a bar with other men from work. I have never seen him have more than a beer in all the years we have been married, but he came home intoxicated last night.

This morning I am angry. So angry I want to hit something. Or someone. But last night, when Harry's friends brought him home, I was too shocked to do anything but direct them to the bedroom where they could put him on the bed. After they left I removed his boots and socks,

but I didn't try to undress him.
He's too heavy for me, especially
now, and he was too drunk to
cooperate with my efforts.

I slept in the children's room.

I thought he was happier since
coming to Bethlehem Springs.
I know he struggled in Thunder
Creek, but I thought he was better
here. Yes, he has worried that he
might lose his job if they let more
men go. But that doesn't explain
his behavior. Nor excuse it.

I wish I could run away and not
deal with it.

God, how can I handle one more
thing? I'm too weak. I can't bear
up under the weight of it. To the
apostle Paul, You said, "My
grace is sufficient for thee: for
my power is made perfect in
weakness." Is that true for me
as well? In my weakness is Your
grace sufficient?

August 19, 1934
Sunday

We had a horrible row yesterday
when Harry finally got out of
bed. We have never fought like
that before. We have had our
disagreements, but never
anything like that. I shouted at
him like a fishwife. Harry said he
couldn't take the sadness and
fear in my eyes one more day,
and that's why he went drinking
with his friends from work.

So his drunkenness is my fault?
The children heard it all.
Charlie isn't old enough to
understand the things we said,
but he is old enough to be upset
by the shouting. He cried. As for
Gladys, she understood far more

than I would like. She was frightened in a different way from her little brother. Her eyes as she looked at us from her bedroom doorway were so big and round.

I feel as if I'm caught in a tornado and have been whirled and whirled and whirled around for years. I'm tired and I'm scared. I can't take much more. But what does that even mean? What choice do I have but to take it?

None of us went to church today.

Chapter 28

Tyler rolled from his left side to his right and looked at the digital clock next to the bed. Almost one in the morning, and he couldn't shut off his thoughts.

"I'd like you to investigate him."

He should have told her right then. He should have said that Peter Ward was a client of the law firm he worked for. He should have admitted that he couldn't take the job because it would be a conflict of interest or something. He should have said any manner of things to make sure she knew he couldn't investigate Peter on her behalf. Maybe he would have said something,

but they'd been interrupted by Victor
Benson about a problem with one of the
speakers. By the time Tyler returned
to the booth, Olivia had gone, a note
waiting on the soundboard.

We'll talk tomorrow. O.

Tomorrow was today, and despite
mulling things over a hundred times,
he couldn't think of a way he could tell
her the truth. Not without permission
from his employer. And even if he got
that, not without making Olivia feel be-
trayed. Could he blame her?

**God, this is a mess. Why didn't I
see it coming?**

He knew the answer, more or less.
The work he did helped people. It pro-
tected people. It found people. It was
good, perhaps even righteous work...
most of the time. But he'd crossed a
line in this case by making himself a
part of Olivia's life. Sure, he'd quit when
he realized the conflict. But not in time.
Not soon enough.

He rolled back to his left side, staring

into the darkness.

It's more than a mess, Lord. It's a disaster. I can't tell the truth without breaking my word. Either way I'm doing the wrong thing.

"How do I make this right? I love her."

He loved her. He'd admitted it to himself for the first time when he'd sat at that table with her parents and daughter on Tuesday. But somehow, only a few days later, the love he felt had deepened. He couldn't explain it. Just knew that it was true. And to lose the chance to win her love in return? He couldn't bear the thought.

Maybe he could tell her that his employer forbade him from taking on private investigations. Only problem was his employer didn't forbid him from private investigations. Not strictly speaking. So that wouldn't be the truth. And a relationship built on a lie? Not the best way to start.

Excuses. Lies. Truth.

He rolled to the other side again. The

time on the clock mocked him.

It was going to be a long, long night.

Somewhere between asleep and awake, Olivia realized she shouldn't wait to tell Emma about her paternal grandfather. Asking Tyler to investigate Peter Ward —was the man anything like Daniel? Was he cruel? Did he only want to make trouble?—had made sense to her yesterday. It didn't make sense this morning.

She rolled her head on her pillow and opened her eyes. On her nightstand sat a pink crystal frog, a gift from Sara several years before. **"F.R.O.G. Fully Rely On God. Try it sometime."** The memory of her friend's words made her breath catch in her chest. The frog had stayed at her bedside all this time, but she hadn't attempted to follow the advice.

It was time she did.

Whispering a prayer for wisdom, she rose and got ready for the day. By the time she stood in the kitchen, preparing her first cup of coffee, an unexpected peace had settled around her heart. "You were right, Sara. It's better when I trust God."

"Talking to yourself, Mom? Isn't that what you do when you get old?"

"That's what they say." She turned to face her daughter. "I didn't expect you to be up this early."

"I got a message from Izzy. The ping woke me."

"I'm surprised she's up this early too."

"She wanted to tell me about Nate Jensen. Did you know?"

Olivia gave her head a slight shake. "Know what?"

"His dad beat him up. Put him in the hospital."

"Oh, Emma. That's awful." She sank onto a chair at the table. How could a parent do such an awful thing?

"I know everybody thinks Nate is the one who pushed over the bookcase. Izzy thinks he's trouble. But he didn't deserve that."

"No, of course he didn't deserve it. No child deserves to be mistreated."

Emma sat opposite her. "I guess I've had it pretty good. I mean, it was hard when you and Dad got divorced and then we moved away." Her brow furrowed. "But I've got lots to be thankful for. Don't I?"

"Yes. We both do." She reached across the table and covered one of Emma's hands with her own. "I love you, sweetheart."

Emma was silent awhile, then replied, "I love you too."

Olivia hadn't known she held her breath until she released it, joy flooding through her. It was the first time her daughter had said those words to her in the two months since Daniel's passing. Longer than that, actually. Much longer.

As if made uncomfortable by the exchange, Emma pulled her hand away and started to rise.

"Emma, wait. There's something I need to talk to you about."

"Now? I was going back to bed."

"It's important."

Emma sighed and plopped back onto the chair. Judging by the girl's expression, the feelings of love she'd felt for her mom had changed to frustration or irritation. Ah, life with a teenager.

"It's about your grandfather."

"What about him?" Genuine concern flashed across Emma's face. "He isn't sick, is he? He looked okay when he was here."

"No. Your **other** grandfather."

"My other—" She shook her head, as if to deny Olivia's words. "You mean Dad's dad?"

"Yes."

"I thought he was dead."

"No. He's very much alive. And he... He would like to meet you."

Emma's eyes narrowed. "Why?"

"Because he's your grandfather."

"He never wanted to meet me before."

"That's not true." She drew a breath and released it. "Apparently he tried, but your dad wouldn't allow it."

"Why not?"

Bitterness tightened Olivia's chest.

Because your dad was selfish. Because he was unkind. Because he always wanted to be in charge. Because he wanted his own way. Because he liked to hurt others. Because he had a cruel streak. Because...

"I don't know," she answered softly. "Your dad never told me why."

"You think I should meet him, don't you?"

"He's part of our family, and family is important."

"But you don't know him either."

"No. I never met him until yesterday."

Surprise widened Emma's eyes. "You did? You met him?"

Olivia nodded.

"Okay." Emma drew out the word, as if still processing her answer. "Then I will too."

Her daughter's consent caught Olivia off guard. She'd expected more resistance. Now it was too late to tell Emma to think about it. Now it was too late to change her mind. And if she was wrong, Emma could get hurt.

Then she remembered Tyler's tender expression last evening as he'd said, **"Seems fair."** He was right. It was fair to let Emma decide.

Trust God.

Funny, that's what she'd said to herself at the moment Emma entered the kitchen. Perhaps this time she would hold on to the thought more than a few minutes.

Emma stood. "Tell him it's okay with me." She stepped toward the kitchen doorway, then stopped. "What should I call him?"

"I suppose that's up to you."

"I'll think about it. Maybe I'll know

when I see him."

"Maybe."

Alone again, Olivia leaned back in the chair and closed her eyes. **Thank You, Lord. That went so much better than I thought it would.**

The coffee in her mug had cooled already, so she popped it into the microwave to reheat it. When it was ready, she carried the mug into her studio, determined to make two phone calls before diving into the day's work.

The first call was to Tyler.

"Morning, Olivia," he answered.

"Good morning. Hope it's not too early to call."

"Not at all. Listen, I'm sorry we got interrupted last night. I never got a chance to answer you about investigating Mr. Ward."

"Actually that's why I'm calling. It was wrong of me to ask it. Emma needs to decide." She paused for a response but was met with silence. It felt strange to her for some reason. After a short wait, she added, "In fact, Emma and I talked a little while ago, and she's agreed to meet her grandfather."

"Sounds like a good decision."

"I'm going to call him next."

"I—" He stopped and cleared his throat. "I'm sure he'll be glad to hear from you."

Did he sound odd, or did she only imagine it? Almost as if he didn't want to talk to her. Maybe she'd called him at a bad time.

"I need to go, Olivia. Will I see you at the theater tonight?"

"I hadn't planned on it. Izzy and Emma are riding their bikes again."

"Then I'll see you at church on Sunday."

Tears stung her eyes. She didn't know why. "Okay. See you then."

After ending the call, Olivia stared at the phone in her hand and replayed the brief exchange. Had she imagined the difference in his voice? That it was missing its usual warmth? It was as if she'd become a stranger to him. As if he'd never looked deeply into her eyes and kissed her. Had he been glad she wouldn't be at the theater? What had she done to cool things between them?

August 21, 1934
Tuesday

We are not speaking. Harry and
I look at each other, but we say
nothing. Even the children are
silent. Like little ghosts haunting
our little house.

August 25, 1934
Saturday

It took almost a week, but Harry and I finally talked about our argument. Oh, the hurtful, angry words we hurled at each other last Sunday. They wound me now to remember them. Not only what Harry said to me, but what I dared to say to him. That I should say such things to the man I love, to the husband I have lived with for over six years and have every reason to treat with respect, to the father of my children. I am very ashamed. It grieves me before the Lord.

    A few weeks ago I wrote in this diary about the mysteries of God. I came upon a verse today in

Colossians that says: "To whom God was pleased to make known what is the riches of the glory of this mystery among the Gentiles, which is Christ in you, the hope of glory."

Christ in me, the hope of glory. That's one of the mysteries. I am God's child. The Holy Spirit indwells me. Should I not be a better representative of His love, grace, and mercy? And while I should let Him shine through me to the world, I should let Him shine even more brilliantly here within the walls of my home.

Gladys and Charlie are the innocent victims of our shouting match.

Forgive me, Father. In Jesus' name. Make this family strong and whole.

Chapter 29

"You want to tell me what's wrong?" Greg asked as he drove his pickup truck down the highway toward Boise.

Tyler turned from the window to look at his friend. "What?"

"You didn't say a dozen words the whole time we loaded up the back of the truck at the Jensen place. Not to mention that scowl on your face. It's been there all morning."

"Sorry."

"Wasn't looking for an apology. Just an explanation. What's up?"

He wasn't sure how to answer his friend, but finally settled for, "I've got what they call a moral dilemma going on."

Greg glanced at him, then back at the road. "Sounds serious." The humor was gone from his voice.

"It is. At least for me." He drew a breath and released it, at the same time searching for the right words, words that wouldn't reveal identities or betray client privacy but could still gain him good advice from his friend. "A couple of months ago, I was assigned a case by the firm. I did what I was hired to do. Found out all the pertinent information and advised the client of my recommendations. Normally that would be the end of it." He stopped, and his mind filled with images of Olivia, slowing when he remembered the kisses they'd shared at the start of the week and ending with the feel of her in his arms as he'd held her during the storm.

"But?" Greg prompted.

"But I let myself get emotionally involved in this particular case. And now...Now the work that I did feels like a betrayal to someone I came to care about. Don't misunderstand me. I didn't do anything unethical. But my work belongs to the firm and its client. What I do is confidential. It has to be. And even if I got permission to talk about it outside the usual parameters, I think the information would...I think it might break something. Maybe beyond repair. Break something for me. For the client. For the person I investigated. Perhaps for all three of us." He sighed as he turned to look out the passenger window again.

For a long while the only sound in the cab was that of tires rolling down the highway at fifty-five miles an hour. Then Greg said, "I don't pretend to understand everything you said, Tyler. But I can tell you're distressed about it. I'd like to pray for you. Is that all right?"

"More than all right."

Churning emotions made it difficult to concentrate on the prayer Greg spoke over him. And yet, by the time his friend said, "Amen," Tyler felt calmer than before, his emotions quieted. He didn't have answers, but he did feel a spark of hope that answers would be found.

Emma made herself sit on the sofa, staring at her phone as she scrolled the feed on her Instagram account. What she wanted to do instead was stand at the window and watch for an unfamiliar car to pull into the driveway. She hadn't felt nervous when Mom told her that morning about the grandfather she'd never met. Now she was nervous. Maybe because she hadn't expected to be meeting him this soon.

Families were complicated. That's what Hailey had told her earlier today. She'd said that God created families, with all their complexities and quirks, and that everybody needed love and grace to make them work well. She'd also said perceptions could make people believe things that weren't true.

What kind of quirks would this grand-father bring to the mix? What kinds of things had Emma believed that weren't true because her perceptions had mud-dled them?

For a long time she'd believed her mom hadn't wanted her, hadn't really loved her, but she'd begun to see how wrong she'd been about that.

Muddled perceptions.

Earlier in the week, when she'd seen Grandma Faith and Grandpa Olin again after so many years, she'd felt happy. Really, really happy. The anger toward them that she'd nursed while in Florida seemed stupid. Why had she been like that? Wrong thinking. Muddled percep-tions.

Then there was Grandpa Peter. Would it be okay to call him that? He was a stranger. He'd never seen her, and she'd never seen him. Did he look like her dad? Was he cool and reserved, or was he warm and outgoing? Did he only want to meet her and then go back to his life as usual, or did he want something more, something long term?

Her phone pinged the arrival of a text, and she checked the message. It was from Hailey. **Praying for you**, it said.

When she was at Blakely, she hadn't known anybody who talked like that. Nobody had ever offered to pray for her. But it seemed to be second nature for Hailey. Izzy, too, although not quite so much or not in the same way.

Thanks, she texted back, feeling the anxiety ease.

Millie MacIver must have been a lot like Hailey. She'd even written short prayers in her diary. She hadn't always understood God or what He was doing, but she'd believed in Him and had trusted Him even when she was hurting.

It was unexpected, the way Emma seemed to understand Millie. From almost the first page of the diary, Emma had felt herself become a part of the story from all those years ago. Was that weird? She'd even made a few notes on her phone of things she wanted to ask Mrs. Simpson when she took back the diary. It would be hard to let go of it. That might be dumb, but it was true. She would miss reaching for it, opening it to older, familiar pages or to ones she hadn't read yet.

She heard the sound of a car's approach in the driveway. Heart and stomach tumbling, she put down her phone and stood, looking out the window as an automobile came to a halt.

Olivia stared at the computer screen, pretending to work while her thoughts bounced between hope and dread. When she'd called Peter Ward with the news that Emma would meet with him, she hadn't expected him to drive up to Bethlehem Springs that same day. She'd thought she and Emma would have a while to prepare. But that hadn't happened.

Did I do the right thing?

She wished she could call Tyler. If not to ask his opinion again, then to wipe away the sense that their budding romance was over for a reason she didn't understand.

"Mom, I think he's here."

Her stomach tightened as she left her desk and went into the living room. She looked out the window in time to see Peter get out of his car. Although his attire was casual, it still suggested a successful man, one used to being in charge. Had she misjudged him? Did he want to take charge of Emma? She hoped not. For her daughter's sake, she hoped not.

She went to the door and opened it as he climbed the steps. "You must have made good time." The words sounded less than welcoming. She tried to change that. "Please. Come on in." She stepped back, holding the door open wide.

"Thank you, Olivia." His gaze moved from her to where Emma stood, her expression tense, uncertainty showing in her eyes. "And you must be Emma."

She nodded.

"I'm grateful you agreed to meet with me."

"Let's sit down." Olivia motioned toward the sofa and chairs. But as she followed behind Peter, she wondered if she should remain in the room. Would it be better to let grandfather and granddaughter become acquainted without a nervous mom looking on? What was the right thing to do?

As if reading her mind, Peter looked over his shoulder and said, "It's good we can all be together." Then he sat in the easy chair nearest the fireplace.

Olivia sank onto the sofa beside Emma.

Silence filled the room. Emma picked up her phone, glanced at the screen, then set it on the coffee table again. Olivia stared at a swirl of dust beneath an end table. She'd missed it when doing her quick cleaning prior to this visit.

The older man cleared his throat. "Emma, is there anything you would like to ask me?"

"Why didn't Dad want you to meet me?"

Olivia's breath caught as she glanced at her daughter, then at Peter. **Please don't say anything that will hurt her.**

"I suppose because I wasn't the kind of father he wanted."

Olivia relaxed, the air leaving her lungs.

"Families are complicated," Emma said softly.

Peter nodded, the hint of a smile on his lips. "That they are."

"My friend says they've all got complexities and quirks."

Olivia wondered which friend had said that.

"Indeed," Peter replied.

"So what do you do?"

"I'm retired. I owned my own construction firm for close to forty years. Built it from the ground up. At one time

I hoped your father would join me, but Daniel had other plans. He preferred wheeling and dealing."

"I never saw Dad use a hammer or stuff like that. He wasn't a manual-labor kind of guy. He'd rather hire somebody to do the work and then tell them what to do so it'd be the way he liked it."

Emma's comment surprised Olivia. She'd known that about Daniel, of course, but she'd assumed Emma believed only the best about her dad.

"What about you, Emma? Tell me about yourself."

She shrugged. "Like what?"

"Well, I know that you like acting. Tell me about your role in the play. **An Ideal Husband**, isn't it?"

Olivia frowned in thought. Had she told Peter about the play? She didn't remember doing so.

Emma seemed happy to comply. She told her grandfather about the theater company, about the director and several of the actors, about being part of the crew for the current production. Her enthusiasm was obvious as she chattered on and on, and Peter's grin broadened as he listened. The grin was very much like Emma's.

"I'll get it and show it to you," Emma said as she got to her feet.

As her daughter ran up the stairs, Olivia wondered how long she'd allowed her thoughts to wander. "What is she getting?"

Peter answered, "The diary she found at the theater."

"Oh."

"I've just about finished it." Emma started down the stairs again, the old book in her hand. "I read a lot at first, but then I slowed down. It's gonna be like losing a friend when I get to the end." She went to a second chair and pulled it closer to the one her grandfather sat in. "Look at how pretty her handwriting is."

"They taught penmanship in school

in those days. My days too. I've heard they don't do that in most schools nowadays."

"You mean cursive, like Millie's? I learned it. That was when I was in elementary school in Boise." Emma looked at Olivia. "Isn't that when?"

Olivia nodded. "Yes."

"But I hardly ever write that way." Emma turned a few pages in the diary now held by her grandfather. "I print or type. But if I could write like this, maybe I would."

"We learn by doing."

"You know what's really gonna be bad? When I get to the end, it won't really be the end. I mean, she lived to be old. Mrs. Simpson, her granddaughter, told me that. She wouldn't tell me much of anything else right then. But when I return the diary, she said she'll tell me more. So I guess I'll find out, but it won't be the way Millie wrote it. Her little girl dying. Having to move again and again. Trouble in her marriage.

The Depression. It was hard." She paused, then added, "I like the prayers she wrote. They've kinda taught me to do the same. You know. Be honest with God."

"It's good when we talk to Him, like a Father and Friend. For some people, writing down prayers is the best way to start." Peter turned a few pages on his own, then closed the diary. "I spent too many years of my life living as if only what I wanted mattered. I certainly never inquired of the Almighty what His opinion might be. Emma, you'll be much better off if you don't make that same mistake."

Olivia had made the right decision, inviting Peter to come to her home and spend time with Emma. She felt it in her heart. All would be well.

August 30, 1934
Thursday

Heat blanketed the town tonight.
The neighbor's dog hid beneath
our front porch, taking refuge on
the cooler earth he found there.
I know because Harry joined me
on the porch after the children
were fast asleep, and he heard
the dog snoring and snuffling.

I won't sleep for a long while
yet. The baby inside me won't
allow it. It is hard enough any
night, but when the air is this still
and sweltering, I won't bother
to try. I long for a cool breeze.
I long for October and the birth
of this child.

Harry sat beside me on the
swing, and he put an arm around

my shoulders, and he said,
"I love you."
    It was enough.

September 5, 1934
Wednesday

It rained today. The heat spell is broken, and the smell of autumn is in the air. The trees seemed to rejoice as water dripped off their branches. I think I even saw a few leaves ready to turn from green to gold. Or perhaps that is only wishful thinking.

We have passed through our first spring and summer in these mountains. Am I ready for autumn and winter? I suppose I shall have to be.

Chapter 30

Olivia put her arm around Emma's back as they watched Peter walk to his car. When he reached it, he turned and waved to them.

"I've gotta text Hailey." Emma returned her grandfather's wave, then went into the house.

Olivia smiled after her daughter, then looked toward the driveway again. As she did so, a familiar black SUV turned off Elkhorn and stopped. Her pulse quickened. Tyler's parting words to her that morning on the phone had been that he would see her on Sunday. But it seemed he'd changed his mind. He was here now.

Her surprise and joy immobilized her. Peter said something as he stepped toward Tyler, who now stood beside his vehicle. Only then did she hurry down the steps so she could introduce the two men.

His back to her, Peter said, "You were right. Thank you."

Tyler's gaze met hers over the older man's shoulder, and something in his eyes made her stomach clench, robbing her of the joy she'd felt moments before.

Peter turned. "Olivia, you have another guest. I'll be on my way."

How she knew, she couldn't say, but these two men needed no introduction. They were already acquainted. "What was Tyler right about?" She pinned Peter with her gaze.

Perhaps it was the resemblance the older man had to her daughter, but she caught the guilty expression before he managed to hide it. She shifted her eyes to Tyler, but he only gave a slow shake of his head. Fear—or something like it—sluiced through her.

"It was my doing," Peter said, his voice low.

"Mr. Ward—" Tyler began.

"No." Peter held up a hand. "I must tell her the truth."

His response sounded jumbled in her ears.

"Olivia, after Daniel died, I hired the firm Mr. Murphy works for to…to make sure Emma had a good home."

Her confusion intensified.

"All I knew at the time was that my son had accused you of being an unfit mother. Back when you divorced. I didn't know if that was true or not. I needed to do the right thing for my granddaughter. I had to make sure she was all right and in a good home."

She took a step back, then another. She looked at Tyler again. "You were **investigating** me?" she whispered, wanting him to deny it, needing him to deny it.

His expression remained stoic, un-readable, and he said nothing.

But his silence said it all.

She turned on her heel and rushed away from them.

Emma looked up from her phone as Olivia entered the house. "Mom?"

She paid her daughter no heed, hurrying on to her bedroom. She closed the door and leaned against it. Then, crushed by the betrayal of the man she'd allowed herself to trust, to care for, perhaps to love, she slid down the door and hid her face in her hands.

"Mom?" Emma's voice came through the door. "What's wrong?"

"I can't talk about it now. Please, Emma." It was nearly impossible to speak around the enormous lump in her throat. "I...I need a little time."

Silence, then, "All right."

Unable to hold them back any longer, Olivia allowed the tears to fall.

Tyler stared at the closed door of the

house, wanting to go after Olivia, needing to explain, and yet knowing he couldn't say anything that would help. Not now. Not yet.

"I'm sorry," Peter said. "I bungled it. I never meant for her to hear me say what I did. Once she asked, what could I do but tell her the truth?"

"Nothing." He just wished it could have been told in a different setting, in a different way. A way that wouldn't hurt her.

"Perhaps I should try to explain." Peter took a step away from Tyler.

"It might be too soon for that, sir."

The older man's shoulders slumped in defeat.

"You read my reports, Mr. Ward. Olivia was hurt by your son. She felt the betrayal for a long, long time. It kept her from trusting men. That now includes the two of us."

Peter faced him again. He searched Tyler with his gaze. After a long silence, he said, "I see."

"Yes." He nodded. "I suppose you do."

"This is why you ended the investigation. You care for Olivia."

There was no point denying it. "I'm in love with her, sir. But that happened after I told you she's a good mother and you should meet her for yourself." He drew a breath and released it. "Not that I imagine she would believe that now."

"I'm sorry," Peter repeated.

The front door opened, drawing their gazes. For a second Tyler hoped it would be Olivia, but he wasn't surprised when Emma came onto the deck. Steeling himself, he walked toward her.

"What happened?" the girl demanded as he drew close.

"Your mom's feelings were hurt over something that was said."

"What?"

He ran the fingers of one hand through his hair. "I think she'll need to tell you that."

"She's in her room crying. I could hear her through the door."

"I'm sorry." He knew it was as useless for him to say it now as it had been for Peter to say it moments before.

Emma scowled at him. "Go tell **her** you're sorry."

"I'd better let it alone for the night. I'll come to see her in the morning. If she'll let me."

The look in her eyes told him what she thought his promise was worth.

"Emma, I wouldn't intentionally hurt your mother. I care for her. More than she knows." He turned away. "I'll be back in the morning." He gave a nod to Peter before getting into his SUV and backing out of the driveway.

To Emma, it felt like an eternity before her mom finally left her bedroom. She appeared out of the short hallway, her eyes puffy and red but her cheeks dry.

"You okay?" Emma asked.

Her mom nodded.

"What did he do?"

"Nothing."

"That's not true."

Her mom sank onto the chair. "No, it isn't."

"He told me he was sorry."

"Maybe he is."

"He said he'll come see you in the morning if you'll let him."

Her mom gazed toward the window, as if looking to see if he was there already.

"And he said he'd never hurt you on purpose. He says he cares for you more than you know."

Silence.

"Mom, I believe him."

"I wish I could."

"He's not like Dad, you know."

Her mom turned to face her, a glimmer of surprise in her eyes.

"I can tell the difference. Dad was... Well, he wasn't like Tyler. Tyler's good to you. Maybe he messed up somehow, but that doesn't mean he's bad or that you should shut him out. Second chances. Isn't that part of what Jesus is about? You know, covering us with His righteousness and all that. Forgiving us so we can forgive others."

A smile tugged at the corners of her mom's mouth. "Yes."

"Then I think you need to hear him out. You didn't give up on me when I messed up."

"That's different. You're my daughter. I love you."

"What's so different? You love him too."

"No, I—" She broke off and her eyes widened a little.

"Okay, maybe you're just starting to feel like that, but it's there. Give him a chance."

The surprise in her mom's eyes vanished, and her smile grew. "When did you get so smart?"

"Not sure. Maybe when I came back home to live."

September 17, 1934
Monday

I have carried the weight of
sadness for too long. For years.
The losses we have suffered—
I have held on to them. Not in
bitterness. At least I think not.
No. It is more like a martyr. I have
written in these pages that we
are better off than many. But in
my heart I have felt put upon.
I have felt too much was asked
of me. I have asked for God's
forgiveness, but have I truly
repented and looked to Him in
trust? I think not.

I have let sadness embed itself
in my heart, in my marriage, in
my home, and in my response to
my heavenly Father. I have let my

hurts and sorrows become what
I project onto the world.

Who am I that I should escape
the hardships of this world?

I will seek to be more like the
apostle Paul who said in
Philippians 4 that he learned the
secret for living in want and in
plenty. He knew how to be
content either way. I want to be
the same.

**Father, only by Your Spirit can
I learn that secret. Change me,
Lord. Renew my mind.**

September 20, 1934
Thursday

Home.
   This world is not my home.
I am a stranger in a strange land.
I am passing through. We are all
passing through.
   God allows me to make my
temporary home with the people
I love. With my husband. With
our children.
   There will be sorrow and
sighing, but He brings joy in the
morning. He brings beauty from
ashes.
   I have begun to see that now.
Beauty from ashes.
   He collects my tears in a
bottle. He knows what is in my
heart.

I cannot quite grasp it all, but I am beginning to.

Chapter 31

Wrapped in a throw against the early-morning chill, Olivia sat on the deck, watching the sunrise. Her Bible and journal lay on the small table beside the chair, but she had yet to open either of them.

"I hired the firm Mr. Murphy works for to...to make sure Emma had a good home."

Those words—and others—had replayed in her mind throughout the night. They replayed in her mind even now, along with questions she didn't know the answers to.

Had Tyler meant anything he'd said

to her in all of these weeks she'd known him? Or had it all been a pretense, done for the sake of a job? She hadn't trusted anyone in such a long time. She'd thought…She'd hoped…

"He says he cares for you more than you know."

Sweet Emma, sounding wise.

"Then I think you need to hear him out. You didn't give up on me when I messed up."

"What if I hadn't let him in?" she whispered as the golden crown of the sun topped the trees to the east.

"He's not like Dad, you know."

No, Tyler was nothing like Daniel had been. Not at all.

"You didn't give up on me when I messed up."

But Emma was her daughter.

"You love him too."

Do I? Do I love him?

She closed her eyes against the bright light, but she couldn't shut out the memories of Tyler Murphy. At the high school track the first time she'd seen him. At the amphitheater, carrying a tray of desserts. At the Gold Mountain, packed with the lunch crowd. On the drive down to Boise. At the Brazilian Grill. At church in the media booth. At the theater in the control booth. At his home, moments after they'd kissed. She saw his smile. Heard his voice. Felt his touch.

"But he isn't who I thought he was."

Isn't he?

The silent question ran through her heart. And as if to provide an answer, she saw his car turn into her driveway. She got to her feet, wrapping the throw more tightly around her. Why had he come so early? It wasn't even 6:30. She considered going inside and closing the door.

But she didn't. She didn't move.

The SUV stopped, but she couldn't see the driver through the windshield. The angle was wrong. It seemed to take forever for the door to open and for

Tyler to step into view. His expression looked as uncertain as she felt.

"Mom, I believe him."

He looked up and their gazes met. Her heart stuttered in response.

"I see I'm not too early," he said.

"Maybe a little."

"I thought I'd have to sit in the car for a while."

She moved to the railing. "I'm not sure you should be here at all."

"I'm not giving up."

She breathed easier, knowing she couldn't drive him away with only a few words.

"Olivia, I know it hurt you, finding out what you did the way you did. I'd like a chance to explain."

"Explanations don't change the facts. You deceived me."

"Mom, I believe him."

He moved up the steps, stopping halfway. "I kept the whole truth from you. But it was for a good reason."

"There's a good reason to lie?"

"I never lied to you." He came up the last few steps.

She wanted to say his denial was a lie in itself. But was it? "Tell me why I should believe anything you say."

"Because..." He took a step toward her. "Because you understand why Peter hired me, even if you don't like it. But more than that, because you know me."

"I don't know you as well as I thought."

"Olivia." He drew out her name. "You **know** me."

When did he step close enough that she had to tip her head back to look into his eyes? Was it possible that she felt his heart beating in time with her own?

"And I know you," he added at long last. "You are a caring mom. You are a faithful friend. You don't give up, even when things are hard. You love God, although you think you've failed Him one too many times. I know you, Olivia. I know the woman I've grown to love."

"Love?"

He hooked a strand of her hair behind her ear. "Love."

"You couldn't possibly—"

"I could. I do."

"But you—"

He silenced her protest with his lips upon hers. A tender kiss. One that didn't demand but encouraged. One that imparted strength. Strength to stand alone, but even more strength to stand together. He'd said he loved her, and miracle of miracles, she believed him. Not only that, Emma believed him.

I'm not afraid. She drew back to meet his gaze again and said the words aloud. "I'm not afraid."

She wasn't afraid to let him love her. She wasn't afraid to love him in return. She wasn't afraid of the windstorms that life might bring her way. She wasn't afraid to put her trust in God.

As if seeing all of that in her eyes, Tyler took hold of her left hand with his right, weaving his fingers through hers.

Then he brought her hand to his lips and kissed the back of it. "I think we have a lot to talk about."

"Yes. Beginning with, I love you too."

September 25, 1934
Tuesday

I have reached the end of this
diary. It isn't a large book, but
it has taken me several years
to fill its pages. It seems fitting
somehow that I should share the
lesson God gave me early this
morning. Last December, I wrote
a passage from the book of Mark
and asked, "Jesus, do You
care?" And here is what I have
come to understand at last.

Mark 4: "And on that day,
when even was come, he saith
unto them, Let us go over unto
the other side. And leaving the
multitude, they take him with
them, even as he was, in the
boat. And other boats were with

him. And there ariseth a great storm of wind, and the waves beat into the boat, insomuch that the boat was now filling. And he himself was in the stern, asleep on the cushion: and they awake him, and say unto him, Teacher, carest thou not that we perish?"

Does He care?

"And he awoke, and rebuked the wind, and said unto the sea, Peace, be still. And the wind ceased, and there was a great calm. And he said unto them, Why are ye fearful? have ye not yet faith? And they feared exceedingly, and said one to another, Who then is this, that even the wind and the sea obey him?"

Yes. He cares.

At last I understand. I have heard Him answer me. He cares. He rebukes the wind because He cares. Even the wind and the sea obey, and He speaks to them on my behalf.

I have read and reread these verses about the storm and the boat in the fourth chapter of Mark, and He has used them to bring me understanding about so many things. We talk of storms in this life. We know that the wind blows, that storms come to everyone. The storm in this chapter of Mark came to the disciples because Jesus told them they were to go to the other side. He must have known there would be a storm, and yet He said they were to go. But He didn't send them alone. Jesus was in the boat too.

I am not alone. No matter how I feel, no matter what storms buffet me, I am not alone. Jesus is in the boat with me.

He cares.

He cares for me.

He cares for Harry.
He cares for our children.
He cares.
Amen.

Epilogue

ELEVEN MONTHS LATER

The sky over Bethlehem Springs was a spotless blue without a single cloud to mar the expanse. The air was pleasant and sweet. A perfect Saturday in June.

From the gazebo in the town park, Olivia looked at the crowd of people who had come to witness Olivia Ward and Tyler Murphy exchange their wedding vows.

Emma—looking far too grown up in her bridesmaid gown of blue, the shade identical to the sky—stood beside Toby Adams. Toby was not the first boy to show interest in Emma since the previous school year had started, but he was the first boy who'd seemed to win her interest in return. And he'd done so, at least in part, by joining the Bethlehem Springs Mountain Theater Company. Smart kid.

Phoebe Simpson, former schoolteacher, and Rachel Hamilton, present school principal, stood talking near the refreshment table, no doubt discussing school matters. Phoebe might have retired, but her heart still belonged in education and with the students. Her kindness to and friendship with Emma were only one indication of that. The two had grown especially close after Emma finished reading Millie's diary and Phoebe had begun sharing many aspects about her grandmother's long life in Bethlehem Springs, including the wonderful devotional books that Millie had written and had published, the last of them only a year before her death at the age of ninety-nine.

Olivia's attention moved on, and she saw Sara Cartwright and her husband deep in conversation with Kathy and Greg Dover. Watching the four of them together, Olivia took a moment to thank God for putting these tried-and-true friends in her life.

Seated in nearby chairs, her parents and Peter Ward laughed over something, and Olivia's joy in this day grew even stronger. Who would have expected Daniel's father to become a beloved member of her family? Not Olivia, that was for certain. And yet that's what he had become.

And so many others. Her gaze swept the guests, and she remembered those times, those moments, as each one had become a part of the tapestry of her life. How sad that she'd closed herself away from them for so long. How glad she was God had changed her heart so she could open herself to them at last.

"Hey." Tyler stepped close to her side,

his arm wrapping around her back, his hand touching her waist. "Who's that smile for?"

"No one in particular. I'm just happy."

His mouth came close to her ear. "Today, I think I want to be the only one who makes you smile. I'm jealous that way."

His breath tickled her neck and she laughed softly, her eyes drifting closed, her head tipping back.

They'd taken their time, she and Tyler, on their way to this wedding day. They'd wanted to know each other and to be known by each other. It had been worth the months of waiting. Olivia knew this man at her side better than she'd known anyone else in her life. Perhaps better than she knew herself. There wasn't a shred of doubt in her heart that she wanted to go through the rest of her life with him.

The musicians returned from a short break, and couples moved to the dance floor that had been assembled near a stand of pines.

"Come on." Tyler withdrew a step and took hold of her hand. "Let's dance again."

They were almost to the wood floor when the band started to play "What a Wonderful World." She recognized the song almost from the first note because Tyler had sung it to her many times over the past eleven months. It was one more thing she'd learned about him. He had a beautiful voice, and he loved to sing love songs to her.

She stepped into his embrace while thinking, **It is a wonderful world**.

Storms would come. The seas would rise and the winds would blow. It would happen because that was part of life. But she and Tyler and Emma would weather the storms together—because they had been rescued already by the One who was with them in the boat.

What a good thing to know as they embarked on a new life together.

A Note from the Author

Dear Friends:

I hope you enjoyed reading **Like the Wind**. The story was inspired by Mark 4. I have been through many storms in my life, and as long as I've remembered that Jesus is in the boat with me, I have never been overwhelmed. If you are in the midst of a storm right now, put your eyes on Jesus. He will see you through. He is faithful.

Longtime readers may have recognized a couple of locations in **Like the Wind** from my previous books. Thunder Creek was the setting for two of my contemporary romances, **You'll Think of Me** and **You're Gonna Love Me**. And, of course, Bethlehem Springs was the setting for my The Sisters of Bethlehem Springs series: **A Vote of Confidence**, **Fit to Be Tied**, and **A Matter of Character**. I hope it was as fun for readers to revisit these small towns as it was for me to envision them in my mind in different time settings.

As I write this note, months before **Like the Wind** will be released, I'm working away on a sequel to **Even Forever**. I hope readers will love a return to Boulder Creek and to reencounter some familiar faces as well as a number of new ones.

And after that, I can't wait to begin writing a new series, which is set around the Yellowstone area in the late 1800s. I came up with the idea for this series over a decade ago, but it got set aside more than once for a variety of reasons. But at last, now is the time. I look forward to telling readers more about the series in a future newsletter. I hope you'll take a moment to subscribe to the newsletter on my website (see URL in my signature) so that you won't miss out.

In the grip of His grace,
Robin

https://robinleehatcher.com

Acknowledgments

Many thanks to the wonderful fiction team at HarperCollins Christian Publishing. I've loved working with various members of the team since 1999, and I treasure the memories made over those many years.

Thanks to Natasha Kern. What a ride we've had, my friend. Life keeps changing, but God is faithful. I so appreciate your advice, wisdom, and guidance throughout my career.

Thanks to my CdA sisters in Christ and the brainstorming we did for this novel. Oh, the sound of the wonderful laughter around that dining room table.

The memory of it always brings a smile.

Finally, to my faithful readers. You make the crazy ups and downs of life as a writer worth it. Thank you for the emails and messages that serve to encourage me, day in and day out.

Discussion Questions

1. Was there a scene in the book that you found particularly meaningful? What was it and why?

2. Which character did you most relate to? Why?

3. Both Olivia (in the present) and Millie (in the past) go through storms in their lives that leave them asking God if He cares about them. Have you ever felt that way? Have you discovered that Jesus is in the boat with you?

4. After the betrayal by Olivia's former husband, she cut herself off from most people in her community. Have you ever isolated yourself after a betrayal? How did you find your way back to fellowship and trust?

5. Was Peter Ward wrong to investigate Olivia to be certain his granddaughter had a good home?

6. Emma was led by her dad to believe that her mom didn't want her. Those types of scars can take a long time to heal. Are there wounds in your life that need healing, even ones from your own childhood or teen years?

7. Tyler's experiences with his mom and sister, followed by years in foster care, filled him with a desire to protect and help at-risk kids and led him to his career as an investigator. Did experiences in your past impact your choice of careers? How?

8. Is there a character in **Like the Wind** that you wish could have his/her own book? Who and why?

About the Author

Robin Lee Hatcher is the author of over eighty novels and novellas with over five million copies of her books in print. She is known for her heartwarming and emotionally charged stories of faith, courage, and love. Her numerous awards include the RITA Award, the Carol Award, the Christy Award, the HOLT Medallion, the National Reader's

Choice Award, and the Faith, Hope & Love Reader's Choice Award. Robin is also the recipient of prestigious Lifetime Achievement Awards from both American Christian Fiction Writers and Romance Writers of America. When not writing, she enjoys being with her family, spending time in the beautiful Idaho outdoors, Bible art journaling, reading books that make her cry, watching romantic movies, and decorative planning. Robin makes her home on the outskirts of Boise, sharing it with a demanding Papillon dog and a persnickety tuxedo cat.